TOURNAMENT OF THE GODS

TOURNAMENT OF THE GODS

A WICKED AND FATED NOVEL

WICKED GODS
BOOK TWO

J. L. JACKOLA

Tivshe
Publishing

Library of Congress Control Number 2023908946

Paperback ISBN 978-1-960784-14-8
Hardback ISBN 978-1-960784-15-5
Electronic ISBN 978-1-960784-16-2

Distributed by Tivshe Publishing
Printed in the United States of America

Cover design by Dark Queen Designs

Visit www.tivshepublishing.com

AUTHOR'S NOTE

Tournament of the Gods is the second book in my Wicked Gods duology, set in my Wicked and Fated series. It is intended for mature readers. Please be aware that it contains content that may not be suitable for all readers, including explicit sexual scenes, language, and violence.

ALSO BY J. L. JACKOLA

CHAPTER 1
GRAHAM

I walked the path from the gravestones as the last rays of my power settled over the cemetery. I'd left flowers as I did every year—pink peonies, Angie's favorite. Over a century had passed since Angie's death. The pain and the endless sadness had faded, brought back as our two children had seen their last days. Neither had had children of their own. It was a blessing, or so my sister, Claire, had told me. An end to the pain my burden of immortality presented. Their deaths had gutted me but so had having to watch them grow old and losing the lives that had been so precious to me.

I returned each year to remind myself of the humanity that sometimes slipped away when I was in my realm, when I was with the other gods. After so many years, it had become habit rather than necessity. My heart had never fully healed. I hadn't found another to take Angie's place, to fill the void she and the children had left. The laws of our existence barred me from loving another mortal, and after experiencing those losses and the fragility of their mortality, I never wanted to love another. If love returned to me, it would be with one of my own kind, the goddesses that made up the vast family that now claimed me.

They weren't truly family, not blood-related aside from my sister, so I could claim any of them if the chance ever came. It hadn't yet. Sure, I'd indulged in the flesh since that time to relieve my needs, but it hadn't been frequent, and I tried to avoid the mortals when I could, preferring to indulge in the flesh of goddesses when the need arose.

Returning to the kingdoms, I decided to visit my sister in the Nightmare realm. Claire and her husband, Jackson, were nowhere to be found, but I discovered Del, Jackson's sister, in the open foyer that connected her wing of their castle to the others. Dellamine, the goddess of delusion. A goddess to rival any of the others, but one I would never allow myself to touch.

She was lying on a long gray chaise, tormenting what looked like a very irritated fairy. Her blonde hair was spread over the back of the chaise, her long thin legs free of the silk dress she'd pulled to her thighs. She was beautiful in a demented yet fragile way. Her soft giggle filled the quiet each time the fairy pouted at her.

I shook my head. "Aren't fairies part of Dream's realm?" I asked, coming around to lean against the chair opposite her.

Her green eyes met mine. The silver slivers that had fascinated me since the first time I'd seen her, danced playfully within them. The soft gold rim of her pupils made the slivers pop against the emerald of her eyes so that they looked like tiny lightning strikes. "Why Graham, you're not going to tattle on me, are you?"

Her voice was silky, with a hint of seduction, but I knew what lay below. The insanity that Delusion held below her delicate features was powerful enough to ravage a mortal's mind with the mere look of those lush eyes.

"Your secret's safe with me. His realm grates on my senses."

"That's the chaos in you. Dream's realm is too perfect, and it bothers you just as it does me. You may be calm and controlled as you bring the rise of each day, Turning, but the chaos you carry from your father flitters below that control."

She bit her lip, those slivers stilling for just a moment. The way she called me Turning, the shortened name of my power, sent a tingle of desire over my skin. I shook it off. She was dangerous in a way that called to that side of my blood, the chaos my father and now my sister ruled. But Del was also delicate, and that part of her left me with a need to protect her, to keep her safe just as I knew Jackson and her other brother, Theo, would. I preferred to think of her like a sister, no matter how my body reacted to her. If I didn't, I risked giving into her, giving into the desire I chose to keep concealed.

She tilted her head as if she could read my thoughts. She'd made no effort to hide the fact that she'd wanted me when we first met, even teasing me as Angie grew older. But she'd stopped suddenly, staying aloof with the flirting, the entrancing looks she'd give me, the inviting comments. I don't know what had changed with her, but I'd been thankful for it at the time. Dealing with Angie's failing health, knowing I'd be forced to face my heritage when she was gone, that I'd have to take my place as my mother's heir, just as Claire had taken my father's place, had been a lot to handle. I hadn't needed the temptation of Del and her curves of perfection at that same time.

She rose from the chaise, my eyes following the flow of her dress as it slid to cover those amazing legs. I couldn't help bringing my gaze up her body and taking in the soft curve of her hips that led to the small waist. I followed the trail to the full breasts that peeked from the long dip in her gown, which fell almost to her belly button and left too much of her skin showing. Any man would be insane not to want that skin against his, those long legs wrapped around him. But I wasn't most men, and I pushed the thoughts aside, no matter how they screamed at me.

The green in her eyes darkened, and the fairy squealed.

"Go. Take my delusions back to your friends and torment my uncle a little, tiny beast," she whispered. I watched as the fairy's small eyes blackened, the pink of her hair turning a shade of wicked red before Del let her go. She disappeared, and I knew Dream would be raging his way through his realm, trying to clean up her damage.

"You are naughty, Del."

"Mmm, I know. It's too fun not to play." She leaned against me, and I could smell the berry scent of her soap on her skin. Her breasts rested on my crossed arm, and for a moment, I had the urge to slip my hand down to tease the nipple below her dress, to cause a sigh to escape those perfect lips. I wondered whether she was a quiet sigher in bed or a screamer. I had a feeling she was very wicked in bed.

Stop it, Graham, I warned myself. Del was off limits to me. She was Jackson's sister and too close to me through that link to take her like I currently wanted.

Her lips parted, the green of her eyes shifting to a soft emerald. "Why, Graham, I do believe those thoughts of yours are dirtier than they usually are."

Damn her and her abilities. "I never said you weren't a turn-on, Del. You're just a turn-on that I can't play with."

"No?" Her hand slid along my arm, her skin soft just like I imagined it would be. "I'm not stopping you."

Shit. This wasn't a situation I wanted to be in. Jackson I could deal with, Claire would handle him, but Theo would have my head if I touched Del.

I don't want to touch her, I told myself, hearing the sudden lie in my mind. I didn't know why she was so alluring today. Who was I kidding? She was alluring any day, I simply turned away from it. I always had, but today I was having trouble.

"Graham," she said, her voice satin against my ears.

"Del," I returned as gruffly as I could, trying to will the hard-on I could feel pressing against my pants to ease before she noticed.

Her eyes twinkled, the slivers bouncing.

"Do you cry out your lover's name when you're coming?" she asked.

Good God, that was enough to break me, but I pushed her away softly. "What the fuck, Del?"

Her laugh was beautiful, filled with the madness I knew she carried. "I do love teasing you, Graham."

Cock-tease was what she was, but I'd never admit that.

I rolled my neck and grimaced at her.

"See, it's that broodiness. Jackson carries that same broodiness, and it's sexy." She must have caught the disgusted look that had overtaken my features. "What? Both my brothers are extremely sexy. I would never touch them, yuck. But that doesn't mean I don't admire their beauty."

"You're insane."

"I'm Delusion. Insanity is my thing."

I shook my head at her. "Where's Claire?" I asked, remembering why I'd come here in the first place.

She plopped back down on the chaise, stretching her long body out. I was drawn to the firm nipples that pressed against her dress with her move. They were the kind that called to be sucked and bitten until she squirmed. Wiping my hand over my face, I cleared the thought away and looked at the ground.

"She and Jacks went to visit Death."

I shuddered. Our aunt's presence was one that disturbed me. She was fond of Claire and Jackson, however.

"Yeah, she gives me the same reaction. She and Jacks have always been close, and she adores Claire."

"Adore? That's not a word I think of when I think of her."

Del laughed, a sound that shimmered through the air. "You'll get used to her. She has a soft side, especially when her life side is present."

Death shifted between two facades, life and death, the two morphing frequently as the life cycles in the mortal world played out. It upset the stability of my powers, but I knew it complimented my sister's. Her chaos fed on the constant change.

"Did you not come to see me?" Del asked, her eyes growing sad, that vulnerability that sat below her power coming through.

"You know the answer, but I'd be happy to stay and play a game if you're bored."

Her eyes lit like two brilliant emeralds, the slivers fading for just that moment. Sliding her hand along her body, she fingered the hem of her dress, slowly lifting it to reveal those gorgeous legs. I could only imagine what they would feel like wrapped tight around me. And I couldn't help but wonder if they quivered when she climaxed. An image filled my mind of the tremor of that soft skin as her scream filled the room.

Narrowing my eyes, I lifted them back to meet hers. "Stop playing in my head, Del." I knew what she was doing. Knew what she wanted, as she sensed my own need. The one I wouldn't act on. "Not that kind of game."

She pouted, a look that didn't help the situation as I pictured taking her bottom lip between my teeth.

"Fuck, Del. Get out of my head!"

Her giggle filled my ears, and I shot her a look. "You're so much fun to torment though. I don't know why you won't indulge. You indulge in others. Why not me?"

"I'm not touching you, Del. Now, do you want to do something...other than that...or not?"

Huffing, she rose from the lounge and crossed her arms. There were so many childlike facets to her; they were what made her so dangerous. That line between childish innocence and unhinged insanity flickered inside of her. It was the latter that tempted the chaos in me, the former that tempted the other side of me. But she was off limits.

"Chess?" she asked, her voice still holding her disappointment.

"Chess works for me."

"Fine."

She rose and started walking to the game room. I moved quickly and grabbed her arm, too curious not to ask her why she was suddenly flirting again. Her body pulled into mine, which hadn't been my intention.

"Why Graham, I thought you didn't want to play that game."

Dammit. There was a rise in my pants again at the flush of her body against mine. "I don't," I said through gritted teeth.

"Mmm, you are sexy when you're irritated. You know, your dick says you want to play." She moved her hand in that direction, and I grabbed it, now realizing I had her by both wrists. Shit, this was not going the way I'd planned.

I pushed her against the wall, unable to resist. The exhale she emitted was like a stimulant. Her heart was pounding below me, and I had every urge to kiss those beautiful pink lips that had parted with her exhale. "What are you doing, Del?"

"Me? What are you doing, Graham? You're the one pressing me against the wall. You know how I like it rough."

"God, no, I didn't know that." And the fact only further enticed me.

"Oh, but I do. It cages the insanity in me, but few can control that side of me. The attempt is the turn-on. A tight hand around my throat, a slap to my ass—"

Her words were like strokes on my now throbbing dick. The

7

image of my hand around her throat as she came undone was almost enough to send me over the edge. I had no doubt that if I ever gave in, she would be everything I imagined, everything I wanted. "Shut up, Del. Why are you teasing me again? You haven't for a very long time."

"Because you're finally open to it."

I let her go and backed away. Rubbing my hand over my face, I turned from her. "No, I'm not."

"You fuck others. Why can't you fuck me?"

Because I don't want to just fuck you, I wanted to say, but I bit the words back.

"Because you are untouchable." She studied me, her eyes seeing too deep into my mind. I sensed her there, like a whisper of seduction. "Get out of my mind, Del."

Her eyes softened as her magic pulled away. "Angie's been gone a long time, Graham," she said, her voice barely audible.

I creased my brow, wondering at the comment, the softness to it. But before I could react, the insanity returned to her eyes, the slivers flittering. "Chess it is, then. And I promise to keep my hands to myself."

She skipped away as if nothing had happened, as if she were a small girl ready to play games with a friend. I sighed, still not understanding what had happened between us and why she was suddenly flirting again.

"Come on, slowpoke. I'm ready to beat your ass again."

I shook my head and laughed, following her path, ready to spend the afternoon playing board games with the hot goddess who had just messed with my head and my body, leaving her imprint this time. I wasn't certain I wanted to erase it, liking the way it settled softly within me.

CHAPTER 2
DEL

Graham. That man had been my obsession since the first time I'd seen him. Before he'd come into his power, before it had simmered over him like a brooding storm that begged me to invade it. I would have gladly brought every bit of my insanity to him and pleasured him with it if he'd let me. But he never had, remaining devoted to his wife, even as her mortality had taken her from him.

I'd stepped away, too fond of Claire to tempt him in his weakened state. And over time, as his heart had healed, I'd stayed away, realizing I didn't want to simply experience his body. I wanted all of him. It was something I'd never admitted about a man before, but there was something about Graham that called to me. Perhaps it was the subtle layer of chaos that clung to his power or the steely control of his more visible powers. Whatever it was, the desire for him had stirred like a festering need deep in my belly, growing with every interaction.

I knew he'd taken others since Angie had died, although it had taken him years to do so. Mortal deaths were hard on immortals, which was why we were forbidden to love them.

Graham had been an exception, marrying his mortal long before we'd discovered he'd been hidden in the mortal world with his sister.

It irked me that he'd fucked the other goddesses and not me. I knew it wasn't many, but there were a few who had succeeded in seducing him, one in particular who loved to rub it in my face. I thanked the Creator there was no more than physical attraction there; otherwise, I would have tormented her with my delusions.

"Pouting again, sis?" Theo said, stepping into my room. "Want me to inflict some pain?"

I smiled at my older brother. He was my constant protector, as was Jacks. I was stuck in the middle of the two of them, wedged between Pain and Terror. It was an ideal place for Delusion to sit, but their overprotective tendencies grated on me.

"I'm fine, Theo. What do you want?"

His eyes lit, the green he shared with mine sparkling with mischief. "The tournament has been announced."

I jumped up, my excitement immediate. "When?"

"In two days' time. I heard from Violence that the Elders have designed an even more challenging course this year."

The tournament was an event that the Elders held every two hundred years. It pitted the children of the Elder gods against each other in grueling challenges across the realms. The cousins, as we all referred to ourselves, were paired up. It was a test of will and strength. The winning pair received the highest esteem and the title of Tournament Gods. Sometimes the pairs would fuck their way through the challenges, exploring their fantasies as the competition progressed. That was when it turned fun. I'd paired with Courage during the last one, and her tongue had left me so depleted that we'd never crossed the finish line. Storm and Thirst had found us, joining in until Jacks had ripped me away, scolding me for my lack of control. It hadn't been my fault that my delusions had slipped through the mortal realm for the days

I'd been occupied. He'd made me clean it all up and refused to talk to me for weeks.

I rubbed my hands together in glee, my delusions whipping about me in long wisps of silver. After that arousing interaction with Graham, I needed a distraction, and the tournament would be the perfect way to get my mind off him. It was clear he wanted me but wouldn't indulge. Another god could satisfy my need. I just needed to make sure the Elders paired me with the right one. Unless...what would happen if they paired me with Graham? I had a feeling nothing would happen, no matter how tempting I was to him.

"What's that look for?" Theo asked, pulling my thoughts back.

"Nothing," I said nonchalantly. The last thing I wanted was for him to know what I'd thought. He and Jacks had both warned me to stay away from Graham. Not that I ever listened to them.

"Yeah, your nothing is always something. You're scheming. I know that look."

I stuck my tongue out, not caring that it was a childish thing to do. He crossed his arms and gave me a look I didn't know how to read.

"Don't even think about pulling something like you did last time. Jacks will have your hide after the mess you left in the mortal world. You know he and Claire now sit with the Elders. He'll have sway over the pairings." My lips pouted. "Don't give me that look, Del. You won't be getting into trouble this time, not with Jacks in control."

I chewed my bottom lip. This wouldn't do. The tournament was only for those gods who weren't bound to another, those who were free to indulge in the pleasures of others. It was a rule that made the games even more exciting. Sex and power went hand in hand with our kind. It made sense that Jacks and Claire would not participate. But then again, Jacks was considered an

Elder now that he had taken our father's place as ruler of our kingdom. Claire, too, was seen as an Elder as the ruler of Chaos. Elders never participated in the tournaments; it was an event designed for the second generation.

I sighed, thinking through my prospects, or, more likely, the prospects Jacks would choose for me. There were quite a few gods whom I found boring and had never touched because they hadn't seemed worth my time. Those would likely be on his list. I supposed if I were stuck with one and I really needed to, I could indulge with them.

"Persuade him to pair me with someone fun at least. If he keeps me from fucking, at least let me have fun."

"That's the spirit. Because you know he will."

"Overprotective ass."

"Just like me. Although you know I don't have the power of persuasion, Persa is your go-to for that." His eyes drifted for just a moment like he was thinking on something. "Now, she's someone I wouldn't mind the Elders pairing me with. She has a mouth like no other, and when she uses those beautiful lips, shit, I lose it within minutes."

I threw a pillow at him. "You're gross. Go take your dirty fantasies somewhere else while I fret over who Jacks will be cursing me with."

He laughed as he disappeared in his power, the sound still touching the air after he was gone.

I remained there, long after he left, thinking of the way Graham had reacted to me today, how his hands had grasped me. Every time I was with him, my body was a mess of arousal. I'd never wanted a man as badly as I wanted him. Just the sound of his voice left me damp. Dropping my head back, I let my hand drift along my body, imagining it was his hand and knowing if it were, there would be a fire behind that touch. The thought sent a flush of tingles through my belly, and I moved my hand lower.

He was fierce, and I knew without a doubt that he would take me to heights no other man had. His touches wouldn't be gentle, they would be rough and aggressive.

I ran my hand below my dress, letting my fingers sink into the moisture that he'd caused and imagining they were his. Biting my lip hard enough to break the skin, I plunged them in, throwing my head back as I lost myself to visions of Graham. My breasts were aching for his touch, and so I pinched my nipple, wishing it were his pinch, and twisted it painfully at the thought. I cried out as I continued to thrust my fingers into me, pulling them out to rub my swollen clit then driving them back in with the force with which I wanted Graham to penetrate me. Within minutes, my body caved to my need for him, and my climax washed over me. My body quaked as it imagined him filling me over and over.

As I settled, the residual waves of my release still drifting through me, I dropped my hands. The moment of pleasure faded, replaced by a melancholy that it hadn't been him. That he'd left me as he always did, needing and wanting, never satisfying me the way I wanted him to satisfy me. The way I knew without a doubt he wanted to satisfy me. I wondered momentarily if he were turning to another goddess to relieve himself after our time together. The thought irritated my delusions, and they snapped wickedly around my head.

Sighing, I rose from my chair and walked across the marble floor of my room, beyond to the balcony that overlooked our kingdom. The silk curtains drifted in the soft breeze that blew in, touching my toes as I walked. A mist hung over the realm, one that never dissipated, hiding the creatures of nightmares that lay below. The twisted demons and beasts that my brother ruled, those who ravaged the dreams of the mortals we oversaw.

Leaning my elbow on the ledge, I sighed again. I should have been in a state of euphoria after my release, but since it hadn't come from the man I wanted, it had seemed hollow, leaving me even emptier than I'd been. My mind drifted back to Graham, wondering if he'd ever break down the barrier he'd built to keep his attraction for me at bay. Desire was there, I'd noticed it today more than I ever had, my mind slipping by it as it called to me. Perhaps one day I would experience him. The thought was tantalizing, but I wasn't certain if experiencing him would rein my delusions in so far that I'd never be able to escape what he did to them and to me.

CHAPTER 3
GRAHAM

I'd spent the afternoon with Del, enjoying her company too much—the scent of berries that drifted from her as she moved, the perk of her nipples below the low-cut gown, the swell of the breasts that teased from the sides of the dip in it, making it hard to think. Harder than most days. I rubbed my face as I entered the great hall of my castle, still pondering why she'd had such an effect on me today.

"You look tired," Penelipen observed as I walked in and sat next to her on the long sofa.

When I'd claimed my mother's kingdom, long after Angie had passed, after I'd buried my children and given my heart time to patch itself, I had continued to share it with Penelipen. She'd won the right to rule the kingdom, to oversee what had been my mother's power—the Turning of the Day, dawn to dusk, dusk to dawn—after my parents had been murdered. She had agreed to train me in my abilities as I'd stepped into the role until I could do the job myself and she could return to overseeing the skies as she had before.

She had not left, however, saying my kingdom suited her

better and that I still needed training, even after all these years. With her presence, rein over the realm had remained hers. I knew she chose to stay for other reasons. That she'd been lonely as had I and that we'd both enjoyed the company. I'd taken her over the years, off and on, as either of us had the need. It was never anything intimate, just dirty fucking that satisfied us both, meeting a need and providing a dull to the ache that still surfaced at times.

She raised her brown eyes to mine, the bronze of her skin shining in the moonlight. I'd turned the day to dusk before I'd returned, and night was now upon the mortal world, reflecting into our realms. She was beautiful, as was every goddess I'd met. Although she didn't hold a flame to Del's beauty, none of them did.

"What are you watching?" I asked, tilting my head to the vision before us.

"Domestic dispute. I'm waiting for her to kick his ass with that frying pan. I can feel Violence lingering in the background, twisting the odds in favor of the wife."

"Nice. You know we really should vie for more entertainment options in our kingdoms." I had never been much of a television watcher but being without one turned out to be torture of its own. The alternative was this, watching glimpses of the mortal world like a reality TV show playing live before us. It did serve as entertainment, but it lacked the finesse of the special effects that the mortal world offered.

"You reek of Delusion. Did you spend the day with Del?" she asked me with a raise of the brow.

"Maybe."

"When are you going to fuck her, Graham?"

"Really, Pen?"

"Really. It's no secret she wants you, you can see it in the movement of those annoying silver flakes in her eyes. Fuck her already and get it over with."

I bit back the retort that those silver flakes were intriguing to me and called to the chaos that stirred below the surface of my power, instead saying, "I'm not sleeping with Del."

"Why not? I've heard she's quite an experience...just don't tell Jacks or Theo I said that."

I chuckled, my mind questioning what that experience would be like. "And that's the reason I won't touch her."

"Seriously? They scare you?"

"No, well maybe, but they're too close to me. So is Del. She's like another sister—"

"That's bullshit if I ever heard it. Fuck her and get it out of your system."

I wasn't about to tell her that I didn't think I could get Del out of my system, especially after today. Nor would I fuck her the same way I did others. No, if it ever came to that, I'd savor every inch of that delectable body and take her like I craved. I had a notion after her comment today that her rough matched the one I wanted to unleash, the one I had never let go for fear of hurting someone. Pen was the closest I'd come, but what I did to her paled in comparison to what I wanted to do to Del.

Damn, I needed to stop.

There was a twinkle in Pen's eyes, the gold in them moving slightly as she brought herself up and straddled me.

"What are you doing, Pen?"

"Mmm, I think you need a good fuck, and I'm in the mood for one."

"I thought we said we weren't doing this anymore after the last time. Aren't you still pining over Cal?"

She narrowed her eyes at me and dug her pelvis low into my length, which twitched in response. I hadn't realized how hard I'd become thinking about Del. She leaned forward, pushing her breasts against my chest and kissed me. If there was anything about Pen, it was that she was irresistible. I didn't love her, nor did she love me, but our bodies went well together, our powers similar enough that when we did have sex, it was dirty and raw.

"Fuck me, Graham, fuck me like you want to fuck Del."

My dick lurched at the thought, but I wouldn't admit that I would never take her the way I wanted to take Del. She leaned back with a knowing smile on her face, and I knew I'd give in. I was in need of a good release, and as I'd discovered, gods liked screwing other gods for the pleasure we brought each other. There were a few, like my sister, who'd bound themselves to another, but for most of them, they were always playing.

Pen lifted her dress from her body, her bronze skin calling to me as her breasts bounced free of it. My hands moved to hold them, my thumb lingering over her thick nipples which hardened at my touch. Damn, she was right; I needed release and in a bad way. I couldn't help thinking how her breasts were slightly smaller than Del's, which I knew would spill over my hands with their size. Del's nipples looked more delicious to me, and my mouth salivated at the thought of licking them. I really needed to stop thinking of Del, so I pulled Pen to me, letting my tongue swirl around her nipple before I sucked her skin into my mouth, continuing to play with her as my hand drifted down her body.

She moaned loudly. She was a screamer, and sex with her was loud and gritty, the way I wanted it. No attachments, just pleasure. My hand dipped low, running the length of her to feel the moisture that was flooding from her. I penetrated her with my fingers, and the cry she emitted was one that sent my dick pulsing against my pants.

"Fill me," she cried, and I thrust my fingers in deeper, holding her waist as my mouth continued to devour her breast.

She grabbed my head and lifted me from her skin, smashing her lips against mine. Her tongue danced with mine in a kiss that set my desire in a frenzy, my body yearning for her, my dick aching to be inside of her.

"Fuck, Pen," I said against her mouth. Her hands had undone my pants and were stroking my length as I continued to pound into her with my fingers.

"Now, Graham, please," she begged me, and I obliged, removing my fingers and lifting her hips so that she sat above my hardness. She pushed against my hold as I pulled from her lips.

"You want it?"

"By the Creator, yes."

"How badly?" I asked, dropping her so that my tip sat just inside her dampness. I was torturing myself, but I loved hearing her beg.

"Desperately. Take me now." Her breaths were short, and I knew from the slight quiver in her body that she was about to break.

I kissed her again, shoving her body down and thrusting into her. The scream she elicited was stifled by my mouth as I continued to kiss her. She rode me, her body writhing on me with a ferocity that had my climax building quickly, so quickly that I squeezed her waist to slow her, hearing her cry as she tipped her head back.

"You're killing me," she yelled.

"Good. Now come for me," I told her.

"Make me," she teased back.

It was the back and forth that made sex with her so enjoyable, and I wondered momentarily if Del would be as flirty with my dick nestled inside of her.

"Stop thinking of Del when I'm riding you, it's bad manners."

"Shut up, Pen, and come for me."

I picked her up and threw her to the couch, spreading her

legs forcefully, my tongue penetrating her fast and hard so that her body lurched against my mouth. Her climax took a matter of minutes to coax forth. A few flicks of my tongue against her swollen clit followed by some deep licks, left her rocking against my mouth so hard I almost came with the movement. As she broke, her cry filled the room, and I rose, driving into her clenching channel. The feel of her convulsing around me was almost enough to send me crashing. I continued to pound into her as her arms came up to pull my face to hers. She kissed me greedily, and my orgasm rushed me with a force that sent currents through me.

"Damn, you're a bitch," I said against her neck as I recovered.

"I know, but you needed that, and so did I."

I moved from her, watching the rise and fall of her breasts as she tried to catch her breath. My own breathing was still hitching slightly.

"You are a good lover, Graham, and I'm going to miss it when Del finally steals you from me."

"What makes you think she'll steal me?" I asked, grabbing my pants and pulling them on.

She rose and walked to me, her bare breasts calling to be touched again. One perk of being a god was the constant ability to have sex. My body refreshed in a matter of minutes, some-times less, as if it hadn't just been drained. The goddesses were the same way, insatiable.

"Because if she ever gets her hands on you, she won't let you go. Del likes to share, but I don't see her sharing you."

"She likes to share?" I asked with a raise of my brow as her hand stroked against my pants.

"She's been known to, but so have most of us."

"Really? I'm not sure how I feel about that." I thought of having Del and Pen at the same time. It would be insanely pleasurable, but I didn't think I'd be able to take my focus from Del long enough to satisfy another woman or to enjoy any touch but hers. Shit, why was I even thinking such a thing? I needed to stop, and Pen needed to stop putting the thoughts in my head.

I grabbed her hand and pushed her across the room until her back hit the wall. "Stop talking about Del and messing with my head."

"That's not one of my abilities. You're messing with your own head, son of Chaos."

I shoved my body against hers, my dick rising in reaction as she lifted her leg to encircle my back.

"Take me again," she said breathlessly.

I couldn't resist. She had me fired up, and the thought of Del again had sparked a need in me. I didn't know why I couldn't stop thinking about her. I couldn't have her, I wouldn't but I could have Pen and as she worked my length out, I kissed her again. My hands grabbed her breasts and kneaded them, pinching her nipples gently until she was screaming out in pleasure.

She had freed my dick, and her strokes along it were firm and torturous. Grabbing her waist, I lifted her, feeling her line me up so that when I dropped her, my hardness filled her. A cry tore from her as I pounded into her harder than I had earlier, my emotions a mess of want and confusion over Del. Desires I couldn't remove now that I'd set them free, ones I couldn't satisfy so I took what I could from Pen, drilling into her with an intensity that had her climaxing quickly. I wasn't ready for release, so I continued to ravage her until my need had built so high that the release crashed over me in waves that sent my body trembling against her.

When I stilled, I dropped my head against her neck, catching my breath. I'd fucked her harder than I ever had, almost losing hold of my aggression. Del had gotten into my mind, and the things I wanted to do to her were not the things I would let myself do with others, not even Pen. I didn't know why, but instinct told me Del would welcome the full extent of my aggression. Her comment about liking it rough had awakened something in me, a part of me to which only she called.

"By the Creator, when you finally take her, it's going to tear the realms apart."

"I won't take her," I said. "I can't."

I drew back, dropping her legs and moving from her, but she grabbed my face. "You can't? Or you won't? You deserve to find someone, Graham. Chaos runs through you, and it's the perfect match to the insanity that runs through her. The calm you have to turn the day is what perfects that match. Del needs someone who can counter her but not contain her."

"And you think I'm that person?"

"I know you are."

"Why would you tell me that after we just had sex?"

She pulled me to her and kissed me again, hungry and powerful, before she pushed me away.

"Because you need to hear it. Now, get dressed and tell me what we're having for dinner tonight. I'm starving."

She sauntered over to where her dress lay and bent to pick it up. Her round ass was up in the air, inviting me to pound into it. I ran my hand through my hair, trying to calm that rising need. No matter how many times I relieved it with Pen, it would return because it was Del who fed that need. And only Del would satisfy it.

"You're too much, you know that?" I said, pinching her ass and grabbing my shirt.

"As are you."

She flopped on the sofa again. "I've decided to refrain from the tournament, as has Cal."

"What tournament?"

She sat up. "You don't know?"

"I have no idea what you're talking about," I replied, pulling my shirt over my head.

"The tournament is a series of challenges that the Elder gods design for the second generation, the cousins. All those who are not bound participate. It's fun, it's dirty, it's often sexy."

"What kind of tournament?" I wasn't really following how tournament, dirty, and sexy all fit together.

"It's a challenge of obstacles designed to test the younger generation. We're paired up, and each team must pass through the different stages that span all of the kingdoms."

"Huh, and what does that have to do with sex?"

Her eyes glinted. "Oh, that's where it gets fun and why the bonded couples don't participate. Often the pairs will take extra time to play with each other and sometimes will play with other couples. The Elders paired me with Jacks once, and let me tell you that man can pleasure—"

My glare stopped her. The last thing I wanted to hear about was her escapades with my brother-in-law before he met my sister.

She shot me a look. "You do realize he's centuries older than either of you and very experienced, as are most of us. You and your sister are babies. Although I will say, you fuck like you've been having sex for centuries."

"Still don't want to hear about what he did before Claire."

"Fine. Anyway, it's been known to happen during the challenge."

I sat and leaned back, thinking about what she'd said. I'd have to participate, I had no doubt. "Do we know who we're paired with?"

"No, the Elders decide. I think they have fun mixing us up, forcing us to work with those cousins we don't usually spend time with. It adds to the spice and the challenge."

"Forces us all to get along," I said. There were many goddesses I hadn't really gotten to know, plenty that I hadn't slept with. Only Pen and a few others had swayed me so far. "When is it?"

"In two days. But Graham, they are grueling. The extracurricular activity gives us a reprieve but make no mistake, you'll get hurt, and you'll bleed."

"Bleed? We're gods."

She sat up, her face turning serious. "Some think the Elders designed the tournament as a precursor for the trials they set in place when we take over another's kingdom or step into a new position. Like when I took your mother's place. Just like the ultimate Trial, we're vulnerable and mortal."

I knew my eyes had grown wide. I was aware of the trials, tests that stripped a god's immortality and tested him to his limits. The ultimate Trial of the Gods was so grueling that it was rarely invoked, and those who were tested didn't often pass. Jackson had been tested with it to claim the Nightmare Kingdom, and from what he had divulged, it had almost killed him. The idea that the Elders subjected their own children to mortality in such a dangerous tournament confounded me.

Pen rose and patted my leg. "You'll be fine. We've never lost one of us. Yet."

Her words didn't reassure me. I watched her walk from the hall, even the sway of her perfect hips couldn't ease the tension that sat in my body. That tension accompanied a worrying notion that this tournament would change everything for me.

CHAPTER 4
DEL

S liding my hands down the tight mortal dress I'd donned, I walked into the bar. It smelled of mortals and that foul ale they drank. But I wasn't here for the ale. I met the eyes of a man in the far corner, drinking alone at a table. His eyes took in the length of me like a hungry wolf targeting his prey. He had no idea he was luring an even deadlier hunter with his invitation. Licking my lips, I draped my fingers across the cleavage the dress had given me, purposely letting them linger.

I hadn't come to the bar for prey, but I'd take him since he was eager for me to feed upon him. There was something else I'd come in search of, and so my prey would have to wait. I had no doubt he would, seeing his hand reach down to adjust himself. Pulling my eyes away, I searched the length of the bar until I found Graham hunkering over a mug of the brown liquid that had turned my stomach the one time I'd tried it. What the mortals referred to as ale was more like piss-water. It was nothing like our ale, and I doubted any mortal could tolerate more than a few sips of what the gods drank.

I studied Graham as I walked toward him. His thick auburn

hair had fallen forward to his forehead. His eyes, cast downward, were focused on his glass. There was tension in his muscles, and I couldn't help imagining the strength of them holding me or the feel of those large hands on my small waist. He was all brute force and aggression, and I knew without a doubt that he would leave marks when he finally broke and took me.

The thought left dampness between my legs. Not that the reaction was anything new around him. He did something to me that stimulated my delusions and my body.

"Why do you continue to frequent the mortal world when you have a paradise at your fingertips?" I asked him, hopping on the stool next to his.

He turned his eyes to me, and for a moment, I lost myself in the brown of them. My pulse quickened at how they followed the curve of my body, lingering on my legs before shifting back to meet mine. The hunger behind those beautiful brown eyes almost broke me.

"Why are you dressed like a hooker, Del?" he said, the corner of his lips curving deliciously.

"I figured I'd dress the part. You know, mortal female in a bar."

His brow raised before he glanced around the bar. "Well, you picked the wrong costume. As you'll notice, the females here are dressed in clothing that doesn't leave all their parts hanging out. Do Theo and Jackson know you leave the realms dressed like this?"

"You're not my big brother, nor is Jackson, so I really don't care what either of you thinks."

"And Theo?"

"Would likely drown me in pain before forcing me to change. But he's not here to do that."

"And what if I do?"

I couldn't help my laugh. "Will you drown me in morning

sun rays, Graham? Or perhaps surround me in dusk until I can't breathe?" The thought of him doing either had the dampness that he'd caused increasing, and I squeezed my thighs inadvertently. I doubted he had any clue about the effect he had on me on any given day. He drove me mad, and I was already mad. I leaned closer to him. "I told you I like it rough. I invite your pain."

He stayed quiet, his eyes studying me with an intense look that had my body tingling. The moment passed as he turned to stare down at his glass, but I noted the tight clench he had on the handle, the tiny fractures beginning to form from the force of his grip. I couldn't help but imagine that grip around my waist as I had earlier, wondering how deep the bruise would be. The thought wouldn't flee until my mind questioned if he gripped Pen's waist that tight when he was fucking her. Jealousy rippled through me like a current I couldn't ignore, and I clenched my fists to keep it at bay. I'd wanted to strangle her when she'd come to see me this morning, flaunting the details of how satisfied Graham had left her.

Trying not to let my jealousy show, I laced my voice with as much seduction as I could, saying, "I heard you had quite the time with Pen last night."

His head whipped toward mine, his eyes a mix of anger and something else. Was it guilt I saw there? Or was I grasping?

"Where did you hear that?"

I let my finger drift through the line of condensation that ran from his drink, taking my time to answer him. "Pen likes to share what you do to her. I hear your tongue is quite erotic."

His glare narrowed, and I couldn't help but send a wisp of my power out to touch his thoughts, sneaking in below the anger to find the thought for which I'd been looking. The thought that he'd wished it had been me, that his tongue had been against my flesh instead of hers. I couldn't help the smile as I drew away.

"I'll have to have a talk with Pen about her own tongue. I don't particularly like her sharing those details."

I leaned into him, loving the strength of his arm against my breasts, and wishing he'd touch them as he'd touched hers, as I now knew he'd wanted to do.

"Why are you here, Del?" he asked grumpily, the tension in his muscles growing beneath my chest. The handle fractured, small pieces of it falling to the bar as his hand clenched around the fragments.

I sighed. He was stubborn and too loyal to my brothers to give me what I needed. But as he turned his eyes back to mine I wasn't certain I knew what I needed anymore. When I'd first met him, I'd only ever wanted to break him, to steal him from his mortal wife and show him what a goddess could do. But now, after knowing him, discovering his undying faithfulness, how hard he loved, and how good of a man he was, I wasn't so certain that was all I wanted.

But what I suspected I wanted wasn't something for me. I was Delusion, someone to revel in madness with, not someone to own, to love. I was either a man's dream or his nightmare, but I was not his to keep. It went against my nature, against the insanity that stirred in my blood and ruled me.

I sat back, pulling the top of my dress up, suddenly self-conscious under the weight of his stare.

"I hear you're stuck with me during the tournament," I said quietly, my eyes cast from his, and feeling suddenly unsure of myself.

"You mean you're stuck with me," he joked, and I glanced back at him.

The gold in his eyes shimmered, and his lips curved into the perfect smile, soft and kissable. So inviting that I almost leaned in and kissed him. The thought was there but mixed with the other thoughts.

"So I am. I do believe I have Jacks to thank for that, although I'm certain Claire added her two cents. Ensuring I'd have a babysitter to stifle my enjoyment of the event."

"Likely. So I get to play babysitter. Should be fun trying to rein you in." He said it playfully, sending me a wink that had my heart purring.

"You know you can't rein me in, Graham. I'm Delusion, I'm meant to be free," I returned teasingly.

His reply came as a quiet whisper, surprising me. "I'd never want to rein you in, Del."

My breath caught because I knew it was the truth. If this man ever loved me, he would love me for who I was, all of me. The thought was almost too much to handle. No man had loved me, no man had dared tame what lay within me. For him, I would willingly tame it, but he would never ask me to.

"You have too much fun in your madness to stifle that," he said, his tone changing as if he realized what he'd said. "I will, however, make sure that fun doesn't get you in trouble."

"So, no orgies this time?" I cooed.

His eyes widened. "You do that?"

The question was innocent and curious, and it stoked the childlike part of me.

"On occasion. Last tournament, I may have indulged for a few days before we turned back to the challenge."

He continued to stare at me until he shook his head. "Not on my watch. No orgies, and no sex." I gave him my best pout, but he ignored it. "If I'm stuck on babysitter duty, you're going to obey my command."

A chill ran through me at the thought. "I don't like to be commanded, it's not usually my thing."

He gave me a coy smile. "I'm not the commanding type, it's more a threat."

My breath hitched because I knew how he liked it. I'd heard

from Pen about his force. The bitch never shut up about it. I wanted to feel that force, to know what he'd do to my body and how my aggression would match his.

"Then we'll get along just fine because I like it rough and hard," I said against his ear.

"So you've told me." I could feel his pulse quicken and sense the image that had entered his mind.

"Well, since you'll be stifling my sex drive for a few days, I plan to get one more good fuck in to hold me over."

His eyes went wide again, a spark of hunger in them.

"I have prey in the corner, and I'm going to give him quite the ride."

If looks could kill, the look Graham shot the man would have left him for dead. He grabbed my wrist before I could rise.

"Oh, I do like that grip you have, Graham. Shame you won't use it on me."

That spark hit his eye again before he shook it off. "You're not going near that man. He looks like a perve. I can sense the foulness in him."

"Exactly. But I plan to get a little pleasure before I get to the fun part." I peeled his fingers from my wrist, adjusted my dress so my breasts were more exposed, and hiked the bottom up more. His eyes watched each move with that ravenous look that had been there earlier.

"You get to have fun with Pen, I get to have my own fun," I whispered into his ear, leaning close enough for his hand to touch my thigh. It sat there as I hung against his neck then slowly moved from my skin but not before his fingers teased just above my hemline. The feel of them caused a flood of arousal that threatened to break me.

"Shit, Del," he murmured.

I pulled away, unsure of the look in his eyes before I turned from him and sashayed to my prey. I didn't want to look back, knowing my resolve would fade, and I'd be content to simply sit with Graham the rest of the day as I'd done the previous day. The thought of him taking Pen after we'd spent the day with each other flickered in my mind, and my resolve grew. Two could play at that game, and my delusions were screaming for me to free them.

I leaned over the table so that my breasts hung before the man's face. His eyes were predatory. He was going to be a fun one. I could sense the insanity within him, the devious past, his sins.

"I'm seriously wet right now, and I need someone to sink his dick into me. Wanna play?"

His eyes lit with excitement, and I didn't have to look to know my words had woken his erection.

"Gladly, but won't your date mind if I take his pussy?"

Oh, he was a dirty one. I couldn't wait to have him pound thoughts of Graham from me.

I glanced back at Graham who was scowling at us.

"He's not my date, he's my brother, and he holds no sway over what I do with my pussy."

The flash of need in his eyes was enough to make me giddy. I loved the hunt, but I also loved the capture, and this man had been easy to capture.

"Well in that case, I will devour every inch of that gorgeous body."

"I bet you will."

He rose, and I led him out of the bar, throwing Graham a wink as I walked by him, dragging the man's hand behind me.

"Your place or mine?" he asked.

"Neither," I answered, shoving him into the closest alleyway.

"You are a nasty one, aren't you?" he said, pressing me against the brick.

"Fuck me," I cried out, wanting someone to fill me, the teasing with Graham driving me almost to madness.

"Gladly." He hiked my skirt up and roughly plunged his fingers into me. There was no softness there, just a need to hurt me, and I reveled in the pain of it.

"Fuck, you're soaked," he said. Of course I was,—it was guaranteed anytime I was with Graham. This man would reap the rewards, thinking he'd been the cause.

Pulling his fingers free, he ripped his pants open. His dick burst out as he tore my dress down with his other hand, pawing at my breasts with squeezes aimed to abuse.

I knew what this man liked, the brutality he brought to his encounters, ones that weren't always consensual. I let him bring it to me. His nails dug into my skin as he pinched my nipples, watching my face for the reflection of anguish he was expecting. He didn't know how much I enjoyed the pain, how it brought me to life, the insanity in me reveling in it. I grabbed his shirt and kissed him with a thirst that he matched before he spread my legs and penetrated me.

From the force of his thrusts, one would have thought he was enormous, but he was nothing more than average. I'd been sleeping with gods for centuries; no mortal ever lived up to their abilities or their size.

"Yes, fuck me harder," I said as he pounded into me.

He obliged, ramming into me with a fury as if every thrust would break me. It wouldn't. I needed more to meet that need— more pain, more torment to feed me. My mind filled with what I wanted Graham to do to me, and the thought sent a moan from my mouth, one he assumed was for him.

"You like it hard, don't you?" he grunted in my ear.

I lifted my legs to take him further and dug my fingers into his shoulders in answer. Groaning, he picked me up, the brick scratching my back and bringing pain that sent currents of pleasure through me. My delusions swirled within me in response.

Not yet, I told them.

A shock of ecstasy tore through me when his hand wrapped around my neck, tightening as he choked me. I screamed out in pleasure, his pace quickening in reaction. I knew what got this man off, his stimulant was the pain he inflicted. But he'd never had someone who enjoyed the pain, who invited it like I did. He dropped his face into my breasts, biting at them roughly, breaking the skin as I turned my head. My eyes met Graham's. He was standing at the end of the alley, his arms crossed, anger etched in his expression. His jaw was clenched so tight, it was a wonder his teeth hadn't broken. He watched, those brown eyes narrowed, but said nothing. I dropped my head back and gave him a sexy smile before I turned my attention to the man who was currently ravaging me and about to fill me.

Let him watch, let him be jealous, he'd taken Pen last night when he should have taken me. The man's grip tightened on my neck, his lips smashing against mine, and I sensed his climax building. The brutality of his actions called to the deepest of my insanity, the delusions ready to strike.

He cried out with his release, pumping into me until he'd finished, and he released my neck.

"You like it that way," I whispered.

"Fuck yes." He kissed me roughly again, squeezing my breast hard, my moan the only answer I gave him. "Will you scream for me now?" he asked, and I knew his intentions.

I glanced to see Graham stoic and on guard still, his expression unchanging. Well, it was time for him to watch and learn what I truly was and what I fed from.

I licked the man's ear, murmuring against it, "No one will ever scream for you again." His hand dropped from my neck, his face coming back to mine.

"You're gonna—" he started, but my power silenced him. I'd given him a false sense of control, but I was the one who called the shots. The only one with the power.

"Shhh, no more will you thrive on their pain." My voice was a demented whisper that poisoned the mind, twisting it to my whim.

He backed away, but my delusions had already slipped from my hold, surrounding him. "For each scream you induce, your own will escape. For the pain you inflict, your own will be twofold."

He had dropped to the ground now, his back pressed against the alley wall as far as it could be. I dropped before him, predatory and in my element as my power swirled, licking against my skin and through my hair.

"You will know all you have done, the damage you have wrought, the lives you have destroyed as their memories play through your head, never stopping until there is no escape but to embrace the insanity I invoke. At every corner, you will see them. With each step you take, they will follow you, haunting you with the truth of your existence, the wickedness, the evil you have brought to your victims."

I released the deluge of my delusions, letting them feed on him. The rush of it coursed through me like an inferno, sending me to my knees. It was ecstasy that sent me over the edge as the insanity fed back to me, my climax rising then drowning me. The cry that fell from my lips echoed through the quiet of the alley until my body calmed, and I called my power back, letting the silky feel of my delusions settle back into my skin.

I dropped my hands to the ground, catching my breath. After letting the quivers of my body calm, I rose. The man who'd given me such brutal pleasure and then fed me to the point of orgasm was huddled in a ball, shaking, his mind ravaged. The faces and the pain of his victims would ravage it further until his mind shattered so far that he would die. A wicked punishment for a wicked man.

Pulling my skirt down and adjusting the top of my dress, I walked toward Graham. His expression was hard to read, his eyes guarded, eyes that had watched me at my most powerful but also my most vulnerable. It was the side of me few witnessed, and even fewer loved me for. I was Delusion, a force that could mangle a man's brain within seconds, one who fed on the terrors my brother invoked, the pain Theo elicited. I was pure madness and I lived for it.

"You climax to their punishment?" he asked as I walked by, a note of curiosity to his voice.

I glanced back at him, knowing the silver slivers in my eyes were still frenzied, the aftershocks of my orgasm still swimming through me.

"It's amazing when my delusions are set free."

"You ever do that when you're having sex?" he asked.

Amused, I gave him a coy smile. "Why, Graham, curious are we?"

"Perhaps."

"No, I never have. I've never had anyone who could take my power, my delusions. The insanity I weave is too much for anyone to handle."

I turned away but not before the wisp of power I'd freed caught his thought. *I could handle them.*

I couldn't help the smile that formed as I continued to walk from him. "Until tomorrow, Graham. Try not to dream too much about me tonight and don't fuck Pen to fill my place again. She doesn't hold a flame to my inferno."

I shifted away, disappearing and leaving him, knowing his eyes were still lingering along with his thoughts long after I'd left him.

CHAPTER 5

GRAHAM

D el had climaxed as she'd tortured the man she'd let ravage her in the alley. I'd never seen anything so tantalizing. My mind couldn't grasp the myriad of emotions that were berating it. I was a mix of horrified and stimulated, and I was seriously thinking about jerking myself off to ease the massive hard-on I'd developed at watching it all unfold. She'd been magnificent.

The entire time she'd sat next to me at the bar in that dress that left nothing to the imagination, I'd fought the need to grab her by the neck and kiss her. And when she'd whispered in my ear, making sure to position her leg against my hand, I'd nearly lost it. Thoughts of slamming her onto the bar and fucking her had flooded my brain. My hand had drifted along the softness of her thigh, and I'd wanted more than anything to reach up and plunge my fingers into the dampness I had no doubt was there waiting for me to take.

But I'd resisted, once again, watching as she'd flirted with that perverted mortal in what I knew was punishment for me choosing Pen over her. I'd trained my eyes on them as they'd left, gritting my teeth at seeing the guy's hand on her ass. The way he'd squeezed it had left me boiling. I'd wanted to rip his hand off before I tore his eyes out for even daring to look at her, let alone touch her.

Instead, I'd followed them, worried about Del when I shouldn't have been. It confounded me that I had this need to protect a goddess who was centuries older than me, who from what I'd just witnessed was terrifying in her own right. The bulge in my pants was aching, my eyes still on the space where she'd disappeared. Her words played through my mind. Telling me not to take Pen in her place. She'd known, and damn Pen for telling her what we'd done. From what it sounded like, she'd been telling her every time I'd taken her. I'd be having a serious talk with her when I returned. Well, when I could walk again.

Shit, my hard-on was raging. If I saw Pen, she'd say she needed to relieve it, and I'd give in with the need I had for Del that was pulsing through me. Del's words were like chains on me. She hadn't used her power, but the command was there: don't touch another woman. The claim she had made on me. But she couldn't claim me. I wouldn't touch her. I couldn't no matter how much I wanted to. No matter how she'd turned me on.

Watching her had been glorious. The way her power seeped from her and ravaged the man who remained behind me, whimpering where she'd left him. She was incredible. What she'd done should have traumatized me, but watching her in action had called to something in me, the chaos that was the weaker of my abilities.

Watching him touch her had called to a different side of me, one that had wanted to beat the shit out of him for daring to touch her. To touch what was mine.

"Damn, Graham, you're losing it," I said, rubbing my hands across my face and cursing the erection that still bulged.

I returned to my kingdom, heading straight to my room,

knowing I couldn't risk seeing Pen and taking her to relieve my need. Wanting for some blasted reason to honor Del's request. I leaned against the wall, my hands going to my length as my mind went back to the moment I'd watched her climax. The quake of those gorgeous legs, the nipples that had pushed so far from her still exposed breasts, the way her breathing had increased before her cry had escaped. The power that had swirled around her at that moment. It was too much, and I freed my dick, knowing I needed release. Knowing I wouldn't be able to think the rest of the night if I didn't relieve it, let alone be ready to face her again in the morning for the tournament.

I let images of her fill my mind and, with each stroke, they brought me closer until my climax hit me. Deep and powerful, it tore through me like a storm as I spilled over the floor. As the residual tremors faded, I rested my head against the wall and wondered why I was tormenting myself so. Why hadn't I just taken her and fucked her against that alley wall, ignoring the fact that she was filled with another man's cum?

Loyalty to her brothers, especially now. Theo had come to me, telling me of the pairings and how Jackson had purposely paired her with me. To protect her, to keep her in check and away from fucking the other gods. It had been hard to hide my irritation at the thought of her with another god. I knew she was far from innocent, but I didn't like to think of another god touching her and doing the things I wanted to do to her.

Jackson had also told me that Claire's chaos had been harder to control lately, that something was bothering her, something even he couldn't simmer. It had them both on edge, which was another reason they'd paired me with Del. I wondered briefly if whatever was affecting Claire was the reason my chaos had been stirring. It rarely did, remaining as more of an undercurrent to my other abilities. I had thought perhaps it was this sudden uncontrollable urge I had for Del, the one that had sprung up after years of burying it. But now I wasn't so certain that it hadn't been the chaos that had woken the urge for her. That part of me that lay below the surface of my power, the part of me that touched her insanity.

That left the question of what had stirred my chaos. Whatever was agitating it was bothering Claire's power so that even Jackson, who was the only man who could keep it in check, couldn't contain it. That thought was one that made every part of my power tense with worry.

MY SLEEP WAS RESTLESS, the release I'd given myself had helped, but the impending tournament and the interaction with Del had kept me tossing and turning. Del continued to stay on my mind as I prepared to leave that morning. It was so bad that I jerked myself off once more before I left, knowing if I didn't have release, I wouldn't be able to resist her this time. I needed to keep my distance from her, but there wouldn't be a way since she'd been paired with me. The alternative wasn't any better. If she'd been paired with another god, I'd be stuck imagining that god fucking her like I wanted to. Although I don't know if any other god could match the aggression I would bring to her if I ever gave in and took her. And I knew if paired with a different goddess, my mind would still be on Del. If Pen couldn't take her from my mind, another wouldn't.

I ran my hand through my hair and tried to clear thoughts of her from my mind for the hundredth time since I'd left my kingdom that morning. Nothing helped and the fact that I kept thinking of her as mine when she wasn't didn't help.

I looked around the hall where the gods met, making decisions that affected the lives of the clueless mortals below. The Elders were all seated on their thrones. The cousins who were bound and had chosen to abstain from the tournament sat alongside them. Claire gave me a wave, and Jackson sent me an expressionless nod. It still seemed funny to see Claire as a goddess even after all these years. She was still my little sister, the one I'd kept safe, and who Jackson now kept safe.

She leaned into Jackson, whose arm was tucked protectively around her. I could feel her chaos pulsing from her as it called to my own, and I furrowed my brow at it. Jackson was right—it was restless in her. It might have been the tournament, but with Jackson's concern, it seemed more likely that it was something we couldn't see. The idea was one that didn't sit well with me. Unknowns were dangerous, and Claire had seen enough danger in her life. We both had.

My thoughts were interrupted when I spotted Del from my periphery. She was hard to miss. She had piled her blonde hair atop her head in a messy yet still stunning way. I'd never seen her hair up, and it revealed the slender neck below that dipped to the revealing shirt she wore. It was a neck made for grasping. The image of the mortal choking her slipped its way into my mind. She'd enjoyed it, her cry clawing at the depths of my need for her. She hadn't been teasing when she'd told me she liked it rough, and my hands clenched at the thought of testing her with how hard I wanted to take her. I could almost feel the delicate skin beneath my hold.

Stop it, Graham. I couldn't let her or even her brothers see how turned on the thought had me. It wouldn't be hard to spot my arousal if I didn't control my mind.

I should have looked away from her, but instead, I perused her attire, devouring every inch of her with my eyes. We were all dressed similar, the gods in black pants and leather vests, our arms left bare. The goddesses dressed in tight pants with matching leather vests that plunged down their chests. We looked like we were heading into some fantasy training mission out of a movie.

Del had changed her gear to fit her personality, and I couldn't help but smile at it, my dick twitching in reaction. The two sides of her personality were clear in it. She'd ripped the bottom of the vest off so that her stomach was free, the ivory skin sitting there waiting to be touched. Her pants hung lower on her waist than the others, her perfect belly button showing and calling for me to lick it. She wore a pink shirt below the vest with cap sleeves that brought out her childlike nature, opposing the sexy swell of her breasts that could be seen from where she'd ripped the vest to a lower dip. I wanted to slip my fingers into that dip and let them feel the voluptuous breasts that were hidden below. Who was I kidding? What I wanted was to rip that shirt from her and devour them. I'd had a glimpse of them yesterday, and they had done nothing but increase my appetite for them.

She was alluring, and as her green eyes met mine, her lush lips curved to a knowing grin. Somehow I'd become her prey, easily climbing into her web and wanting her to devour me. I didn't know how I was going to make it through this tournament without falling for her spell, one I wanted to let touch every part of me, to take me and own me.

Fuck, what had come over me?

"I tried to talk her out of the smutty look, but it's Del," Theo said, coming behind me. I yanked my eyes from Del and hoped he didn't notice the bulge she'd caused in my pants.

"Yeah, it is. No arguing with her when her mind is made up." As I said the words, I recognized the truth in them. She wanted me, she had since the first time we'd met. And I wanted her, with a need that had now overtaken all of my senses. Who was I to deny her? To deny myself?

Theo's hand on my shoulder brought me back, reminding me

of why I was denying myself. "Did you notice Claire's eyes?" he asked, and I looked back at my sister. She was close to Jackson; their faces lowered in a whisper. It was an intimate moment, but there were rarely any moments that weren't intimate with them. They couldn't resist being close to each other. She looked up and caught my gaze. The gold rims of her eyes were thick today, spreading into the brown, the flickers of gold that sparkled within doing so at a rapid pace.

"Yeah, what is that?"

"Her power is pressing to be released. Chaos is yearning to be freed, and that's never a good thing."

I glanced back at Del, seeing the slivers in her eyes that were more active than they usually were. "As is Delusion."

"Noticed that, huh? Yeah, Del's particularly worked up today. I thought maybe it was the tournament, but the slivers are moving in ways they only do when her insanity is being taunted. She needs to release it, or the others will have her to worry about out there, too."

"She released it yesterday."

"What?" he asked, his eyes concerned.

"I watched her ravage a guy in the mortal world yesterday. Quite the scene, and trust me, she was very sated."

He raised a brow. "Should I be concerned that you seem pleased at having watched my sister release her power and do what I know follows when she's in her element?"

"You mean the orgasm?"

His eyes narrowed. "Not many see that part of her. Keep it to yourself. The other gods know she's volatile, that she prefers to feed up close. They don't know that she does it for release. They already see her as a freak. They fear her on a level that's different than how they fear your sister. One that could easily tip them to condemn her."

"Secret's safe with me. I promised to protect her, and I will."

"Good. Because Del is too fragile to be hurt. One wrong move and mortality will suffer as they have never suffered. If she loses it, there will be no bringing her back, and the others will banish her in their fear. Our realm will suffer, and Jacks and I will weaken. If Jacks is weakened, the nightmares lose their power."

I stared at him, knowing my jaw had dropped at the power of his statement. The idea that their entire realm could collapse if just one of them faltered was unfathomable.

"The three of us balance each other, Graham. Siblings do that, just like you and Claire do. Without Del, Jacks is vulnerable as is our standing in the realms."

My mind was hurtling, never having understood the delicate balance the three of them had, the line he and Jackson walked to keep Del stable so that their kingdom didn't collapse. I looked over at Del, watching as she talked with Vanity, her green eyes sparkling with excitement, the slivers flitting around. No wonder they wanted her protected; she was vulnerable in ways I'd never seen, only seeing the strength in her powers, in her presence, the occasional childlike ways that made her frightening when set against the insanity she held.

Death's voice broke my thoughts, pulling my eyes from her to the Elders.

"Keep her safe and in check," Theo said. "I don't know what's coming, but if both she and Claire are agitated, it can't be a good thing, and I guarantee it's not something the Elders have brewed up for us."

He walked away before I could respond, leaving me with the stark reality that not only did I need to keep Del safe from herself, I needed to keep her protected from some unseen threat that had yet to reveal itself.

CHAPTER 6
DEL

B y the Creator did Graham look sexy in that leather vest. I wanted to eat him up and steal him from the glances of the other goddesses. I was tired of sharing him, of having them taste what I wanted to taste, what I'd patiently waited for him to give me.

His eyes fell on me, and I saw it there, that same hunger that I'd seen the prior days. His hold on that need for me, the one he kept restrained, was breaking. It was only a matter of time and I'd have him. I watched as his eyes took me in, trailing over every part of my body like hands touching my skin. My delusions stirred, my power aching for release, tempted by his thought the prior day that he could handle them. How they longed for someone who could.

Theo drew Graham's attention from me, and my breath returned. Theo had seemed especially on edge this morning, standing guard while we waited for the summons to call us to the tournament. He'd griped about my tweaks to the uniform, but I'd ignored him. I didn't care what the Elders thought or what he thought for that matter. The uniform was bland, and it needed a touch of me to make it lie comfortably on my skin. My delusions were unusually distracting today, and the last thing I needed was an uncomfortable outfit to trigger my power, freeing the insanity I held close to me.

My aunt, Death began to speak, signaling the beginning of the tournament. There was excitement in the air. I pulled at it, bringing it against my skin and letting it feed me. The others began moving to their partners, but I waited for Graham, meeting his eyes again. He crossed his arms, something that only made me long for those accentuated arm muscles to bring me to ecstasy. He expected me to come to him, but I held my stance, letting him know I wasn't budging. His lips twitched as he forced the smile back that I knew was building; I could see it in the twinkle of those luscious brown eyes. The gold in them was more prominent today, flickering within the brown in a mesmerizing way.

He moved his hand and brought his finger out, gesturing with it for me to move to him. Sly demon. He wanted to control me, the way Jacks controlled Claire. But I wasn't chaos; I was the force that fed chaos, that instigated it.

He stared me down. "Any day now, Del," Jacks' voice came from the thrones. Damn him and his commands.

I turned my eyes to him. His look was hard, his gaze unwavering, and I knew then that he was not in a playful mood. Still, I teased him. "I told you before, I'm not Claire, Jacks. You may command her, but I don't have to heed your commands."

His eyes became daggers, but mine were drawn to Claire. The gold in her eyes was flittering as mine would. Streams of it were coming from the gold that lined them. It was startling and uncharacteristic. That's why Jacks was being so stern, he was worried. I drew my eyes from hers and crinkled mine when they met Jacks' again. He wore his worry like a cloak. His love for

Claire was palpable as was his fear that anything would happen to her again.

I stuck my tongue out at him and skipped over to Graham, knowing Jacks wasn't in the mood to be pushed. Jacks and I were close enough for me to read him easily, to understand his moods, ones that were usually brooding. He was someone to take seriously most days, but when his mood was heavy like it was now, he was to be greatly feared.

I stopped in front of Graham, bouncing on my toes and reveling in the way his eyes followed the corresponding bounce of my breasts.

"'Bout time you got over here," he grumbled, his gaze moving to Jacks. He gave a nod of his head before his lips pursed as his eyes fell to Claire. So, he had noticed as well.

"Ready to have some fun with me?" I asked, pulling his gaze back to mine.

My knees went weak from the intensity in that gaze. He studied me, following the flitters of my slivers, his brow creasing further before he gave me a gruff, "If I must." The gruffness did nothing but tempt my arousal, and I bit my lip at the sensation of it as it stirred between my legs. His eyes fell to my lip, and I saw the twitch in his jaw. Not one to let him off easily, I slowly released my bottom lip, dragging my teeth over it in an exaggerated fashion. I left my mouth parted before I swept my tongue over my top lip. That jaw tightened, and his eyes flew back to mine. I saw the longing there before he scrunched his eyes at me to hide it.

The horns blew to announce the start of the tournament, drawing his focus from me. Magic coated the hall. The Elders would remain here, sequestered for the entirety of the tourna- ment so that none could give advantage to their own children or siblings.

"Let the games begin!" my aunt, goddess of heart, shouted as the floor shimmered and the hall disappeared.

I grabbed hold of Graham's arm as we shifted to the first kingdom. The hard terrain below my feet informed me we were in Death's realm before my vision settled.

"What the hell?" Graham asked. I found it cute that he still used mortal terms, even after finding that the mortal world was not governed by the gods with which he'd been raised.

"Death's kingdom," I said, looking around at the darkness that surrounded us.

It wouldn't all be darkness. Her realm was a blend of her two sides, death living in the darkness, life in the light. Looking down from her castle, one could see the splashes of light that sporadically covered her realm, but from this vantage point, there was nothing but night.

"Great. So we need to make our way through this kingdom? That's our challenge? The first ones out take the prize?" Graham asked.

I raised my brow to him. "Were you too busy fucking Pen to find out what you were in for?"

He gave me a look of irritation. "No."

"Huh." I turned and pressed closer to him, sniffing along his neck. Pushing me away, he gave a low growl that had my legs clenching. "You smell too satisfied to have stayed from her bed." Jealousy clawed at me. "Did she *come* for you?"

His jaw was clenched, and he looked for a moment like he wanted to smack me. Mmm, I would have welcomed it. I had a distinct feeling roughness from him would set me ablaze the way no other man had.

"I said, I didn't fuck her. Now back off."

I tilted my head, evaluating him. "Who did you fuck last night in place of me, Graham?"

I was pushing it, but I wanted to. I wanted to know who he'd

47

replaced me with. It irritated me that he hadn't heeded my request, that he'd once again shared a night of passion with someone other than me.

"Who did you fuck yesterday, Del?" he snapped back. "Because I distinctly remember watching you fuck a stranger in an alley before you came, very sensually, to his unraveling."

He pushed me aside and walked away, leaving me to wonder at how angry he sounded at my act. And questioning how this had turned around on me.

Dammit. How had he taken the upper hand from me?

"Where are the others?" he asked gruffly as if the prior conversation hadn't happened.

"They're spread throughout the kingdom. The Elders don't like us together, keeps it more challenging if they separate the pairs."

"Otherwise you fuck in groups." The snarl that accompanied the words had me dripping, and I was tempted to strip and throw myself at him to satisfy the burning that sat in my belly.

"No," I replied, pulling myself together. "That usually doesn't happen until later in the challenge. The first few days, we're usually just in our pairs."

His head spun to me. "Few days?"

"Good Creator, if you'd gotten your head out of Pen's pussy for two seconds, you'd know this lasts for days."

His nostrils flared and he grabbed my arms, stepping close. So close I could feel his breath against me. "I did not touch Pen last night. I took care of myself if you really need to know. Now, stop talking like a dirty whore and explain what you mean."

Damn, he'd jerked himself off instead of seeking her out like I'd thought he would. My heart pounded, and I wondered if he heard it. "You know, I would have willingly helped with that. I'm sure I feel better than your hand, especially right now."

The flicker of desire that swept through his eyes almost

melted me, and I had to force my legs to continue holding me up. Creator, how I wanted this man to take me and make me his.

"Besides, I hear my dirty talk drives men crazy."

There was the flare in his nostrils again, matched with the clench of his jaw. His grip on my arms softened, and I missed the pain it had brought. Those rich eyes searched mine, and we stayed there, looking into each other's eyes, his face drawing closer to mine for just a second before he narrowed his eyes and let me go.

"Why does it take days?"

And just like that, the moment was gone, as if it hadn't happened. I wanted to stomp my feet and yell for him to act on his desires, but he wouldn't. He was too stubborn, too determined to deny me.

Sighing, I answered, "Because each realm has its own challenges that we must face. Making our way through each can take two days, add on the vast number of kingdoms and you have multiple days. We must travel on foot or on beast. Our ability to travel by magic is dampened like our immortality."

"Shit, I thought you said this was fun."

I gave him my impish smile. "I never said what kind of fun it was."

He didn't respond, turning instead and walking forward. "Come on. Let's get this over with."

I mumbled a few expletives, and he jerked his head around to give me a scolding look. I was certain he didn't know it did nothing but soak me more. It was that fierce broodiness I craved. Following reluctantly, I tried not to watch the movements of his ass and those thick leg muscles that I could see against his pants with each step he took, not to mention those arms that looked like they could bring me to climax with the mere squeeze of them around my body. Images of the pain they could give me tormented me so that I was having trouble walking I'd grown so wet.

I could see the light of a patch of life ahead of us. They'd dropped us in the middle of Death's kingdom, which meant fewer obstacles. The light patches were always the pleasant part of the kingdom, so I picked up my pace, walking ahead of Graham.

"Tired of me already?" he grumbled.

"Never," I replied as I heard a rumble that hadn't come from him.

It was one I should have recognized—this wasn't my first tournament. But grappling with my lust for Graham made me slow, and as the ground exploded around me, I cursed. Graham grabbed my arm, yanking me back as a black monolith lifted from the ground in front of us.

"Dammit! Jump!" I yanked free and jumped to the flat top.

Graham didn't question and followed me. "Why are we up here, Del?"

"Because we have to be. Now, get ready to jump again."

He gave me a puzzled look as another monolith burst from the ground to the left of us.

"Now!" I yelled, throwing myself to the second one and sliding as it continued to rise.

Graham grabbed my leg as he landed behind me. I would have enjoyed that tight hold on my calf if I hadn't been close to sliding off the edge of the damned monolith.

"What the hell is going on?" he demanded, helping me up.

The monolith behind us shattered, collapsing, and his eyes grew wide.

"We have to keep moving as they emerge. It's the only way to get to the next part of the kingdom." I nodded to the light from the life patch.

"Fuck," he muttered as another one exploded from the ground in front of us.

We both jumped, but Graham landed hard on his stomach, his legs dangling over the edge. I heard the distinct *oof* he made and knew it had hurt.

"Don't damage that," I said, pulling him up and eyeing his lower half.

"Seriously?" he groused.

"I haven't had a turn with it yet. I want it to be in prime shape when I do."

The stone behind us shattered, and a new one emerged, stopping his chance to come back at me. We continued to jump as the monoliths moved us closer to where I knew we'd be safe.

"What are these things?" he asked as we pulled ourselves up again.

"The edge of life and death. The balance a mortal holds within him. As death's hold grips them they must fight to make it back to life. It's not an easy fight—" I jumped again. "It's a struggle against nature to stay alive."

"You've got to be kidding me. Do we have to be so literal as gods?"

I laughed and pointed to a slow-moving stone. "That's the last one but make it fast, this one won't hold up as long."

I jumped, teetering as I landed, the ground below messing with my delusions. Graham's hold kept me standing, and I took the moment to look back at him.

"Ready?"

"For what?"

"For the fun part."

"Do I want to know?" he asked, his face crinkled in concern.

"Probably not but too bad." I held tight to the arm he had wrapped around my waist, enjoying his closeness for just that moment. "In about ten seconds, this one is going to fall backwards. Follow me and don't stop."

"What?" he asked as it started to wobble.

"Come on!" I moved his arm and took his hand. Running, I jumped as the monolith began to fall, landing on its side as solidly as I could since it was still at a sharp angle. Then I ran, his hand in mine the entire time. I let out an excited giggle, my delusions reveling in the madness of the action. As its base grew closer, I heard the shattering begin.

"Del!"

"Trust me, Graham," I yelled back, letting his hand go.

I eyed the cracks and found the line I was looking for, following its path as the sides of the monolith began crumbling.

"Now slide!" I yelled, dropping as the crack split to reveal a long tunnel. I slid along, the speed whipping my hair around.

At the bottom of the slide, I tumbled, coming to a stop on my back. I couldn't help laughing at the thrill of it. Graham tumbled after me, landing on top of me, his face inches from mine.

I stopped laughing but kept my gleeful smile. His eyes were locked on mine, and I was too lost in them to breathe.

"You call that fun?" he asked, raising himself onto his arms.

"It put you on top of me, didn't it?" I teased, loving how his body felt against mine. "Do you prefer it this way?"

He narrowed his eyes.

"I have a feeling we wouldn't make it to this point, would we?"

"No, we wouldn't," he growled.

"Because you'd take me before we even got close to the ground."

His grimace was perfect, but it couldn't hide the fire in his eyes. I knew it was the truth. Knew he'd take me wherever we were when he finally gave himself permission. And I couldn't wait. The thought sent a flood of arousal flushing through me. I drew my leg up, moving it along his, a move that pushed the hard length that had formed further into me.

I searched his eyes, parting my lips and giving him the sign that I was ready and more than willing. But as he did each time, he pursed his lips and refused me. Picking himself up, he ran his hands through his hair then reached his hand down to help me from the ground.

Sighing, I took it and let him pull me up. I landed in his arms, that firmness so tempting that I had to force myself not to reach down and touch it.

"If that's uncomfortable, I can relieve it for you," I said playfully.

His look was a mix of surprise and desire, and it killed me when he let go of me and walked away.

"So, anything else you want to warn me about in this realm?" he asked as if I hadn't said anything.

"Plenty. I'm the least of the dangers," I said, giving him a wink.

I was trying to play, to ignore the fact that each time he turned away from me it gutted me. I hated it, and I hated admitting what he did to me.

"Even in that sunny space?"

I looked over to the patch of light. "No, those are clear."

"Then let's go. I could use a little calm. That was too intense. I was like being back in my uncle's training courses."

"Your uncle trained you?" I asked as we started walking again. I had met his uncle the day I'd met Graham. He'd been a Chaser, a weapon of the gods, but had died protecting Claire and Graham.

"Yes, quite aggressively from an early age. Protecting Claire was paramount."

I was about to respond when a thin black rock erupted from

the ground in front of me, and I smashed into it before I could react.

"Ouch," I complained, rubbing my nose.

"You okay?" he asked, turning me to look at my face.

"I'm fine," I snapped, not meaning to, but I was annoyed that I hadn't seen the thing and still slightly frustrated that he'd once again thwarted my constant need for him.

I turned from him and studied the thin wall that now stood as a barrier between us and the next part of the kingdom.

"Dammit," I said, putting my hand up against it just as another erupted behind Graham, pushing him against my back.

"What the fuck is this, Del? I thought we were done."

He was so close it was driving my delusions into a frenzy.

"I forgot about this," I said as he tried to move from behind me.

The wall shoved him further into me, and I couldn't stop the soft moan that it forced from me. The resulting jerk in his pants had my delusions pummeling my mind so that it was hard to think.

"What is it that you forgot about?" he said with a gruff.

"Well...the walls symbolize the last struggle a dying mortal faces to return to life."

"I thought the shit we just went through symbolized that."

"It did, in a way. That was the fight to free oneself from death. That doesn't always return a mortal permanently. The fight is twofold, and this is the final step. It won't let us go easily, just as life doesn't come easily."

"Can't we just go that way?" he said, his hand pointing down the thin tunnel that had formed.

"No, every move we make will squish us more."

He dropped his hand. We were so close it landed on my hip. I tipped my head up and looked up at him.

"Since we're stuck here, feel free to make that hand more comfortable."

"Stop it, Del," he grumbled, but his hand didn't move.

I leaned my head back further into his chest as his fingers spread to encompass my hip then tightened.

"Don't tease me, Turning." I groaned, and the bulge in his pants twitched again.

He squeezed tighter, the pain tantalizing me. My sigh was louder than I'd intended.

"Dammit, Del," he said with a hoarse quality to his voice.

"You do it to yourself. I'm ready...very ready now."

"How do we get out of this?"

"Do I want out of this? Your hand is stirring my delusions, and that hard-on that's trying its best to reach me is making me so wet, I'm surprised my pants aren't drenched...or maybe they are."

The rumble in his chest resonated against my back, sending a distinct flurry of electric currents through my body.

His hand fell from my hip, and I missed the pressure of it immediately.

"Now, Del. No more playing. Get us out of here."

Huffing, I finally gave in to him, knowing no matter how hard I tried, he wouldn't give in to me.

"Fine. The only way past is to think as if you are dying. Think of the one thing that would keep you alive, that you would fight to live for."

"Really?" He sounded irritated, but that was the trick to escaping Death's Lock. "Do we have to do this each time we pass into a section of life?"

"No, once we prove worthy, the realm recognizes that you've passed its test."

"We both need to think?"

"Yes. Now hush and just think of that one thing that would make you fight to take another breath."

I closed my eyes, knowing I would fight for his touch. That I'd struggle against my aunt's hold to feel his lips against mine, to have his body pressed on mine, to have him.

As the tension slipped from his body, I could tell he was thinking about his motivation to live. His hand met the skin of my hip again, his fingers softly brushing my flesh. He lowered his head so that his face was in my hair, and that's when I knew I was the one for whom he would fight to survive. My heart jumped, my pulse racing as I sent my matching thoughts out.

The two stones crumbled, the fragments dissolving into a plume of smoke around us. We didn't move. Instead, his other hand came around my waist and pressed flat against my stomach.

"Graham," I whispered, leaning my head back further and relaxing completely into his arms.

I wanted him so desperately, wanted him to take me right there with the dust swirling around me. Time seemed to stop as I let myself go to the feel of having him so close, but the moment was over sooner than I wanted.

He drew away, waking me from my reverie and grumbling as he walked from me.

"Let's go."

I stood there, staring at his back as he walked away. Leaving me as if nothing had happened, as if he hadn't just told me how he felt in that touch, in the thoughts that had broken us free. Leaving me once again to wonder why he was so persistent about ignoring his feelings. Ignoring me.

Knowing it would do me no good to argue or complain, I followed, pushing my hurt away like I did each time he turned from me.

WE MADE our way quickly through the brighter space of life, and I enjoyed the reprieve. I brushed aside the incident from earlier but distanced myself from Graham. I trailed behind as I had earlier in the day, not sure I wanted to be that close to him. I didn't know if I could behave myself, and his mood hadn't lifted. He was broody, something that didn't help me. In fact, I couldn't take my eyes off his ass and couldn't stop the constant moisture that the damned broody aura around him was giving me.

Even after we'd left the calm of life and entered back into the darkness of death, he remained a distraction. No matter how I tried to keep my mind from him, it wouldn't listen. My eyes drifted up his back, watching the muscles below his leather shirt, the ones that ran through his shoulders and down those powerful arms. My delusions fluttered as I remembered how his hand had felt on my hip and imagined how it would feel wrapped around my neck.

Stop it, Del, I scolded myself as a wail broke the silence and my torturous thoughts.

"What was that?" Graham asked, stopping and throwing his hand out to stop my forward motion. It settled on the skin of my stomach, sending a million flutters coursing along my body. His muscles clenched when his fingers wrapped their way around my waist, lingering there before they tightened. The feel sent my heart racing; his grip was exquisite. I held my breath, waiting for them to move, to bring my body to pleasure, but he pulled his hand away quickly. He mumbled something under his breath, but I couldn't make it out as another high-pitched wail filled the air.

"Banshees," I said, hearing the shake in my voice.

His touch had left me weak, the delusions lurching for the freedom to touch him as he touched me.

"Banshees? Is that something I need to worry about?"

"Definitely," I answered, trying to focus. "They're vicious pets of Death. They don't play for fun like I do."

I saw the shiver. He tried to hide it, but there was enough of it to reassure me that he would be mine before these games were over.

The trees around us swayed in a sudden gust of wind, and Graham tensed further.

"Stay behind me," he said, and he pulled out two silver rods from his pockets. With the flick of his wrists, they lengthened to weapons. His grip on them was so tight the muscles of his arms bulged.

"That's a sexy move, Graham. Do you use those in the bedroom?"

He glanced back at me, his brow lifting. "Would *you*?"

"I told you I like it rough."

There it was, that hunger that sparked behind his eyes. His mouth dropped open just slightly enough, beckoning me to grab him and kiss him. I had no doubt this man was my equal in every way possible, and my heart fluttered at the thought, my power crashing within my mind to drown him in it as he drowned me.

Another shriek broke the moment, and I cursed it as Graham whipped his head away.

"Holy shit," he said, seeing the banshee break through the trees.

It was a delicious mix of terror and pain, a gift my father had given Death long before my brothers were born. Banshees held a piece of our kingdom. They were a living nightmare that warped the spirit of the dead to a monstrous spirit that hunted its prey then drove them to insanity before feasting on their soul.

"You are glorious," I said, taking it in.

"Glorious? That thing is terrifying."

"Embrace your chaos, Graham. You'll start to see the beauty in the darkness." I put my hand on his, lowering his weapon. "You won't be needing those. There's a reason Death and Nightmare were the closest Elders. A reason Terror is favored by Death."

I walked past him as the thing shrieked again, its long, shadowed arms coming from the dark spectral body to strike. Graham grabbed my waist, a move that sent a current of excitement through me. I had to bite back the moan that threatened to break free.

"Del, don't go near that thing." I could hear the worry in his voice, and it gave me comfort.

Flashing him a smile, I said, "Watch and learn. You might find this to be quite the turn-on though. I know I do."

I freed myself from his grasp as the creature opened its mouth again to shriek. It was massive, stretching well above me and even Graham who was well over six feet. Within the sinewy black body lay a torturous death that no mortal would ever invite.

The delusions that had been pushing for release fled my body, not to cause harm but to dance with the demented beast before me. They swirled around it, calling to it, seducing it to succumb to their hold, to partake in the insanity only my power could invoke. The beast shrieked again, but this time the pleasure in the sound encased my body, driving me to release more of my power. We were engulfed in the darkness of that power, the seduction of it. I sensed it touch Graham, his curiosity at the feel of it stoking the fire within me as his chaos fought his restraint. I knew it was only a matter of time before I broke that restraint, and he let his chaos dance with my delusions.

As the creature fell further to the seduction of my delusions, it began to break apart until only long tendrils of mist were left to play with my power. They swept around the space, twisting within my delusions until they faded. My power had drawn from it, feeding from the sheer essence of the banshee. I called my power back, gasping when it settled back in my skin, bringing me a touch of ecstasy that left me aching for release. Knowing I would find none from Graham, I let wisps of my power surround me, touching me as my hands followed them up my body. The tingle of their elation and the remnants of the banshee's horror took me over the edge. I fell to my knees as my climax hit, my head tipping back while the waves flowed through me.

I sat there on my knees, knowing Graham had watched, knowing he'd seen me at my weakest twice now. That he'd witnessed me succumbing to the power I owned in ways no other god or goddess had. I was madness incarnate, and I reveled in it to the point of climax. It was a secret my brothers protected, my parents had kept safe, and one I now trusted him to hold for me. No others knew. I never exposed myself this way to them, never let my power go so far but somehow I knew he needed to see this part of me. To understand that there was no separation between me and my power. To know that when I was with others, I held it at bay, kept that part of me restrained, never revealing the depths of my insanity. The monster I truly was.

CHAPTER 7
GRAHAM

I couldn't move. I was too enraptured by the beauty of Del as she released her power on the banshee. She was gorgeous, and as I watched her delusions dance before us, their touch drifting over my skin while they circled us, I fought the urge to step to her body and touch her. I wanted her in that moment worse than I ever had. She was powerful with a ferocity that called to the very core of my being. Her power broke the banshee apart in a delicate, sensual way that mesmerized me. As it returned to her, I couldn't pull my eyes from her. The way the strands of her magic touched her body like I wanted to had me rock hard and that was before she'd broken, climaxing with an entrancing quiver of her body in a way that almost made me lose it.

I stared at her as she bent forward, her cry still echoing in my ears. That sound was one I wanted to elicit from her. I wanted desperately to hear it as I made her come undone with my kisses and my touches. And I was jealous of her delusions because they'd done what I longed to do.

I rubbed my hand down my face, trying to calm the hard-on

that was pushing uncomfortably against my pants. This was torture. There was no way I could spend days alone with her and not take her like I wanted.

She lifted her head, her eyes seeking mine out. A vulnerability sat within them, and I remembered what Theo had told me. This was a side of her others didn't see, only her family. A side she was revealing to me, trusting me to keep safe. She looked so innocent and childlike that all I wanted was to pick her up and hold her, reassure her that I would never hurt her in that way. That I would never betray her.

I swallowed, giving my neck a roll before I walked over to her. Extending my hand to her, I said, "You get off like that every time you torment something, regardless of if it's living?"

The innocence faded, her eyes lighting as a mischievous smile played on her face. "My power has that effect. I'd be happy to let it touch you and watch as you break for me."

She was something. "It takes a lot to break me, Del."

Her eyes studied me, the slivers calm but larger than they usually were. She leaned into me, and it took all my strength not to pull her closer and kiss her. "I can break you, Graham, like no one ever has."

And I knew she could. There was no doubt in my mind that she would break me so that no other woman would ever compare. The slivers began to move again, playfully dancing in her eyes. I brought my finger to the corner of her eye, hearing the hitch in her breath. Gently, I traced the curve of her face, lingering at her lips and forcing myself to stop before I lost control. I brought my hand back, and she gave me a curious look.

"That's much too gentle, Graham. You don't strike me as the gentle type."

I laughed. "I can do gentle, trust me."

"Mmm, but I don't think you want to. I think you're like me. I think you want to take me hard and relentlessly."

Shit, she needed to stop, and I needed to walk away, or I would do just that. Unable to stop myself, I said, "Did you ever think you might need gentle for once? There are two sides to you, Del. Maybe someone needs to treat that other side of you the right way for a change."

Her mouth dropped, and I knew what she was thinking. That I had understood there was more to her than the insanity, that there was a softer side to her. The vulnerable one I'd just seen, the girl who needed protection, who needed someone to hold her when that insanity wasn't being fed. I knew she wanted me for the chaos in me, but the other side in me wanted to see that soft side of her... Well, after I ravaged her.

I walked away, shaking my head to clear those thoughts and leaving her there.

"Catch up," I commanded. "We need to get out of this blasted realm."

THE DAY WAS LONG, and we faced more banshees, ones I did my best to wrangle in with my powers so I didn't have to watch her climax again. Not that I didn't find it incredibly hot, I just didn't think I could resist her if I had to watch that again. It had been hard enough to keep it together when I'd watched her in the alley. It had taken me two times of jerking off to deal with it. Now I was stuck out here with no ability for release and the hottest goddess created, one who would readily give me the body I'd craved for ages. There was no way I could watch her again without giving in.

"Hey you two!" Theo's voice broke through my thoughts. "Damn, we took a wrong turn. I knew that last banshee got us twisted around."

"Your dumb ass got us twisted around," Persa complained.

Persuasion. Yet another goddess who oozed sensuality. She greeted me with a sexy grin, calling me by my power. "Turning."

"Persa." I gave her a nod.

Making no attempt to hide her annoyance, Del asked, "Why are you two here?"

"Well, little sister. This one took us the wrong way."

"I did not! I told you we needed to head west, but you ignored me."

"Aren't you supposed to have power over decisions, Persa?" Del asked. There was a distinct snarky sound to her voice, and I glanced over at her.

She had her hands on her hips, and the silver in her eyes was bouncing wildly.

"She's right. Damn, Persa, why didn't you just use your powers?"

"Maybe I did," she said, giving me those bedroom eyes that she'd drawn me in with the last time I'd been alone with her. "No one says we can't have a little fun this early in the tournament."

"You're joking, right?" Theo asked with a distinctly disturbed expression etched on his face.

"She better be," Del snarled.

Persa let out a laugh that slithered through me like a light touch. "Why don't we have a little fun, settle down for the night."

"If that weren't my sister, I'd be fine with that. But that's not gonna happen. Graham won't be touching Del, and I sure as hell won't." The scowl he wore turned to a horrified look. "That's just gross, Persa."

"Del can watch while I play. There's enough of me for both of you."

I raised my brow and gave her a head shake, pushing the subtle hold of her power from me. "We tried that once, Persa. You're not my type, remember."

"I'm always up for another try, Turning."

"Nah, I'm good." It was tempting and would have taken my mind from Del, giving me release from the ache she'd brought me all day. But I was so fired up from Del that I didn't think anyone could handle me at this point. Anyone but Del and that wasn't going to happen.

"I'm not enough for you, Persa?" Theo said, pulling her to him. "I was enough last time I was pounding you."

"Mmm, you're enough, but Turning is—"

"Not your speed," Del snapped.

She was in a mood, her delusions leaking from her so that small wisps of white drifted from her skin.

Persa glared at her then looked between us, a knowing smile curving her lips. "Well, well, finally staking your claim, Del. You could have warned us you'd finally be taking him off the market."

"What?" Theo said. He turned his eyes to me. "Did you touch my sister?"

"Shut up, Theo. There's been no touching, unfortunately. Now go somewhere else and play. We don't want to be part of it...ewww. And it's definitely not something I want to see."

Theo moved closer to me. "Protect, Graham. That's all you're doing."

Persa yanked him away. "Leave him be. There's no stopping that when it happens."

"Nothing is happening," I argued, noticing how my mind wasn't agreeing.

"We'll see. I'm just sorry I never got a full taste of that." Her tongue made a sweep over her lip.

"Like I told you, you're too soft for me, Persa."

She studied me as Theo grumbled more. "Maybe, but it would have been worth another try."

"Come on," Theo said, and his irritation was clear. "Graham, hands off. Persa, get him out of your mind. You're stuck with me, and you better not have him in your mind when I'm fucking you later."

"You're such a romantic, Theo."

He grabbed her arm and moved her from us. "I'll show you how romantic I can be later, after I clear my mind from the fact that you just suggested a threesome with my little sister watching. Have you been spending time with Perversion again? That's seriously messed up."

She shrugged. "It was worth a try. Just be glad I didn't use my power on you." She blew me a kiss and ran off.

"She's going to be a handful to deal with," Theo mumbled. He started to run after her then turned back to us. "Don't even think about it, Del." His look was serious, but Del being Del, she merely released a flick of her magic at him and stuck her tongue out. "You're a child, Del."

He turned and ran after Persa, leaving me with what I suspected was a very fired up Del. She affirmed my suspicion when she turned to me quickly.

"You fucked Persa? Really?"

"I didn't, but even if I did, it's none of your business who I sleep with. And stop saying fuck." It was turning me on too much. Every time she talked dirty, it did something to me.

Her eyes were glaring, the silver in a frenzy.

"Like I said, she's not my type. Too soft."

I pushed by her, not caring to deal with her little jealous pout. Although I wasn't entirely certain if it was jealousy or anger at me for choosing the others over her. I'd already heard it from her about Pen and that had been enough to make it clear she'd been upset by my actions. Raking my hand through my hair, I cursed myself for not just taking her when I'd wanted to all those years ago, for thinking another goddess would fill that need for her. They'd all been worth it, sex with a goddess was erotic in ways mortals couldn't touch. But none of them had been Del.

"Are you going to stand there glaring at me while I leave your ass behind?"

I heard the pouty sigh, the one that made my balls tighten as I imagined that sound coming from her as my tongue tormented her. She trudged up to me, her arms crossed. The huff she made stopped me.

I yanked her against me, scolding myself as soon as her chest met mine. She was alluring, her power still casting a white aura around parts of her body.

"I didn't have sex with Persa. We fooled around enough for me to realize she couldn't handle me, and I turned her away."

She narrowed her eyes. "Did you touch her?"

"What the hell, Del? Is your mind okay right now? You really want to know how I touched Persa?"

She didn't drop her gaze.

"Damn, you are something. She's got nice tits, but they're not made for biting."

I saw the reaction, the flash in her eyes that told me hers were, just as I'd imagined they were. I brought her closer, seeing her lips part in anticipation of the kiss she expected. The one I desperately wanted to give her.

"I need a woman who likes to be bitten," I said, loving the way her breath hitched. "And she wasn't one of those." Just to rile her up, I added, "Pen is," and shoved her away from me.

The anger in her eyes was adorable, and I couldn't hide my smile as I turned away from her. She was fuming and damn if that didn't call to me even more. I could only imagine what sex with Delusion was like when she was angry.

I needed to stop and get us both focused again. I couldn't have her power out of control; there were too many obstacles to face. Knowing her emotions needed calming, I glanced back, saying, "But she wasn't one who'd enjoy me breaking the skin. That's the kind of goddess I need. One who likes my teeth tearing into her while my dick is."

A slight cry escaped her as her body lurched slightly. Damn, I didn't want to picture how wet she was right now, and I turned away quickly. That reaction had been enough to break my resolve and if I didn't keep moving, I'd slam her to the ground and take her.

Rolling my neck, I continued to walk, not saying any more when she caught back up with me. She stayed quiet and my need finally calmed, the tightness in my pants finally relaxing.

As time passed, we picked up the light conversation again, the banter that was laced with subtle sexual tension. It was a rhythm we'd developed over the years, one that teased and tempted but never provided release.

I couldn't tell if it was night or day, but Del's yawns were an indicator that we needed to rest. Jackson had warned me that she needed sleep, that she grew cranky, and her delusions would grow restless if she didn't get it. Especially if she'd used her powers, and she had.

"We need to look for someplace to camp for the night," I said, looking around in the darkness for someplace that would work.

"I think we're almost to the next kingdom. We should continue," she argued.

"Nah, you need to sleep."

"Will you be sleeping with me? If so, I'd be happy to lay down for you...do you prefer me on my back or with my ass in the air?"

I stared at her, unable to think of a comeback because my dick had jerked so hard it had been painful. The image of her body bent over with that tight ass in the air, legs spread and ready for me to plunge into was tantalizing. I'd been watching her ass most of the day in those tight pants, and it had been driving me crazy.

"Hmmm, I peg you for an ass guy so maybe the latter."

She turned away and started walking again, leaving me to battle the visions in my mind.

Finally waking up, I said, "I'm more of a leg guy." And her legs were the best I'd seen, long and thin with small defined muscles, just delicate enough to know they'd wrap around me tight as I pounded her against a wall. They'd also feel good around my neck as I took her below me. Fuck, I needed to stop. She was killing me, and I was tormenting myself.

"I have all the leg you need, and I can guarantee they'll clasp around you so tight you'll come just from the pain they'll bring you."

There was that lurch in my dick again. It was like a dog she commanded, coming to her at every word. I wanted it to come *for* her, too, and my resolve was breaking quickly. She turned and stopped.

"I don't know why you deny yourself, Graham. I'm here, I'm more than willing, and I will make you see stars—"

"Del—"

"No, hear me out—"

"Del, shut up and don't move." I'd watched as she'd slowly started sinking, lowering with each word, and was surprised that she hadn't seen the fear in my eyes. Or perhaps she had and had read it wrong because what she was suggesting was what I wanted, and I did fear it. Feared making her mine, claiming her like I wanted for multiple reasons, including her brothers.

She looked down and cursed.

"What is it? Quicksand?" I asked as she sank another inch.

"No, it's much worse."

"Worse than quicksand? Are you kidding?"

Bringing her eyes back to mine, I saw the fear. The confidence she carried was gone.

"What is it, Del, and how do I get you out?"

"You don't. I have to."

I creased my brow, not understanding.

"It's Death's Grip. There's no escaping it. It pulls you under and forces you to face all your fears in life, your regrets, every burden you've carried."

She dropped lower, all the way to her waist.

"You're not going under there," I said, running to her and dropping to take her hands.

"There's no escaping it."

"The hell there's not. Now hold on."

I pulled, using my feet as leverage, but she slipped further down.

"Graham, it's fine. I'm a child of the Nightmare Kingdom. This doesn't frighten me."

"I promised I wouldn't let you out of my sight or my protection. I will not watch this pit take you from me." The words had slipped out, and I hadn't realized the power of their meaning until they were out. Her eyes softened, and she held tighter to my hands.

"Fine, you stubborn man. And how do you suppose you're going to get me out of here?"

She slipped down another inch, and my mind whirled through the possibilities. I couldn't pull her; the hold below was too tight. We were locked in the realm of Death, in a pocket of darkness. But I held sway over the darkness, calling it to rest over the world when dusk fell. And I held sway over the light, calling dawn to the mortal realm. I just didn't know which side of me to use.

Unless those weren't the sides of my power that needed to save her. "Chaos," I muttered.

I glanced at her again, seeing her eyes light, the slivers flutter in anticipation. I never called on that side of my powers. The side my sister ruled. I lived in the calm, controlled side of my magic. But there were times when I sensed the chaos. There were parts of me I knew it drove, the aggression, the sexual intensity, the brutality that I held.

I thought about what I wanted to do to Del, the way I wanted to hear her scream for me, wanted to take her so hard it called her delusions, how I wanted to feed her need for pain and pleasure. My chaos bucked within me at the thoughts, clear and ready for me to use. I closed my eyes and set it free, letting it rampage through my body, pushing aside the clarity, the control my other powers had.

Opening my eyes, I met Del's wide eyes, the green bright and excited, I could feel her power as it fought within her to break free. But this was not a task for her powers, this was meant for mine. I released my hold on the chaos, and it tore from me, plunging into death's grip and tearing it apart. Shrieks and howls of the phantoms that lay below filled my ears as my chaos ripped through them. The hold on Del released and I yanked her to me, falling back, her body landing on mine.

"By the Creator, you are delectable," she said breathlessly, the slivers in her eyes shooting around in a frenzy. "Either take me now or call your chaos back before it stimulates me more."

I was so out of control in that moment that I almost gave in, almost pulled her lips against mine and gripped her hair like I wanted to, but instead, I stayed faithful to my promise. Calling my chaos home, I relaxed as it settled back to its resting place, my other power overshadowing it again. I didn't move, relishing in the feel of her body against mine and cursing my dick, which I knew was pushing hard against her.

She pursed her lips then rolled from me, laying on the ground next to me. "So, you don't want to lose me, huh?"

"That's not quite what I said," I argued, knowing she'd spoken the truth. I didn't want to ever lose her, but I didn't know how to keep her. How to let myself have her.

"I like your chaos, Graham. You should set it free more often. It's very sexy."

She rose, using her magic to clean the muck from her clothes. I continued to lay there after she walked away, thinking through her words, remembering how the chaos had felt, uncontrolled, unhinged, frightening. I wasn't sure how Claire dealt with it, but I was beginning to see just why Jackson had been so important to it. Just like with Del's powers, Claire's needed a control, someone to keep her in check. Jackson was it for Claire, but I didn't know if I could be that for Del. Even the small amount of chaos in me led me to believe I'd only make her more volatile.

I FINALLY CONVINCED Del to camp for the night. She was tired. Using her powers had exhausted her, and I could sense the diminishing in her control of them. I found a small shelter and sat against the stone, lighting a fire with my magic to bring light to the space. Del created a blanket, and I expected her to lie down and sleep, but instead, she came over to me.

My resolve was low, and in the firelight, she looked so

intriguing that I would have given in if she'd tempted me, but she didn't. Instead, she sat next to me and leaned against my chest. The feeling of her against me was perfect, and I brought my arm around her. She reached up and set her hair free, the long golden locks tumbling around her small face. Her eyes, a rich emerald in the light looked up at me. How I longed to kiss her in the moment, to lay her down and make love to her—not the hard, rough way I'd been fantasizing about but soft and slow so I could relish in each touch I gave her, each stroke of my fingers against her skin.

She laid her head down and I pulled her in so that she rested comfortably in my hold. It was a delicate moment, one the two of us rarely had, one I doubted she gave anyone else. A reflection of the innocent woman inside of her, the one the insanity shadowed.

Resting my head on hers, I took in the berry scent that drifted from her hair, laying a light kiss on her head as her arm wrapped around my waist. She fit perfectly against me, and I wondered at the sensation.

"What would have been your greatest fear if you'd been pulled under?" I asked her.

She stayed quiet for a moment, her body moving gently with the rise and fall of her breaths.

"Being seen," she said softly.

Two small words that held such power. I wasn't certain how to respond.

"You see me...and you don't judge me. Not like the others would." Her voice was barely a mumble.

"I do see you, Del. And there's nothing to judge. You're beautiful and delicate with a power that can ravage even the most brutal enemy. You are incredible."

The tension fled her body, and she relaxed further into my hold.

"What would have been your biggest regret?" I asked, curious as to her answer. What regrets did a woman who'd lived countless ages have?

The silence lasted longer this time, her breathing slowing until she drowsily said, "Never having you love me." The words were so soft I almost didn't hear them.

I froze, not sure how to respond, knowing this was her soft side, the vulnerable one that she never exposed. She'd shown me part of it and now had handed all of it to me, setting it in my hands to either destroy or protect. I closed my eyes and brought my head back against the stone.

"What would your biggest regret be?" she asked as if she hadn't just said those words.

I didn't answer. Instead, I continued to hold her until sleep took her, her body melting into mine. I held her there for a long time, feeling the subtle movements of her breathing, the soft purr of her chest, keeping her close and protected.

When I knew she was deep in sleep, I brought the blanket around her and rested my head against hers again, whispering, "That I never let myself love you," before I slipped into my own sleep.

CHAPTER 8

DEL

Graham's arm was still wrapped around me when I woke. He was sound asleep, breathing softly, and I took the time to look at him. Studying this man I'd given my heart to hold and protect. His thick auburn hair was tussled, and he had a day's growth on his face. Both looks only managed to make him more attractive. I had every inclination to straddle him and wake him up the way I'd dreamed of, but I didn't. I was awake now, my devious side back, after having depleted myself the prior day. I hadn't realized how I'd drained myself, and I wondered if the constant restraint on my hunger for Graham had been a factor.

Slipping from his hold, I rose and stretched. Yes, I was back, my delusions frittering delectably through my head. I hadn't meant to be so open with Graham, to answer him the way I had, but that side of me had been present, and part of me knew he would keep my secrets safe. I never heard the answer to my question, and he'd never responded to my answer. I wasn't sure how to read the reaction, but it made me nervous. I'd never given anyone else insight into the person I was under my delusions, the side of me that my brothers protected. Opening myself to someone like that scared me, and nothing scared me.

Stretching, I wandered to see where we were. We'd covered a lot of ground the day before, and I could sense we were close to Heart's border. Stepping through the trees, I discovered I was right. The terrain opened to a lake with a waterfall, the perfect spot for two lovers. I wasn't sure Heart's kingdom was meant to be the second kingdom to surpass. It never had been in the past; it was usually one later in the tournament, when we were all in need of some leisurely activity to rest our powers and bodies. The route usually guided us through the kingdom west of Death, Nature, which bordered Death and Chaos, touching Heart at the point where the other two kingdoms were separated. Only then would it loop us back to Heart before sending us through my realm. Theo had said the Elders had made changes. Maybe this was one. And it would explain why Theo and Persa would have been confused about what direction to take.

Persa. I didn't have any qualms about her, but it had rubbed me wrong that she was yet another goddess Graham had indulged in. And the way she called him by his power had been annoying. She'd layered it with her persuasion, trying to tempt him. I preferred to think that was the reason he'd succumbed to her in the first place. Even if he hadn't had sex with her, he'd still touched her and not me.

I watched as the water splashed into the lake, stirring up the water below. Persa was beautiful, not as pretty as Pen or me, but she was still a paramount of perfection like all of us were. Theo had been smitten with her for years, he made no attempt to hide it. Nor did he keep silent about the times that he'd had her. Their relationship ran hot and cold. My brother was a handful, every bit of a pain in the ass as his power implied. He was arrogant, brutish, and callous at times, but under it all was a big softy. From what Graham had said about Persa, I could see why she kept returning to his bed. I had no doubt that Theo was nothing like his exterior in the bedroom, even if he boasted differently. The goddesses with the more subtle powers, like Persa's, swayed him. Not like Graham who was drawn to the fiery ones like me.

With Graham on my mind again, I dipped my toe in the lake. It was inviting, and that waterfall was beckoning me. Unable to pass it up, I stripped and hopped into the lake. The water was the perfect temperature, and I dunked myself under to wash the grime from me. Refreshing wasn't the word for how it felt as I made my way to the waterfall. Rising, I let it wash the rest of the prior day's dirt away, relishing in how the water splashed upon my skin. I don't know how long I stood there before I sensed his eyes on me.

I gazed his way, seeing the grip in his hands, the lump in his pants, the one I'd felt against me when he'd pulled me from Death's Grip. He wanted me. I just couldn't figure out how he kept resisting me or why. If it was my brothers, they wouldn't have minded as long as he didn't hurt me. Well, I'd let him hurt me because that's what I craved from him, but I didn't think he'd hurt my heart.

I knew he used my brothers as an excuse, but I suspected there was more to it, another reason he wouldn't let me in. The real reason he chose to fuck other goddesses and not me. The thought of Pen with him sent a jolt of jealousy thrashing within me, and I glanced away from his gaze, not wanting him to see it.

"You should join me," I called, feeling his eyes peruse my body. "There's plenty of room for both of us."

"I washed up in the stream. Get dressed and let's move."

I rotated my body, letting him see all of me, and enjoying the lust that sat in his eyes and the clench of his jaw. He was beautiful, and I wanted him so badly it ached between my legs. I wanted him to relieve that ache, to feel him buried deep inside of me, to know how his tongue would press against me as it took that ache from me and brought me to the cliffs of ecstasy.

He walked away, leaving me drenched in all aspects of the word. Reluctantly, I dressed, leaving the water on my skin and in my hair. I found him on the other side of the lake, his back to me. Tapping his shoulder, I watched his eyes as they took me in, seeing how they settled on the drops of water that lay on my chest and followed their path downward as the droplets settled in my cleavage.

He furrowed his brow and said in a gruff voice, "Don't wander off without me again."

"I thought you didn't want to play, so I figured I'd play with myself."

His eyes widened, his expression curious. "Did you?" he asked in a softer voice.

"No, you didn't give me time to, but I'll gladly show you if you want."

The grimace returned, and he turned his back on me, walking away. "Where are we?"

Damn him for denying me again. I ground my teeth and replied, "We're in Heart's kingdom."

"Great," he grumbled.

That was it, I couldn't take anymore, so I stormed up to him and stopped him. His eyes held a fury that I'd never seen in him, and it caused the arousal to flood in me. I almost toppled from it. But I didn't, and I matched his fury.

"Why won't you take me? What do I need to do to have you give me what you gave Pen? Am I not good enough for you? Too deranged for you to touch, so you'll touch other goddesses? Experiment with Persa, fuck Pen?"

He snapped, slamming me against the closest tree and holding my wrists tight to my sides. His body pressed against mine, his desire for me reaching for release.

"You want me, Graham. And I want you to take me, to hurt me, to make me come so hard that you break me."

There was a twitch in his jaw, and he stepped closer, my body smashed against his.

"You push, Del. You push and push, and you won't stop."

"Because I know you want me, Graham."

"Of course I want you. Who in their right mind wouldn't?"

"Then take me."

"I can't take you."

"Dammit, yes you can."

"No, I can't. I promised your brothers I would keep you safe, that I wouldn't let anything hurt you. And what I want to do to you, Del, is hurt you. I want to take you so hard that your screams cut the air. I want to bite you and spank you and hear you cry out in pleasure. I want to leave my mark on you so no other man will ever touch you, leave bruises so they know you're mine."

My heart was pounding, my body lurching with every word because it was exactly what I wanted him to do to me. I wanted him to bring me to ecstasy the way I knew only he could ever do.

"Then do those things," I said, leaning further into him. "I want you to hurt me, to bring me that pain so that it brings me pleasure, the kind of pleasure I know only you can give me."

He released me and walked away.

"I won't because I gave them my word."

"Fuck you, Graham. You'll give that to Pen, to other goddesses and not the one you want for some guilt that my brothers will care? She's nothing compared to me—"

He had me pinned against the tree again before I could finish, his face so close to mine that his lips almost brushed against mine. "I don't want Pen. She's nothing to me, just a release, a way to satisfy my need for you. No other goddess compares to you, Del. No other comes close to what I know you'll do to me."

"Then let me satisfy you," I said, hearing the desperation in my voice. I almost crossed the remaining distance between us, but I refrained, needing him to make the first move.

"No."

I wanted to cry, to scream, to break down, but I didn't. Instead, I lowered my head, and his lips drifted across my hair. The need he had for me poured from him, the need he wouldn't heed no matter how much he wanted it.

My hands were still pinned above me, and he lowered them with what seemed like reluctance. His fingers sank in between mine, and he squeezed my hands before he pulled away, releasing me. I wondered if it was a final release of his desire for me, a final push to distance himself from me, from what we both wanted.

"Let's go," he said without looking back.

His head was hung low, his shoulders drooped, and for the first time since I'd met him, he looked defeated. My heart broke because I knew there was more to his denial than the excuse he gave, something underneath it that he wouldn't move past.

Begrudgingly, I followed, staying behind him and keeping silent until my delusions were knocking around so badly that I let them take over the soft side I'd revealed for him, letting them shelter it so he wouldn't hurt it any further.

ON AND ON, we walked, my power stirring in my mood as I watched Graham's back. My eyes drifted occasionally to how his ass looked in those black pants. But each time they did, I forced them away, remembering how he'd turned me down once again.

"Does this blasted kingdom ever end?" he grumbled.

"Of course it does."

It had been a boring walk. Although this kingdom did turn my stomach, there were aspects that I enjoyed, ones that enticed my delusions—the lush greenery, the flowers that bloomed in vibrant reds and pinks, creatures that were soft and easy to manipulate, their pink fur inviting to touch. But today, my eyes continued their vacant stare, refusing to look beyond the unusual heaviness that sat in my chest.

As my delusions licked at my mind, my eyes trailed to the ground, and I ran smack into Graham's back.

"Ouch," I complained, rubbing my forehead.

He shot me a look. "Pay attention to where you're walking."

"Well, if you hadn't stopped in front of me, I would have been just fine." My words were terse, and I knew I'd been sharp, but he'd been sharp with me first. "Why did you stop?"

"Other than the overpowering pink all around us, I stopped because the ground didn't seem right."

I gave him a curious look. "Have my delusions slipped to you?"

There was a slight tug at his lip. "You'd know if they had."

My heart danced again but quickly fell as the sparkle in his eye clouded over, and his expression soured again.

Huffing, I pushed him out of the way. "The ground is fine. It's just a meadow of pink wishing willows. They're my aunt's favo—"

"Del, don't—"

"Oh stop being such a moody overprotective ass. It's fine." I bounced up and down on my toes. "See." But as the word left my mouth, I heard the crack.

"Dammit, Del," he said as he launched forward to grab my waist.

By then it was too late, and the crack had spread, the ground falling from under us both. He pulled me to him as we fell, and my body awoke, ignoring the free fall until we landed with a hard thud.

"Oof," he mumbled as I rolled from him.

Our landing was softened by the plethora of wishing willows that were spread around us.

Standing, he glared at me. "I told you to be careful."

"And I don't take commands from you. I keep telling Jacks the same thing. I'm not Claire, I don't bend."

If looks could cause pain, I would have gladly taken the ache his look would have given me. Just the look alone dampened my pants, and I wondered if my judgment to go without a lining of panties was a good call or not. In my defense, I'd been hoping he would have ripped them from me by now.

"You're a menace."

"Well, you're an asshole. And I enjoy being a menace. Don't forget who I am, Graham. I revel in my insanity and spreading it to others. Not my fault you don't want to partake in my revelry."

I walked away, hearing him grumble under his breath. For curiosity, I let a wisp of power slip to his mind, hearing it whisper that he'd gladly partake if it made me come the way I had with the banshee. My laugh escaped before I could catch it.

"What was that for?" he asked.

He needed needling, so I said, "Because I come way better when I have the right god pounding me."

His eyes widened, a flash of desire flickering through them before they turned angry. "Stay out of my head, Del."

"Then voice those dirty thoughts about me. You might make me come just hearing them."

Before he could respond, I skipped away, my power happily frolicking in my mind and spreading around me. It called the wishing blooms to me, their tiny petals dancing around me as I giggled. I let the thoughts and the worries of him go and embraced my madness. My power encased me as the pink underground world that surrounded us came to life. I was in my element, and it was wonderful.

The ground shook, the wishing blooms floating away with a gust of wind.

"Del!" Graham shouted and ran to me, pulling my back against his chest as glass encased us, light cascading in rainbows around us. It was like we'd been imprisoned in a prism.

My heart was pounding hard, my power stuttering to a halt. His hand was still around me, and for just a moment, I couldn't help but lean against him. I felt his heartbeat increase, and his length grow, pressing to have me. A sigh slipped from my lips as his fingers spread across my bare stomach, slowly inching to run along the bottom of my shirt.

"Del," he whispered against my hair, his finger brushing below the material touching the bottom flesh of my breast.

"Please, Graham," I pleaded, wanting him so badly that every part of me trembled.

His fingers tightened, squeezing my skin and I could tell he was fighting his need for me. The pain it caused forced the moan I'd been holding to free from me, and he yanked his hand away, pushing me from him.

I pressed my head against the crystal, trying to calm my body, trying not to fall apart from just that brief touch.

"How do we get out of here?" he asked, his voice hoarse.

I turned and leaned on the glass, my breathing still ragged. His eyes looked pained, and he seemed frazzled. I hated that I was the one doing this to him, that I was causing him pain he didn't welcome, confusion that I hadn't intended.

"I don't know. I don't know this challenge. It wasn't part of the last tournament. Theo said the Elders had made some changes and added more difficulties. This must be one."

"Great. Stuck in a prism with you for who knows how long."

"I could offer a few things to keep us busy, but you'll just turn them down," I teased.

"Nice. Why don't you work on getting us out of here?"

I threw him an annoyed look. He was killing me. Every touch he fought to keep from me was a taunt to the overpowering hunger I had for him. I wanted this man more than any before him. I would have given him all of me, something I'd never done. He'd already seen more than any man, seen my other side, the one I kept hidden. But I would give him the rest of me—my mind, body, and heart. All of them his because I knew he would keep them safe, he would keep every part of me safe.

"Standing there staring at me won't help, Del."

"Mmm, it will help the clenching between my legs that wants your dick to relieve it."

"That's ladylike."

"What gave you the impression that I was some delicate lady who didn't have a mouth or a body on her? I have both, and I use both impressively, or so I've been told."

Those brown eyes filled with a blend of anger and jealousy. "And how many men have you used them on?"

I let a laugh free, and it bounced around our prison. "Plenty but then again, you're no virgin, Graham."

"Never claimed to be."

I wanted to make a quip about Pen again, but he'd reacted so violently to it the last time that I bit back my retort.

"Then why don't you show me how experienced you are, and I'll impress you. Or, if you'd prefer I can just show you what my mouth can do, and you can try my body later."

"Why do you do that, Del?"

"Do what?"

He came closer, his expression guarded. "Tease me."

"Because it feels good to make you react. You won't touch me so I can at least get pleasure from my teasing."

There was silence as he studied me, his eyes seeing into my soul. I parted my lips, ready for him to kiss me, but he didn't.

"Just kiss me already," I challenged him.

He gave me a crooked smile, one that made my knees weak.

"If I kiss you, I won't stop."

"And what's the harm in that?"

"A lot." He pushed away, and my breath released, my heart dropping like it did each time he turned away from me.

"So, what's the challenge then?"

"Aside from you," I mumbled.

"Yes." I hadn't realized I'd said it loud enough for him to hear, but the space we were trapped in was a small, enclosed space. I should have known better.

"Not sure. We must have to do something, though."

"That's observant," he said playfully.

Ignoring him, I groped around on the crystal, wondering what we were meant to do. There were four triangles that leaned in to enclose us, each thick with streams of color running through them like rainbows.

I touched one of the rainbows and watched as it spread.

"Graham," I called him, sensing him step behind me to watch.

The space around us darkened, and the colors swirled to form an image, blurry at first until it became distinct. I stepped back in reaction, bumping into Graham but not having the same response as I'd had the last time his body had been pressed into mine. Before me was an image of me, a memory playing out, one I didn't want anyone seeing, one that my delusions shielded me from and to which I never wanted to return.

CHAPTER 9

GRAHAM

Del was about to push me over the edge. I'd resisted for so long, holding onto my strength to deny her, to deny myself. I'd almost lost it before we'd been plunged into this trap. Almost given in, her incessant need to throw Pen in my face taking me closer. I'd never realized that it had bothered her, never wanted to hurt her by taking Pen or any of the handful of goddesses I'd let appease my appetite. I would never have willingly hurt her like that, but I had. I'd only taken them to ease my need for her and in doing so, I'd inadvertently hurt her. It killed me, but I couldn't take it back. Shit, I didn't know if I would. Pen had been an incredible fuck, the best out of the ones I'd tasted. She met my fury without hesitation, in a way I imagined Del would, only I knew Del would not only match it but unleash it in a way I'd never allowed it to be released. Each time I'd taken her, I'd imagined it was Del. That it was her in my grasp and her cry that held my name.

Seeing Del in the waterfall had been like a dream. I'd never seen her naked, only envisioned what she would look like based on the skin I had seen from her. She was immeasurably more beautiful than I'd imagined, and my strength had almost wavered, especially after holding her through the night. When she'd turned to me, the water pouring over those perfect breasts, traveling to the small patch of blonde between her legs then working along those glorious legs my dick had jerked so hard that I almost climaxed from just looking at her. She was glorious, and I wanted her to be mine. I didn't want to have another god or another mortal touch her again.

I'd forced myself to turn from her, letting her invitation go, knowing I needed to move, to leave her be or I would lose my resolve completely.

Now we were stuck together, and the teasing and taunting had reached its apex. I was one step from smashing her against the glass and ravaging her, but something she'd done triggered an image to appear. She backed into me, a tremble that was not sexually induced shivering through her body. She was afraid, and I'd never seen Del afraid.

I watched the image, realizing it was a memory. A young Del sat on the marble floor, her blonde hair in long braids, her green eyes confirming to me that it was her. She couldn't have been more than six years old in human terms. Her beauty even at such a young age was striking.

She was bouncing a ball in front of her. Lines of her power, delusions, were whipping around it and moving it chaotically around the room. The action had her giggling maniacally. I found it adorable, but then I'd always found the dichotomy of her to be attractive. The silver in her eyes wasn't visible, and I wondered why it wasn't distinct back then.

Two children came running in, both stopping in front of her. One whispered in the other's ear, and they both laughed.

"Why are you so crazy, Dellamine?" the boy asked, squatting down in front of Del and using her given goddess name. It had come out in a tease that bordered on malice, and I wanted to reach into the glass and strangle him for it.

"Leave me alone, Ger," she said, pushing him aside and trying to grab her ball.

Hunger, now I recognized the vulture. He was one I tried to avoid, his gaunt eyes too creepy to hold for more than a few seconds. He was a god who kept to himself, aside from the times I'd seen him with his sister, Thirst. The girl in the memory wasn't his sister, however.

"I don't think so," the girl said. She looked familiar, and I thought she might be a young Violence.

She and the boy were several years older than Del was, and I had the urge to give them both a sharp spanking. They were brats.

"You don't have a real power, Dellamine. You're a waste of space. Your brothers have terror and pain, and you? What do you have?"

"I have delusion," she said in a small voice. It was laced with insecurity and doubt, neither of which I'd ever seen in the Del I knew.

"Delusion? What good is that? You can't protect yourself with delusions. You can't hurt mortals with delusions."

The boy was vicious, getting right in her face and pushing her to the ground. I could see the tears in her eyes, the slight shimmer of silver that was forming within the green of her eyes.

"They don't know yet," I said, and she trembled against me. They didn't realize how deadly she truly was, underestimating the delicate child she was and not knowing they were playing with a ticking time bomb. One that I had a distinct suspicion was about to show them how wrong they were in a very unpleasant way.

I put my arm around her, ignoring the feel of her skin and

only wanting to protect her from the memory she so wanted to escape.

"Make it stop," she whispered, her voice shaking, and I could hear the tears in her eyes. I hated how vulnerable she sounded, how unlike herself. How fearful she was of the event that was unfolding before us.

I wanted to stop it. I wanted to break the glass and protect her from the memory, but it kept playing.

The girl, who I was now certain was Violence, had smashed the ball, sending shatters of glass scattering across the floor.

"You don't count, Dellamine. You are nothing but a crazy girl who no one likes. Always chattering away with your delusions and your ramblings. You have no power, and you have no place here."

I gripped Del tighter, my heart breaking as I saw why she was so fractured now. Why there were two sides to her. The fragile child who had broken that day, hidden behind the madness that ruled her.

The slivers exploded in her eyes, sharp fragments of silver in the sage. Her delusions escaped, no longer frolicking but angry and looking to cause pain. Neither child noticed them as they continued to taunt her, to create the woman she was today. Bullying her with their words and their actions until she broke. Her delusions took form, long lines of white that attacked the two children, silencing their words. The slivers in Del's eyes were fluttering in a storm of power as the insanity seeped from her in a cloud of gray that covered the floor. The room shook as she chanted over and over, "You hold no power over me. You are weaker than I am. You will always fear me."

She stood. The two children were screaming, and I saw two young boys race into the room, stopping as they observed the storm. The older one I was certain was Theo, making the small boy with him Jackson. Theo looked stunned, the features on his teenage face morphed into an expression of astonishment. Jackson's eyes were wide but filled with what I could only describe as pride.

"You will fear me. My delusions will bring you only pain when you fail to remember that you fear me because I am your worst nightmare." Her voice was layered in power as she weaved her spell. The innocent child who had sat delightedly playing with her toys had disappeared, hidden below the lethal goddess who had emerged. "Never again doubt that I am a child of the Nightmare Kingdom. I am my father's daughter. I am madness incarnate."

Her voice was haunting, and even through the memory, I felt the power in those words.

"Dellamine!" a booming voice broke through her power, her delusions and the insanity collapsing in a wave of dust that settled quickly to the ground.

The two children were curled in balls with their hands over their heads. Del stood over them, a wicked glean in her eye, her lips curved to a dangerous smile. The silver bounced through her eyes. Then, just as quickly as she'd turned, her expression softened, the childlike features reappearing. Her eyes returned to the bright green they'd been. The slivers, however, remained. She turned to the man who I now saw was her father, the god of nightmares, and he took a step back.

"Papa?" she asked, moving toward him.

But he stepped back again, uncertainty in his eyes before Jacks and Theo swept in. Theo picked her up, talking cheerfully to her, leaving the room with her in his arms. Her smile lit the space. Jackson, who couldn't have been more than five, stared at the two children then at his father. Even as young as he was, he looked like one to be feared. I could see it in his eyes, in his demeanor.

"Call your mother and have her fix them," his father commanded. "I need to think on this."

The memory faded, the prison turning to its former look, the light returning. Del remained shivering in my hold. I brought my other arm around and pulled her back to me, closer to my chest. Resting my head against hers, I stayed quiet, knowing it wasn't my place to talk.

"That was the first time anyone feared me," she said eventually, her voice timid. "They never dared taunt me again, but none of them played with me. None of them would even look at me. They still fear me to this day. They say they don't. We made amends, and Violence and Hunger joke about it now, but they all still look at me as if there's something wrong with me. And my father...never held me close again after that. I was lethal, deadly."

"So are Jackson and Theo. Shit, any of you are."

"But I can't be controlled." She turned and faced me, remaining in my arms. Her eyes held such sadness that all I wanted to do was take it from her. "I'm lethal because I'm unhinged, uncontrollable, madness itself. I am something they don't understand."

"No, you're something they don't truly see. There are two sides to you, Del, just as there are to me. Your brothers see it, I see it."

Her eyes searched mine. "Do you?"

"Yes, all the time. You don't frighten me."

"No?"

"Never."

She looked like she wanted to say something more, but she hesitated. I wanted nothing more than to kiss her, but I dropped my arms and kissed her forehead instead. The feel of her skin against my lips and the smell of her hair was enough to drive me mad, but I resisted and stepped away. I turned and rested my head against the crystal, trying to calm the emotions that were pummeling me.

"Graham." The worry in her voice caused me to lift my head.

Colors streamed through the glass I rested against, an image slowly becoming clear as giggles I remembered all too well echoed around us. My heart wrenched as the image defined, and my two children came running across the yard, catching fireflies while Angie and I watched. It was then that I understood the challenge, the test Heart's kingdom was giving us. And it was one I didn't want to face, one I didn't think I was strong enough to handle.

CHAPTER 10
DEL

Having to watch the moment that had unleashed my power, waking it to become what it was today, had been torturous. It had brought an ache to my chest that I didn't invite. But Graham had been there, holding me through it, a force of support while I braved the moment that had defined me. I'd wanted to run from it, to turn my eyes, but I couldn't.

Hearing Graham say that he didn't fear me like the others did, in a voice that held no judgment, had fortified me. I knew then that he was the one who would protect my heart, protect the part of me that only my brothers understood. I'd wanted to kiss him then, and I could see that he wanted to kiss me, but damn if he hadn't stopped himself again. The brush of his lips across my forehead had only been a temporary salve to the need I had for those lips to be against mine.

The moment fled and now, as I watched the crystal he'd rested his head upon morph, the image I saw there broke my heart. The challenge was clear then: we had to both face our pasts, face the incidents that had defined who we were today. But where having to witness my memory had been hurtful, the one for Graham was cruel.

I saw the defeat in him as his eyes took it in. I'd always known how much he loved his wife, but seeing it there in his eyes hurt more than I could have imagined. I saw then why he couldn't love me, his heart still held too much of her.

I watched as the memory played. Graham was leaning behind her while they watched their children play. It was an intimate moment, one I didn't understand why I would be privy to and one I wasn't certain he'd want me to see. Angie turned to him. I'd forgotten how pretty she was. Her blue eyes searched his, her auburn hair drifting in the evening breeze. The love that was in her eyes was tangible, hurting me more. I wanted that love to be mine now that she was gone, ached to look at him that way, but I never could. Ours was a volatile dance of power and seduction. I didn't know if there was room for something that soft if anything ever did come to fruition between us.

"I've been thinking about your decision," she said softly.

"There is no thinking about it. The decision has been made."

"But, Graham, you're a god. You need to be with your people now that the truth is out."

"I am with my people. You and the kids—"

"What about Claire?"

"She has Jackson, and trust me, he'll keep her safe and controlled."

"Mmm, I can only imagine from those stories she told us."

He nuzzled her face, the move causing me to drop my eyes. I never wanted to take the love he had for her away. I'd always respected it, but I didn't want to witness it.

"Feeling adventurous?" he asked Angie, his voice calling to me but not in the same way it did to her. I lifted my eyes back to the image, seeing then how different Angie was to me.

"Maybe but about the decision—"

"No buts. I'm not going anywhere. I want to be here with you and the kids."

"You're immortal, Graham. We are not."

He was quiet, and she brought her hand to his cheek. I watched him lean into it, a twang of envy in my gut at the intimacy.

"I stay here."

"To do what? Watch me grow old and die? To watch them do the same?"

"Yes."

"No, I don't want that life for you. Promise me that if you stay, you'll go home when I get old. That you'll move on, take a goddess who can match your immortality, your power."

"I won't take another, Angie."

She laughed, a beautiful soft laugh. "I know you well enough to know you'll be too frisky to go an eternity without sex. There's a side of you I can't match, Graham. I've always known that. You'll need an outlet for that."

He grimaced. "Okay, fine. Maybe I'll give in to one or two, but it will only be sex." He pulled her close and leaned his forehead against hers. "I will never love another. I promise you that."

"Don't—"

"Yes, there is no other. There's only you, and my promise will stand."

"It's one that can't stand, and I won't accept."

"Enough, Angie."

Her eyes were sad until he kissed her, and I watched the man I loved give his first love all of himself, locking his heart away with those few words.

The image faded, and he dropped his head back to the crystal. I saw it clearly now, the thing I hadn't seen before. The one hidden under the excuse that my brothers would be angry if he touched me.

"You don't have to love me, Graham." But I wanted him to.

He picked his head up and turned to me, the sadness in his eyes was almost unbearable. "I made a promise."

"One she didn't accept. One you couldn't make, shouldn't have made because it wasn't yours to make." He looked questionably at me. "You are a god, an immortal god who has an eternity to live. We don't love mortals for a reason. It's forbidden because our love isn't meant for them. It's too volatile, too powerful when we do love."

"I loved her, Del."

"I know, and you always will, but keeping yourself from touching me isn't the solution."

He picked his head up and moved closer to me. "I can't touch you."

"But you can. Sex isn't love."

He brought his hand out to my hair, pulling a lock of it forward and letting it drift through his fingers.

"Take me, Graham. Like I know you want to. She was right. There's a part of you she couldn't match, but I can. Bring me pain and ecstasy like no man has before because I know it's there waiting for me."

The gold in his eyes shimmered seductively. "I don't want to hurt you, Del."

"Oh, but I want you to hurt me. In every way possible." And Creator how I did. My body was alive at the thought.

"I can't," his face drew closer, "touch you without loving you."

There it was, the piece he struggled with, and my heart leapt as my delusions swept around my mind.

"Then love me and take me. She never accepted that promise. I'm not Angie, I never will be. I'm not fragile, I don't need that softness from you. I need your power, your strength, the force you have. Bring it to me and let me love you back. Because

I do, Graham. I love you with every spark of insanity that fuels my body. And if you don't take me, if you refuse me again, I don't know that I'll be able to stand it."

He stared at me, his eyes shifting, and I saw the desire, the hunger he had to take me, to own me, to make me his. It clashed with the side of him that wanted to honor his promise, to not accept the chaos I knew ran through him.

"Give me your chaos and let it run free," I whispered against his lips. My body was trembling at the heat that was pouring from him, the anticipation of his touch.

His fingers drifted along my face. He brushed his thumb over my lip so that a soft cry slipped from me. I saw the effect it had on him in the stir of the gold in his eyes. Bringing his fingers to my hair, he softly tugged it.

"Harder," I moaned in expectation, and his eyes flared.

His chaos slipped free, my delusions reaching out to meet it as his hand drifted to my neck, gripping it so tight the moisture flooded between my legs, and my moan was loud and feral. His head lowered to mine as he pressed his body into me. He was so hard, and it pulsed through his pants trying to reach for me.

"Dellamine," he said hoarsely against my lips, and I reached for his chest, pulling him as close to me as I could. The anticipation of his kiss, of his touch had my legs squeezing so tight that I thought my climax wouldn't wait. This man had the power to break me with just his presence, and I knew when he took me that he would own me for eternity.

"I want you," he mumbled, his lips brushing against mine.

"I'm yours, I always have been."

My words triggered something in him, and his hesitation broke. His lips crashed into mine with an intensity that took my breath away. My body came alive, my delusions breaking free as I caved to his kiss, meeting his demand with a ferocity that sent my blood rushing. He tore my shirt from me in a move that took me to the height of ecstasy. His hands were everywhere at once, squeezing and touching, bringing me pain and pleasure in a symphony of sensation. I ripped at his shirt, taking it from him so I could feel his muscles, the strength I'd longed to run my hands over. They were tense and powerful as he continued to devour my mouth.

My hands reached for his pants, but he grabbed them, pinning them painfully against the wall of glass. Dropping his mouth to my breasts, he fed on them as if he was fulfilling a fantasy he'd had. The way he bit at my nipples, sucking then nipping had my body quivering for release. He dropped his hands, running them along my body, squeezing, bruising with the force and with each bruise my climax grew. A cry escaped me when he spread my thighs and tore my pants from me. His fingers entered me with a thrust that broke me, my scream filling the space. I heard his groan rumble through his chest before he returned to kissing me.

As my body quaked against him, and he picked me up, pushing me so hard against the crystal that it fractured, pieces of it piercing my skin. The pain rippled through me like a wave of ecstasy, and I groped at his pants, longing to have him fill me. He shoved my hand away and freed himself, lifting me higher before he lowered me, penetrating me so hard that my body came undone with the force. Another climax tore through me, leaving me gasping for breath. With each thrust of him, my back scraped against the uneven shards, further stimulating me. I tried to throw my head back with a cry, but he forced my lips to his, his fingers twisting in my hair so tight that strands ripped.

He was every mix of fantasy I'd ever had, and my delusions cascaded through the room, taunting his chaos forth until the two were rushing over my skin in a sensual dance of their own that tantalized me. He yanked my head back, a jolt of pain threading through me, meeting the rush of my climbing need so that I was trembling for release again. His mouth was on my neck, and his hand held my ass so tight I prayed he'd leave a handprint, that I'd feel his touch for hours after he stopped.

"Come with me," I moaned, my voice sounding distant as arousal whipped through me so badly that my legs tightened.

His grunt was animalistic, and I knew I'd caused him pain, pain he embraced just like I did. I dragged my nails across his back, loving how he drove into me with more intensity the deeper I dug.

Around us was a fury of our power, chaos, delusion, insanity in beautiful harmony that pressed against the crystal as he broke, his cry rumbling through the space. It called to my own climax which unraveled me, breaking me the way no man had ever broken me before. The crystal shattered, giving way from behind my back, but he held me tight, thrusting the last of his climax into me. My own still battered me in waves that drowned me then swept me in before pulling me under again.

As I calmed, his grip loosened, still tight, but the ache of it lessened. He drew his head from my neck, and his brown eyes, vibrant with the circle of gold, searched mine. The look said everything, and I brought my lips to his ears, saying, "Take me again. I want you to take me to the cliffs again and jump with me so hard that every part of me shatters."

The groan that slipped from him started in his chest, reverberating against me until it released. It called to me, reigniting the fire that still sparked in my belly. His fingers were still tangled in my hair, and he pulled it, forcing my head back. I purred, welcoming the ache it caused, the one that was clawing between my thighs as he sat still nestled in me.

"Only if you scream like that again for me," he growled, and the fire ignited.

"Always."

I kissed him, biting at his lips while he dropped us to the

ground. I'd expected the crystal shards to pierce me but instead a bed of wishing willows softly greeted me.

"Damn," I gritted against his mouth.

He pulled back to question me, and I couldn't help but bring my hand down his chest, admiring the build I'd only dreamed of touching.

"What?" he asked, stilling his movement.

I looked sharply at him. "I expected pain when we dropped. I'm disappointed."

His eyes glinted fiendishly. "I can bring you pain, Del." He dropped his mouth to my neck, biting me hard. My resulting cry was one of pleasure. "As much as you can tolerate."

Drawing his mouth to mine, I whispered against his lips, "I embrace pain, now fuck me until my screams fill this kingdom."

"Gladly," he said, smashing his mouth against mine and driving into me so hard that it sent my body trembling.

He took me again with the ferocity of a man who hadn't just had me, bringing me more pain and pleasure than I'd ever had, more climaxes than I'd thought possible. I broke so easily for him, and each groan, each jarring flash of pain sent me cresting. He was insatiable in every way and my equal like no other. As my body rose toward a final release, he tumbled, taking me with him so that we both fell into the abyss, shattered like I knew neither of us had ever been.

CHAPTER 11
GRAHAM

The coming sunrise called to my power, waking me softly. The turning of the day was natural, but it still needed coaxing just as the dusk did. I'd wondered how it was continuing if we were here, and Pen was sequestered, all of the gods locked away for the duration of the tournament, but Del had explained that the Elders cast spells to balance the world in times like these. Their combined powers were enough to hold the mortals to their routines and experiences while we were engaged in other matters.

Del. She was curled into me, my arms still around her while her head nestled into my chest. I hadn't intended to give in, to break the resolve, but the challenge thought I needed to do otherwise and had shown me the memory. Shown her the memory. Her own memory had given me insight into how she'd come to be the way she was, her fragile side shielded from the delusions, from the insanity her mind created. Both protecting the child within, the one who had broken that day. I loved both sides of her, I always had. To be honest I think I fell for her that first day

I saw her, although I had been protecting my children from her at the time. She called to me then, that part of me that was slight, overshadowed by the power that drove the turning of the sun cycles.

I took her in. There was an innocence to her that she only showed a rare few and I had been given privy to it. It rested on her now in the peaceful way she lay against me, the slight smile on her pink lips, the sparkle of the setting moon that drifted into our cavern on her golden hair. She was beautiful. She was mine. And she was everything I'd fantasized. I'd never taken a woman the way I had her, never left a bruise, never brought pain to them the way my chaos wanted. But I'd wanted to hurt her, to watch as she reveled in my aggression, and had she ever. I should have been embarrassed at the way I'd taken her. Sure, I'd fucked Pen hard, but that had been nothing like I took Del, and it had only been hard because I'd wanted her to be Del. Somehow I'd known Del would embrace that side of my power. She'd climaxed to the ravaging of a mortal, my girl would invite the sting of a smack to her ass or the pull of her hair. My girl. She was no girl, but she was mine.

I loved her, and I could tell her now, admit it. The barrier, the weight of the words I'd told Angie had been lifted. Endless life was a long time to be without love. Angie had told me that, and I hadn't listened. My heart still held her, keeping her memories safe. But now there was space for Del who I knew would fill every inch that she could. She already did, bringing out a side of me I'd never known, one Angie would have run from, but Del encouraged.

I kissed her head and she moved, a slight sigh escaping her mouth as her lips parted. She lifted her head, the innocence of her overwhelming me in that moment. The slivers of silver were faded, hidden behind the green that shimmered when she met my eyes. There was a flicker of nervousness and fear, so I brought my hand up and ran it through her hair.

"I'm not going anywhere," I said, rolling over so that our bodies touched. The hitch of her breath accompanied by the fleeing of the fear had my heart thumping louder.

The smile she gave me was gorgeous, and it lit every space in my body. "I knew you were worth the wait, but that…that was glorious," she said.

"Glorious that I hurt you?" I asked, wanting reassurance from her that I'd correctly understood the invitations she'd given me.

"Mmm, I think you need to hurt me more next time. My delusions like pain, especially from you."

The silver flecks grew, bouncing around as the insanity stepped in to replace the innocence. I gave her a devious smile, knowing she'd just made my dick twitch with those words.

Smoothing my fingers over her arms, I noted the bruises, my brow scrunching. They layered her arms, my fingerprints dark on her waist. I let my fingers drift to her back feeling the scratches the crystal had made and seeing the flash of arousal in her eyes at the hurt they gave her with my touch.

"Shit, you're not healing."

"We don't heal in the tournament. Remember? No immortality."

"Well, that's a problem."

She pressed further into me, and my need for her grew. "Not for me. I like the lingering pain."

"Nope, put your insanity away. I'm not hurting you again."

She pouted, her eyes growing sad. "I'm not the only one with marks. And I'd be happy to give you more." Her fingers pressed against the scratches her nails had made, sending a rush of ache through them that only further managed to turn me on. There was something seriously wrong with us and I had a feeling we went well together for a reason.

"No, not until we're done here, and you can heal again."

I went to rise, and the look in her eyes crushed me.

"You're not going to touch me again until this is over?"

I cocked my head at her, giving her a sly grin. "I didn't say that."

Hovering above her body, I let my lips drift down her neck. My hand caressed her breast, and I watched her nipple rise in response, my thumb teasing it further. She had the most amazing breasts, and I craved them just as I craved having those luscious legs wrapped around me. Now I could touch them any time I wanted, and the thought was a thrilling one.

"We're going to play gentle this time."

"That's no fun."

I raised a brow at her. "Have you ever let your other side come out during sex, Del? The one that hides behind your delusions."

Her lips parted, and the slivers stilled. "No," she said with a softness that called to the part of me that wanted to protect her, to keep her safe from anyone who might hurt her.

"I think it's time she gets a turn. Let your delusions sleep while my chaos sleeps."

I kissed her softly, her body responding with the arch of her back and the press of her breasts against me. Bringing my hand around her waist, I pulled her closer.

"But I want you to fuck me again," she whined, and I heard the bit of fear in her voice. I was forcing her to be vulnerable, and it was a place she didn't like to be.

"No, I'm going to make love to you. Now stop talking dirty before you make me change my mind, and I bend you over and smack you."

The shiver that ran through her threatened to break me. "By the Creator, please do that."

"Fuck, Del, you're not making this easy." Visions of her bent over with that tight ass in the air filled my head, my dick throbbing in response.

"Then take me how I know you want to."

"You're a deviant. Now shut up and let me make love to you. I'll ravage you when I'm done."

"And bend me over."

"Good God, yes I will definitely do that. Now silence your power and your mouth."

The delusions stilled, the slivers in her eyes doing the same. Her eyes looked into mine expectantly, hesitantly.

"Do you love me, Del?" I asked her, holding her gaze.

The green in them shined. "Yes." The word was like a lifeline to my heart, waking it to the possibilities of what life with her could be.

"Good," I said, nuzzling her neck before kissing it. "Because I'm going to love every inch of you, delicately, intentionally until you know how much I have loved you for far too long."

Her chest rose with her inhale, and I took the opportunity to run my hand across her breast, hearing the sigh that fell from her mouth as her body curved into my hand. I continued to kiss her neck, moving down slowly to her shoulder, my hand gently touching her other breast and lightly pinching her nipple. I let my tongue follow the dip of her neck to her breast, taunting that nipple while my other hand dipped to her stomach. My thumb grazed her skin while my fingers wrapped just slightly around her waist squeezing but not hurting. Her heart thumped below me, her chest rising as she pushed her breast further into my mouth, her body reaching into mine.

I took my time, tasting every inch of those delicious breasts until I had worked my way down to her waist. By now she was squirming. Sounds like mews were coming from her lips. It was taking all my effort not to satisfy the pounding in my own length with each lurch of her body, each sound she emitted. She was driving me as crazy as I was driving her. I dropped my head to her stomach, trying to control myself and steady my breaths. My fingers were holding her hips, and I tried with all my might not to squeeze them hard like I wanted to. I had promised her gentle. I wanted to take her in her vulnerable state, to have her trust me to protect it, just as she had trusted me to watch her at those moments.

I kissed her belly button, slipping my tongue over it as I'd envisioned doing a million times, before making my way down her hips. Spreading her legs, I brushed my lips over her inner thigh, basking in the softness of her skin. Those legs I'd longed to touch, to feel around me were just as I'd imagined they would —they were incredible. I kissed her down to her delicate feet and up her other leg. My hand ran along the curve of her calf, then along her thigh, trailing my lips until I settled between her thighs. Sinking my tongue deep into her, I tasted the sweetness of her. She was wet, and it lingered in my mouth, stimulating my desire. My dick ached at the scent of it, the taste of her as my senses came alive. She was more delicious than I could ever have imagined, and I devoured her until she was clenching those beautiful legs so tight around me that I almost came. Her body writhed as my hands held her hips in my firm grasp. It was glorious, and I relished the way she wrenched my hair as she came undone against my mouth. Her muscles quivered uncontrollably, her cry filling my ears in delectable tones.

As she descended from her high, I moved up her body, brushing my mouth along every inch that I'd just kissed until her mouth met mine. Her kiss melted me. It was a kiss layered with sensuality and love, unrestrained and unguarded. She was everything I'd ever dared to imagine, and as I entered her, I held her against me, our bodies moving as one. Gone was the madness induced chaos we'd had the night before, replaced by only us. Our bodies and our souls, exposed for each other in ways I knew she'd never been exposed, in ways I didn't even think I'd ever been exposed. Not even Angie had ever had all sides of me. She'd seen the gentle side, but I'd kept her from the chaos, from the man who craved the hard brutal side of passion, the side Del fed. The goddess of madness who held the blend of nightmare and passion within her that twisted beautifully to create the insanity she imbued—only she could meet both sides of me, and I saw that as I made love to her, keeping her heart safe, her emotions protected. My desire climbed with each sigh she emitted, each tremor of her body as her climax built again, and I let mine soar. It clawed its way to the peak where I knew I would dive into the abyss with her once again. As it crashed through me, I held her tight and she broke with me, our bodies lost in the throes of our release so that we became one in that moment.

Her breathing calmed as the last of my orgasm filled her, and I laid my head against hers. My heart was hammering, my breath ragged. Her hand came to my cheeks, and she picked my head up, her large emerald eyes searching mine.

"I didn't think it was possible to love you more than I did," she said, her fingers tracing my face delicately.

I turned my head into her hand and kissed her fingers. "I love both sides of you, Del. You never have to hide them from me. You never had to, I've always protected them."

Her smile was genuine, and a pink color settled in her cheeks. I furrowed my brow. "That's a first."

"What?" she asked, a sense of innocence in her voice.

"You blushing."

"I don't blush."

"The hell you don't. That is a blush, and it's beautiful just like you."

The color deepened. "You need to stop breaking me, or I won't be able to function, Graham."

I nipped at her bottom lip. "I like breaking you."

"Mmm, well don't make it a habit." She gave me a flirty smile, and my heart fluttered. "Now, I think you promised to bend me over and spank me." The slivers returned to her eyes, and the reaction in my dick was immediate. "I'm ready to be owned by you again."

"I never stopped owning you."

"Fuck me, Graham," she commanded, and her words elicited a growl from me at the reaction they stirred in my body.

"Now that I can oblige. Turn that tight ass around and let me have it."

"I told you I don't take commands. You'll have to make me."

The flames whipped through me, and I knew there would be more bruises on both of us before we were through, no matter how much I'd hoped to avoid it. Grabbing her hips, I flipped her before yanking them forward so that she was on her knees. I reveled in the squeal she let out, losing myself to her body once again. Her power broke free with a fury, calling my chaos and dancing with it in harmony along with our bodies.

I SPENT the morning exploring every part of Del I'd longed to discover, memorizing each curve, the sound of each moan, the different cries she made, and the way her screams brought me closer to climax. As the afternoon sun warmed the air, I knew it was time to move. I rose to her complaints, dragging her from the ground and pulling her to me.

"Take me again," she purred.

"Aren't you exhausted yet?" I asked, nibbling at her neck.

"Madness never rests, Graham."

"Hmm, not sure if that's a perk or a nightmare."

Her laugh was maniacal, her eyes shimmering with that madness. "It's both," she said, biting my lip.

"Well, as much as I'd love to hear you scream more, we have a tournament to finish."

I pushed her away and grabbed my pants, but she didn't move.

"Del, dress now."

"I told you I don't heed commands. That's Jacks' thing."

I cringed, knowing those commands were for my sister and having witnessed firsthand how they owned her.

"Oh you're such an overprotective brother. Claire loves every bit of it."

"That's what irritates me. Now get dressed." I buttoned my pants and threw her clothes at her. "Otherwise, I'll show you what happens when you don't heed my command."

A moan came from her that stirred my blood, and I cursed myself for having put that thought in her head. Del was not someone to threaten with punishment; she welcomed it too readily. Commands were not going to be our thing, but I had never thought they would be. Punishments, however, might be in our future. The growth in my pants stirred at the thought.

The slivers in her eyes fluttered as if she'd thought the same thing. They were hyper today, more so than they had been although I'd noticed they'd been more active since we'd started the tournament.

She lifted her pants to reveal the two pieces I'd ripped them into in my haste to touch her the prior night.

"You know, you could have just used your magic to remove my clothes."

I'd never thought of that. "Not as much fun."

She repaired them with her magic, and I watched her put them on, covering those legs that I longed to run my hands over again. "I'm not keen on the pants," I said. "I prefer the dresses, they offer easier access."

The look she gave me wasn't the one I'd expected. "You've never been up my skirts, Graham. How many goddesses have you fucked in their dresses?"

The jealousy that glared in her eyes left me with a mixed reaction of annoyance and excitement. I moved to her, yanking her body against mine forcefully so that her breath escaped. "I told you why I've never been up your skirts, Del. Are we going to go back to this again?"

She pursed her lips as I let my hand brush against her breast. "I can be jealous."

"Jealousy isn't your power."

"No, but you fucked Pen the day you spent with me. The same day I wanted you to sink into me. You left me hungry and fed her instead."

"Didn't you satisfy that hunger?"

"Mmm, the same way you did the night before the tournament."

"Shit, did you really?" I couldn't get the image of her touching herself out of my head now.

"Yes, and each time I plunged my fingers in, I imagined it was you." She was going to drive me mad. My dick was full again, pushing painfully against my pants. "So while you were plunging into her, I had to pretend."

I bit her lip hard, her cry maddening me further. "Should I fuck her again and watch you do that next time?"

Her eyes darkened, the silver almost covering all of the emerald and her power whipped around me.

"Oh, Del, jealousy may not be your power, but maybe it should have been." I pinched her breast, her power calming immediately. "I'm not touching another goddess, and if I'd known you were doing that, I would have stayed and watched, letting my hand and that fantasy satisfy my need for you instead."

Her demeanor changed so quickly it was astounding. The fragile little girl was back, her eyes a clear crystal green. Just as suddenly, it was gone, replaced with her delusions, the fragmented silver returning. I kissed her, my love for her increasing, confirmation resounding in me that she was mine to protect. That anyone who dared to hurt that fragile side of her would feel my wrath and I would let the chaos free as I never had.

I dropped my head to hers. "Finish dressing before I ravage you again."

"But I want you to ravage me."

Kissing her nose, I released my hold on her and turned away to pick up my shirt. "Oh I will. There's no doubt I will stop every chance I can and ravage you. Now put that damned shirt on and cover those gorgeous tits of yours before I'm tempted to devour them again."

I pulled my shirt over my head and stared her down, calling to the part of me that held control, the turning in me that held sway over my chaos. Her eyes evaluated me, a small curve forming on her lips before she held her ripped shirt and vest up.

"Again, magic is easier," she said.

"And again, it's not as fun."

There was a twinkle in her eyes while she pulled the pink shirt on, repairing it so it covered her breasts, the parts that weren't spilling over the top of the shirt. Damn, she was hot, and

I questioned how I'd ever had the strength to not touch her before now.

She tossed the leather vest aside.

"Don't you need that?"

"Nah, it's only for the creatures in my realm."

I raised my brow in question.

"The nightmare realm is the only kingdom that has creatures that will tear you apart. The Molinard in particular has pinchers that will rip right through your chest. Viscous little shits…well, they're not little but they're still shits. Anyway, they'll recognize the nightmare in my blood and won't attack me. You, however, they will attack, so keep that leather on. They don't like the smell of it for some reason."

She skipped off, her blonde locks bouncing over the pink shirt, her ass bouncing seductively in those pants. Maybe the pants weren't that bad after all. It took me a minute to draw my eyes from the movement before I urged myself to catch up with her.

"Don't walk ahead of me. I'm your protection, remember," I scolded her when I finally reached her. I needed to focus and keep her body off my mind. She'd been a distraction before we'd had sex, but now it was even harder.

"Are you going to get all broody on me again?" she asked, peeking over at me. "Because it's sexy and won't do anything to rein me in."

"Who said I wanted to rein you in?" That was the last thing I wanted to do. Her instability was what drove me crazy, the insanity in her. The delusions messed with me in a way no other woman had.

"All men want to rein me in."

I grabbed her arm, jerking her against my body for no other reason than to feel her there. Her lips parted seductively, her green eyes were rich with sensuality.

"I will never restrain you. I want that side of you present, I want it free when I fuck you, and I'll only ever silence it when I want to make love to you."

Her breaths were short, her eyes needy, and I couldn't resist bringing her mouth to mine and kissing her fiercely.

"Graham." My name came out as a breath against my mouth, calling to me.

I dug my fingers into her waist, her responding moan only further coaxing my length to grow. Damn, I'd just gotten us dressed and moving again, but the need to tear her clothes off once more was clawing at me. Her fingers clenched on my arms, and I slipped my hand up her shirt, the feel of her breast against my skin like an aphrodisiac. I couldn't believe I was this worked up when I'd had her so many times, but I was, and I knew then that she was my drug. I would never have my fill of her, she owned me, ruled me with the same control she ruled her delusions.

I pinched her nipple, and her head fell back, her cry like a stroke along my dick. I needed her again, needed to see her fall apart for me so I tore the material from her shirt, setting her breasts free and taking one in my mouth. Another cry escaped her, and I continued to suck, teasing her nipple while my other hand slid down her pants. She was drenched and as my fingers sank into her moisture my arousal pushed harder against her.

I shoved her against the nearest wall of the cavern we remained in, all thought of leaving it gone with my need for her. It was overwhelming. My body was acting as if I hadn't just taken her. She ripped at my pants, freeing me. Her hand surrounded me, tugging in an erotic way that almost had me exploding into it.

"If you keep that up, I'll be coming in your hand," I said against her breast before biting it hard and tasting the blood. Her hand dropped in reaction, her scream accompanying it. "Take those blasted pants off before I rip them again."

Her delusions escaped, long tendrils of them like wisps of white shadows surrounding us, calling to my chaos which heeded their call. Her pants disappeared, and I growled at the feel of her skin against me. Picking her up, I sank into her, pumping hard as the madness of our power caressed my skin.

"Come for me, Del," I whispered against her ear, wanting desperately to see her fall apart for me, to feel her muscles clenching down around me.

Against my body's desires, I slowed, pushing her harder against the wall and removing myself from her warmth. The move ached, and my dick jerked in reaction as she tugged at my arms to bring me back into her.

"No," I said, sliding myself through her dampness but not entering.

"Please," she begged, a sound that only further excited me. She moved her body seductively against me, my length sliding in and out of her folds in a way that tormented me just as much as it did her. But I stopped her with a bite to her neck.

"Do you want release, Del?"

"Yes, please, Graham. I need you inside of me." Her voice was hoarse and needy.

Ignoring my own body, I dropped my mouth to her breast again. Freeing one hand, I slipped it between us, my thumb rubbing her clit as I stilled my length. She began to move again, riding me as if I were deep inside of her. It was erotic to watch, and I peeked up at her as I continued to bite and pull at her nipple. Her climax was building, I sensed it in the quiver of her body, her clit hard and swollen against my fingers. The dampness around my cock grew so that it was covered with her arousal, and it twitched as she continued to ride out her oncoming release. Within moments, her body bucked against me and broke. I didn't stop touching and licking until her scream subsided. Only then did I shift my position and thrust deep into her still spasming muscles. The feel of her surrounding me was so stimulating that within minutes I crashed, my orgasm hitting me like a storm that wouldn't subside.

As I held tight to her, she came a second time, her body squeezing so tight around me that it coaxed the last of my climax from me, filling her so that it was spilling around me. Waves of residual tremors tore through me and all I could do was hold her. My breathing was so ragged that I wasn't certain I wasn't dying.

"Fuck, we are never going to get out of this blasted realm if you don't stop taunting me woman." My voice was barely a murmur, my breath still too heavy to speak.

"Don't blame that on me. That one was all you."

I nuzzled my face in her neck, keeping her ass in my hold and not wanting to release her. The position was too good to move from. She wrapped her arms around my neck, and I lifted my head to look at her. Her cheeks were flushed with the remnants of her climax, her hair wild around her. Her delusions, not completely settled into her, gave her a halo effect. She looked angelic, although I knew she was anything but that.

"Is this what you've been denying me all these years?" she asked, nipping at my lip.

"Mmm, I think this is what I've been denying us both. I'm inclined to think I had a bit of your insanity in me to have kept myself from it for so long."

"Maybe it wasn't the right time until now."

"You think I needed to get those other goddesses out of my system first?" Her eyes grew dark, the halo around her darkening to a gray haze. "Are you certain you don't have a bit of jealousy's power in you?"

"I'm certain. Now no more mention of any other goddess but me, or I'll bring my insanity down around you."

"Watch out, I might just enjoy that."

She tilted her head and studied me. "Yeah, I think you would."

I kissed her again, unable to resist the taste of her before I released my hold on her and let her legs drop. I fixed my pants as I watched her shake her head at her ripped shirt.

"Should I forgo the pants and just put a dress on so I can stop repairing my clothing?" she asked with a beautiful raise of her brow.

"I'd likely rip the dress as well. You do something to me, Del. I lose all control with you, and that material needs to come off your body as fast as it can. Maybe you should just walk around naked to make it easier." She gave me a wicked smile. "On second thought, forget I said that, or we won't get anywhere because I will not stop touching you."

"And that's bad?" she asked with a glimmer in her eyes.

"Very bad. Leave the pants. I like watching your ass in them."

I caught the slight clench of her legs and the low moan she let out, the sound causing a rumble deep in my chest. Shit, this was going to be more challenging than when I wasn't touching her. At least then we got somewhere.

"Put the clothes back on," I said, tearing my eyes from her and pulling my shirt on. I hated the constricting feel of the leather against my skin but unlike Del, I didn't have nightmare running through me. Getting impaled by those beasts she'd spoken of sounded highly unpleasant.

I walked on, leaving her to dress, not daring to watch for fear of taking her again. Rolling my neck, I inspected the tunnel before us. I couldn't see an end to it. All around was a brightness that irritated my senses like an itch that couldn't find relief. The cave reminded me of something from a sci-fi movie. Crystals could be seen in some spots, surrounded by the fluffy patches of wishing willows that floated into the air when our feet stirred them. The walls hummed with a pink and purple glow as if they were living, reminding me of the inside of an actual heart.

"I find Heart's kingdom bile-inducing," Del said, catching up to me.

I glanced at her pink shirt and gave her a questioning look.

"That's a dab of pink. This place is drowning in it. No black or gray, only brightness. The only balance to it is where it's situated."

"What do you mean?" I asked.

"Death, Chaos, and Nightmare border Heart's kingdom. Only a small corner touches Nature."

"Wow, that's quite a combination."

"Heart is a mix of emotions that involve the heart," she said, running her hand along the cavern wall. "She's love but also heartache. Most of her kingdom has love embedded in it—the colors, the brightness, the uplifting feeling—but the heartache can be found where our borders touch hers. The blend of the three seeps into the bliss and morphs it, infecting it so that it embodies the elements of heartache. Theo's pain, mixed with my delusion, Death's endless sorrow."

"Huh, that's warped on so many levels. Where does Chaos fit into it? Claire's kingdom doesn't seem to go with the rest."

"It didn't always sit there," she said nonchalantly.

Her power slinked from her, tendrils of mist that invaded the wall so that the colors shifted, fading until they turned a dreary gray, the ground above them collapsing. I snatched her away as her power morphed the fallen ground into a slope.

"Found us a way out," she said happily before prancing up the slope. "Come on, slow poke."

I shook my head and followed. The world around us was cast in the glow of the midday sun. "What do you mean the Chaos Kingdom didn't always sit there?"

She looked around and started walking in the direction of the sun. I had no idea where we were, but she seemed to know, so I continued to follow.

"It used to be Discord's kingdom, but when he was banished, the Elders gave his kingdom to Claire."

Discord was a name that elicited an indescribable reaction within me, uncontrollable and intense. It was a grip of anger that ripped from one end of my body to the other. He'd been responsible for the murder of my parents and had almost killed Claire and me. None of the gods spoke his name often, especially me.

"But Claire doesn't rule that power," I said, not fully understanding. Claire had accepted her place in the kingdoms much earlier than I had. I'd waited until after I'd lost Angie, delaying it further until the kids had finally passed. At that point, there was no further delaying it.

"No, but when he was banished, his kingdom was left empty. Your father's kingdom had been dismantled to honor him when he was murdered. Your mother's, as you know remained intact, Pen stepping in to take her place." I noted the grit of her teeth when she said Pen's name. "Chaos was split, a piece layered into each kingdom as a reminder of them both. When Claire claimed her place here, the Elders all returned the pieces, blending them into the kingdom Discord had once ruled, changing it to the kingdom of Chaos. All but a small piece she asked to leave in our kingdom as a reminder of her place in Jacks' heart. Sweet in a slightly stomach-turning way."

I couldn't help the smile her last comment had brought to my face. My mind was a bit overwhelmed with the information she'd given me. Our parents had fallen to the one weapon created to kill us, Claire destroying the final two weapons in existence when we'd been attacked. My father, Chaos, and my mother, Turning of the Day, had not fared as well, having been murdered by the same weapon decades before. Their murders were the reason Claire and I hadn't been raised among the gods, and the reason I still felt like an outsider at times, torn between two worlds. And Discord had been behind it all. A traitor amidst the family of gods who had no idea what he'd done or that we even existed until Jackson exposed him.

His punishment had been banishment, but his name still left a distaste in my mouth, his deeds scars on both me and Claire.

"So Claire's kingdom, isn't really Claire's kingdom?" I asked, trying to wrap my head around what Del was telling me.

"Not truly, the original kingdom is still below it. See Discord and Chaos run from the same power. They are very similar and so the merging of the two was possible. It's one of the reasons they never called a replacement for Chaos when he died. Discord was similar enough, and when active with my powers, Chaos is created."

"That's headache-inducing on so many levels," I said, scratching my head.

"Mmm, it is but so is anything god related. As Jacks says, we're not meant to be understood, we're gods."

"Point taken," I replied, deciding not to think on it any further.

"So what kingdom do we pass into next? Chaos or Nightmare?" I was hoping it would be Chaos, knowing my tie to it would make it an easy one to pass through. Nightmare was one I wanted to avoid regardless of whether Del held sway over the creatures of the realm or not. I knew enough to know there was a reason Jackson had been named ruler of the kingdom. He was the one with the true power over those creatures and the nightmares they spawned, not Del.

"Nightmare," she said with a giggle, crushing my hope.

"Fantastic. So I guess we enjoy this piece of cake kingdom until we face the horrors that feed you and your family?"

She stopped abruptly and turned to me.

"What?" I asked, wondering at the look.

"You think Heart is easy?"

"So far…" But then I thought of what I'd had to face, the memories, the images. "Well, not easy but not any kind of physical challenge."

"You want physical challenge, Turning?" I swiveled to see Angst and Violence strolling toward us. Angst had a cocky grin on his face that I wanted to remove with my fist.

"I don't mind a physical challenge, Angst."

"You don't strike me as one who would succeed at such a challenge," he taunted.

I narrowed my eyes at him, my hands curving to fists.

"Plus you have the plaything of madness at your side," Violence said. I remembered how hard she'd been on Del when they were children and the repercussions. She clearly hadn't learned her lesson. "Must be hard having to fight everything for her."

"I think Del can handle herself."

I could feel the stir of Del's power, but as Violence's eyes blackened, I didn't know if this was a fight I wanted her picking.

"Back off, Lencie, I don't think you want to be reminded of what my powers can do."

I saw the slight flinch before Angst said, "Are you going to tickle us with your delusions? Make us see butterflies and dance in fields? Maybe talk to ghosts? And what's Turning going to do? Shine the sun in my eyes?"

I wanted to punch him, but I didn't think he was worth the time. They were up to something, egging us on for a reason. I just couldn't figure out what that reason was.

"Did you two fuck, and you want us to join?" I said. "Because last time I checked, neither of you was my type. I think I told you that the last time I had your ass bent over, Lence, or don't you remember?"

She hissed, and I felt the daggers from Del's eyes. Yes, I'd had my turn with Violence, but she was a letdown. I'd thought she'd satisfy that side of me, but she'd been weak, and at the first sign of roughness, she'd whimpered. I'd let off, knowing she was not the one to take my mind off Del. She was all talk and barely any movement in bed. I still took her, but only once and not the way I had Pen and definitely not the way I took Del. I'd never taken anyone the way I took Del.

"You slept with Turning?" Angst said, flipping around to her. Nothing like riling up a current lover.

I couldn't help my smirk. "Just once, she's all yours. As I said, not my type and definitely not up to my par in the bedroom."

He shot a look back at me, and I sensed the power rise in him.

"Come on, Ang. We did what we intended to do. Let's leave them to fight their way out."

"Seriously. You fucked him?"

"Shut up and let's go. If you're lucky I'll go down on you when we stop." She said it with a flirtatious smile, but there was no seduction to it.

Her words, however, affected Angst, and he trailed behind her like a puppy dog.

"Have fun finding your way out of that mess, Turning. Is Del up to your par? I hear she's meek in the bedroom, just like her powers. I'm a better fuck any day over that piece of lunacy."

She was on the ground before she could turn back, a tendril of Del's power whipping from her and tossing her on her ass. The delusion slivered over her body, and Violence backed away. The fear was there, the nightmare returning from that day Del had bested her. I could see it in her eyes.

Angst grabbed her by the elbow and hoisted her up, but I could see the shake in her legs.

"You might want to keep your mouth shut. There aren't many of us who play well with her delusions. And trust me, she's a better fuck than you any day," I retorted.

Her eyes grew wide with surprise. Crossing my arms, I watched them scurry away. I glanced at De. She looked vulnerable, the child below still hurt by the comments even though her delusions had protected her.

Her eyes narrowed and a deep growl came from her. "You slept with Violence?"

Shit, there it was. "Seriously should consider moving in with Jealousy, Del."

"I'm serious, Graham!" She started to move toward me, but her body jerked back with the movement.

"What the hell?" I looked down at her legs. Vines had wrapped around them and were slowly moving up her thighs.

"Uh oh," she said.

"Uh oh what and what are those?"

"Violence was taunting both of us, but I think she was really aiming for me. Jealousy is Heart's daughter, Graham."

"These are from you?"

"Maybe—"

"Fuck, Del! What do you have to be jealous of Violence for?"

"I've always been jealous of her," she said the words so quietly I almost didn't hear her.

"Why? She has nothing on you."

"She's strong, powerful, and beautiful."

I crossed my arms and scowled at her.

"I know, I'm beautiful. And to be honest, sexier than she is, but she's still more powerful."

I continued to glare at her.

"She is!"

"I've seen what your powers do."

She dropped her eyes, guilt on her face.

"Dammit. She played you. She knew you were jealous of her. I doubt she knew the extent...and of course, I made it worse."

"Damn right you did. Why would you have sex with her?"

The fire was back in her eyes, the guilt gone.

"I was finding an outlet—"

"An outlet? I thought Pen was your outlet."

"What did I tell you about bringing her up again?"

That fire turned, and hunger replaced the anger. But then her eyes flared again.

"Violence?" she hissed. And I knew why that one bothered her so much—the memory that haunted her.

I stepped closer to her, knowing she couldn't move and noticing the vines had made it to her hips.

"Keep it up, Del. Eventually you'll be completely tied up, and I may just torture you as promised."

She sucked in a breath, her chest heaving slightly. Those breasts were pouring over her shirt, and I let my finger drift along them.

"She was miserable, by the way. Doesn't live up to her name," I said, dipping my finger down to brush across her nipple.

She tried to stop me, but as she jerked her arm, I saw that the vines had captured her wrists. "Oh, this is going to be so much fun," I said, rolling her nipple between my fingers.

"You're an ass," she said, her voice slightly huskier than it normally was.

"Mmm, I am. You know, I tried to take her from behind first, thinking she'd be that kind of woman, but damn if she didn't whimper when I squeezed her waist. That firm ass was sitting there primed for me, and that bitch whimpered."

The vine had climbed higher but stopped on my last words. I

dropped my hand and let my finger slide along the waistband of her pants.

"I want someone who can scream for me, Del. Whimpers do nothing but turn me off. I flipped her and took her missionary, glad she hadn't completely destroyed my hard-on."

The vine climbed again, now around her forearms. "You still had sex with her."

"Eh, it did the job, but the name doesn't fit the product," I told her with a wink. "Now, this other goddess I had. She was a screamer." I pushed her pants lower on her hips my eyes on her expression as it flipped from anger to expectation then back to anger. I dipped my fingers in, stepping closer to her and sliding my other hand up her shirt, biting my moan back as my hand engulfed her breast.

Her lips parted, her own moan matching mine.

"I have to say I like you like this, Del. I'm going to want you tied up more often."

A shiver went through her. The slivers in her eyes were stirring in a frenzy by now, her delusions slipping from her, unsure whether to strike me or pleasure me. I could feel their confusion.

"So who did you fuck who was a screamer?" she said, her teeth gritting as she asked the question, those vines tightening around her arms and legs this time. A cry escaped her, and my dick twitched, knowing those vines were getting her as wet as my words were.

I let my fingers drop, thanking the vines for forcing her legs apart. The wetness that greeted me almost broke me, and the groan she released pushed my erection further. I forced back my reaction, not wanting her to see what she was doing to me.

My fingers played, spreading moisture between her clit and her opening, the warmth calling me as I tried to ignore it. She was biting her lip so hard the skin broke, the swell of blood waking my chaos. I leaned into her and licked it up.

"Graham." My name was a ragged, desperate whimper.

"Now that kind of whimper I like," I said, knowing it wasn't fear or unwelcomed pain, it was a plea to have me bring her release. There was a difference, and this whimper clawed at my need for her.

Damn, I'd started this to torture her, but I was killing myself. I rolled my neck and tried to grab hold of my own desire.

"That screamer was my favorite," I continued, watching how her expression shifted again. As the vines grew tighter, ecstasy overcame the flare of jealousy in her eyes.

I glanced at them, making sure they weren't growing too tight. I wanted to play, but I didn't want her to be harmed. I had a little leeway and with the gush of moisture that had just surrounded my fingers, I didn't think she'd last much longer.

"She was gorgeous, and there were no whimpers when I fucked her so hard that she came around me." There was the flicker again, those slivers so chaotic that her power flared, striking me.

I welcomed it, the feel of it only increasing my arousal. I teased her clit faster, then plunged my fingers in as the vines grew tighter. Her nipples were so hard between my fingers that I had to hold myself back from lowering my head to bite them. I kept my eyes on her as the flush of her cresting climax took hold. I stepped so that I was pressed against her, dropping my hand from her breast and wrapping it around her cinched arms to squeeze her ass as my fingers thrust harder.

I bit her lip then kissed her, whispering, "And the way she comes for me is the most amazing thing I've ever witnessed."

Her scream filled the air as the vines went deeper and her orgasm struck. She was clenched so tight around my hand that the pain it brought me elicited a groan from me that I couldn't restrain. I kissed her, smashing my lips against hers. Her body shook against me, the quivers falling within her frantic kiss.

"You are the only one who screams that way for me, Del," I said against her lips. "The only one I want coming for me, the only one who will ever satisfy both sides of me. There is no other, there will be no other, and…there never has been another. You were meant to be mine, and you own me as no other woman has."

Her sigh lit the fire in me, and the vines slipped from her body, freeing her as my words confirmed my love for her. She fell against me, and I held her as the waves of her orgasm continued to pulse through her. I brought my hand against her hair, running along the softness of her long locks and ignored the bulge that had formed in my pants. This had been about her and only her. I'd taken advantage of her entangled limbs and enjoyed every minute of her torture. I hadn't known it would free her, but to my surprise, it had.

She lifted her head, her eyes hazy with contentment, the slivers stilled.

"You are a bastard."

I brought my fingers to my mouth and licked them, savoring the taste of her and enjoying the sparkle in her eyes. "And you are a delicious screamer," I said before kissing her nose.

Her smile lit my heart, and I picked her up, bringing her into my arms.

"Why are you carrying me?"

"Because I'm not taking a chance that your jealous ass doesn't get yourself tangled up again. Although I'd welcome the ability to soak those pants another time."

She giggled and snuggled her face into my neck, her teeth biting into me.

"Stop that. I'm having a difficult enough time trying to relax this raging hard-on."

"I can take care of that for you."

"No, you will not. You will focus and get us out of this realm so I can deal with your nightmare creatures."

She huffed. "Why are you still carrying me?"

"Because I like it, and you'll deal with it until I'm ready to put you down."

She snuggled deeper into my hold, and I rested my chin against her head. Continuing down the path, I didn't want to release my hold on her, fearing I might lose her if I did.

CHAPTER 12
DEL

Graham continued to carry me. His strong arms were protective and comforting. What he'd done to me when I'd been entangled in the vines had been wonderful. Everything he did to me was that way—a bliss that filled my body, calling to me in ways no one ever had. It was like he knew exactly how I worked, saw me for who I was, and embraced me. Only my brothers had ever seen me that way. The others only saw the madness, even those gods I'd slept with in the past. The fear was under the surface, driving the action. None ever invited my madness, my need for pain, my need for the insanity that fed me.

None but Graham.

He dropped me, and I gave him a sad whine.

"Don't give me that and put those puppy dog eyes away. You can walk." He pushed past me, broody and sexy like I preferred him.

When he was like that it kept me in a constant state of need for him. Now that I knew what that broodiness brought to his sexuality, it only worsened the state. It still irked me that he'd slept with Violence, that he'd wanted to take her with that brutal side of him. I supposed it helped to know what a dud she was in the bedroom, although knowing him, I was sure it hadn't taken place in the bedroom.

"Del." His voice cut through my thoughts.

"Hmm?"

"Why are your delusions whipping around you in a frenzy?" He'd stopped walking, and his brown eyes were assessing me.

I summoned my delusions back, not having realized they'd fled me.

"No reason."

He cocked his brow at me, his lips curving slyly. "What were you thinking about?"

"Nothing." I brushed past him, not wanting to admit my mind had wandered back to that. But it had. Violence and I played a game where we walked the tightrope of friend to enemy. I had never liked her since that moment when we were young, but in time, she'd started approaching me, talking to me again. There were times when I thought she might be a friend, but then she'd turn on me, just as she had today.

His hand encircled my waist, and he pulled me back to him. He stood there, waiting for my answer.

"Let it go, Graham. It's nothing you want to hear."

His eyes darkened, and he furrowed his brow at me. "Are you seriously obsessing about who I've slept with again? What the hell, Del? How many gods have you slept with? You're how many centuries older than me? I think if anyone should be jealous, it's me."

He pushed me away and stormed off, saying, "Focus on something else, or I'll take you gently next time as punishment."

My body jerked at his words. While I had enjoyed him that way, the other side of me, the one he'd taken to places she'd never been, loved his roughness.

"I wasn't being jealous. That was annoyance."

He stopped and turned back to me, crossing his arms. The muscles in them bulged, and I so wanted to grab one and bite it. He waited for me to speak.

"I told you I wanted you when we first met. I waited, respecting Angie, respecting what you had. I could have seduced you, could have forced you to take me then, but I didn't. I continued to wait, and you knew how desperately I wanted you. Yet you took others…you took Violence who is not my friend, no matter how she pretends when she's not teasing me. You took Pen…and good Creator did you take her. Every damn time you did, she told me about it. I don't know why, but she did, and it burned me up. And trust me, she didn't leave out any details. I know how hard you took her."

He shook his head.

"And I know you took them because you wanted me and thought you couldn't have me. You bound yourself to that prom-ise, but it still hurts that they had you first when I was the one who loved you."

His face softened, but he didn't move. I could feel his chaos, had been noticing it more since we'd started the tournament. It swirled around him, calling to my madness. The softness in his face fled, his expression hardening as he stormed over to me. His hand twisted in my hair, and he pulled it, the sensation sending a flood of currents through me. Roughly, he yanked me closer, jerking my head back.

"I will deal with Pen when we're done here for tormenting you. Now, if you don't settle your delusions and convince them to stop this madness, so help me I will bend you over my knee and spank you so hard you won't be able to sit for days."

I couldn't stop the moan that his words caused, the shiver they sent that touched every part of me to the depths only his touch reached.

"Now, I will tell you this once more and only once more. I have loved you since that first day. You called to my chaos then, and you still do. I wanted you then, and I wanted you when I stepped into my powers. I think I've always desired you, even when you were simply the whisper of delusion that slipped into my mind at times. You are the only one who matches my intensity, the only one I have ever taken the way I take you. And yes, I misread Violence, thinking I could have what I wanted with you, with her. Thinking I could feed that need I had for you through her, but I couldn't because only you feed that need, Dellamine. Only you embrace the pain the way I do. You are the only one I want to ever watch fall apart again, the only one I will ever love again, the only one I have ever made scream the way you do." He yanked so hard the pain flashed through my skull, but with it, my delusions danced in delight.

Releasing me, he walked away, leaving me drenched and wanting him again. Who was I fooling, there was never a time when I didn't want him, even when I was fully satisfied.

"Get your ass moving before I leave a handprint on it," he grumbled.

A smile pulled at my lips. He was mine, this side of him was the one he only reserved for me because it was only mine. I didn't care what he'd done with Violence or even Pen, because he'd never done the things he did with me to them. There was no one who could handle him the way I did, and no one who could handle me the way he did. A rush of warmth flushed through me as my heart leapt again.

"And if you don't stop wasting my time reassuring your insecure mania, so help me, Del, I will tie you down and torture you for hours before I finally give you release," I heard him threaten as he continued to walk away.

My delusions swarmed in the excitement that only he brought to them. I laughed and ran to him, jumping on his back.

Instinctively, he caught me, his arms encircling my legs, and I wrapped my arms around his neck.

"I thought I said I wasn't carrying you anymore," he groused.

I tightened my grip on his neck, and he stopped walking. Biting his ear, I whispered, "You'll carry me, so this damned wetness soaks into your back like it's currently soaking my pants."

A low growl rumbled through his chest, and I groaned at the sound, gripping his neck tighter and knowing I was making it very hard for him to breathe on multiple levels.

"Fuck, Del. We won't ever leave this realm if you don't stop." I released his neck and dropped my hand to feel his firmness, which was pressing against his pants. "I'm serious, Del," he said as I stroked him.

"You didn't have any release, and I know you want it."

"And I won't have it until we've moved more than the few feet we have."

I bit at his neck and squeezed his dick before stroking upward again. He had a fantastic dick, and I wanted nothing more than to sink my mouth around it and let my tongue dance over the length of it.

"I bet you taste phenomenal," I whispered, and he twitched in my hand in response.

"Cut it out, Del." He jerked me up, adjusting his hold on my legs and began walking again, a move that forced my hand from him.

"You're no fun."

"Not now I'm not, but I will hold you to that invitation when we stop again."

"What invitation?" I asked with a slight coo to my voice.

"Your mouth around my dick as I fill it."

His words were hard and dirty, and a flush of arousal soaked me more.

"Mmm, I am a bit hungry," I mumbled against his ear.

"Dammit, Del, I'm serious. Stop turning me on and let's finish this damned tournament so I can ravage you for days, and you can let me fuck that gorgeous mouth of yours a few times."

My moan was feral, ripping through me like a thousand claws shredding my body. I couldn't help the quiver it caused.

"You need to stop talking dirty like that, Graham. It's going to make me come on your back."

He stopped, turning his neck to look at me. His eyes were a rich brown, the gold in them vibrant. "You're naughty," he said.

"And you love every bit of my naughtiness."

"Damned right I do." He began walking again, and I settled my head in his neck, content to feel the movement of his muscles with his steps.

He didn't seem to mind carrying me, didn't complain, and we fell into a contented silence. With the rhythm of his steps, I drifted off, my dreams filled with him until his voice woke me.

"Del," he said in a hushed tone.

"Mmm."

"What is that?"

I blinked my eyes against the grogginess and saw the change in terrain, the way the nightmare realm cast its shadows into Heart's realm.

"We're almost home. That's the Nightmare Kingdom."

He let my legs slide down, still holding tight to my waist and keeping me close to him.

"No. That." He inclined his head in the other direction, and I followed with my eyes.

A massive creature, one I'd never seen the likes of, was watching us intently. It reminded me of a beetle with its rounded shell and small head. But this beetle was as large as my castle and its wings, as they spread open, spanned as wide as its body.

"I...I don't know."

"That's not one of your brother's creatures?"

"No, that's not a creature of the nightmare realm. It's too colorful. See the red against the black spots. We don't do color in our realm."

"It looks like a ladybug on steroids," he said, but I wasn't certain what either of those things were.

"It looks like a beetle," I argued.

He shot me a look. "A ladybug. It's red with black spots. It's a fucking enormous ladybug."

I glared at him. "Well, do ladybugs eat people?"

"When they're that size? I'd imagine they eat whatever the hell they want."

It let out a roar that shook the ground, and I debated whether I'd be able to tame something that angry and that large, something that wasn't from my kingdom. But it wasn't from Heart's either. I'd been in my aunt's kingdom enough, in all of the kingdoms enough, to know what creatures wandered the lands. This was not one of them.

"I don't know what that is or where it comes from, Graham," I said, my power pushing for release.

"It's not Heart's?" He looked at me with surprise, his eyes wide.

"No, nor is it from your sister's realm."

"No, she doesn't like bugs. Her chaos is also less physical."

"Right. So, if it's not from any of the surrounding realms..." I trailed off, trying to make sense of the creature and where it had come from.

"What?" he asked as I studied it.

Its color was reminiscent of Heart's kingdom, but the black of it was gnarled and uneven. Its expression was terrifying, calling to my delusions and my connection to my brothers and to our realm. But it didn't belong there, I knew that without a doubt. As it drew closer, I saw the swirl of chaos in its beady eyes, and my confusion grew.

"Does it call to your chaos, Graham?" I asked him, curious to know if the thing called to both of us. If so, it was more worrisome than it looked. No creature called to a god unless it belonged to that god's realm.

He was quiet for a moment, and the beast moved closer. As it let out another deafening roar, he said, "Yes, strangely enough."

"That's not good."

"No, it keeps coming closer."

"Not that, although that's not a good thing either. It's not distinctly from any realm. It's a blend of Heart, Nightmare, and Chaos. As if all three realms were melding together. No, all four realms, beetles would hail from Nature's realm. Shit, that's why it looks like an innocent beetle."

He turned sharply to look at me. "That thing is not innocent looking."

"No, but in Nature's realm it would be. All the realms that touch Chaos and Heart are represented in that beast. What in the Creator's name are the Elders up to?"

"I don't know," he answered, his voice sounding as confused as mine.

We stared at each other, but from the corner of my eye, I saw the beast begin to charge. I brought my hands to Graham's face and turned his eyes back to the rapidly approaching creature.

"Fuck, that's one angry mutant." He pushed me behind him, and when I tried to move back, he yelled, "Stay behind me, this one's mine. He doesn't feel like he wants to play with your power, nor does he look like he plays nice."

Graham whipped the two silver rods out, and in one thrust of his arms, they expanded. I couldn't help but stare as he ran toward the beast, no power drawn, just sheer force and muscle. Good Creator but he was something to look at, and as he met the beast head on, I remained frozen in place, my body on fire as I watched in wonder. This man was mine. He was pure physical power that put the other gods to shame.

He brought his metal weapons to its legs, slashing as the creature jutted its jaw down to bite at him. Leaping from its grasp, he rolled beneath it, avoiding its collapsing body. The beast roared again, its wing coming down to catch him and throwing him.

My heart hammered in fear. We were mortal in the tournament, and he could easily be wounded or even killed. Death had never happened, our powers offered enough protection, but against this beast, I wasn't so sure. There had never been a creature from a myriad of realms, and I wasn't certain what that made it.

Graham had landed on his feet. I remembered Claire once saying he'd been a fighter, training her when they were younger. I supposed he'd always been a fighter, never raised to depend on his powers. His physical strength was his power. It made me wonder if he'd never given up that part of himself when he'd taken his place as a god. If he'd continued training, he was far deadlier than any of the others gave him credit for. Without our powers, we were weak. But not Graham, he would remain a force to be reckoned with.

He lunged at the wings, which, to my horror, separated from the beast's body and sped from it, engaging Graham in a one-on-one battle. Flashes of red and silver were all I could see, the movements were so fast. The body of the beast rose and turned its attention to me.

"Well, damn," I muttered. "Looks like you're ready to have some fun."

I called my delusions, feeling their strength as they fled from me in long white and silver streaks. Reaching for the nightmare within the creature, I summoned it, waiting for it to heed my command, but it ignored me. Jacks was the more commanding of the three of us, the only one who truly had control over the creatures in our realm. But this wasn't a creature from our realm, the power of the connected realms lay fragmented within it. I didn't know if even Jacks could manage to control this creature.

It screeched as my delusions slammed into it, seeking out its mind but bouncing back on the impact. I stumbled back. Never had I met a creature that I could not corrupt, and it unnerved me. The beast began its run again, this time toward me. I reached further in, summoning my powers to the fullest. The air around me swirled with the force of my insanity. I unleashed it upon the beast only to have it break right through.

"Del!" Graham screamed, and I saw him slash through the wings, the creature letting out a ground-shaking squeal but not stopping its path.

I didn't know what to do, and for the first time in my existence, terror touched me—my brother's power. And I had no doubt he would feel it slice through me. Our connection was too strong for Jacks not to notice. I knew just as he would that our kingdom would quake from the impact of the corrosion its daughter was facing from one of its own children. Pain I welcomed. Theo's connection to me was not as close as Jacks'. Madness and Terror went hand in hand; we were the closest of the three of us. Pain was like a salve to my insanity, distanced enough. Terror, however, would be my undoing.

The infection the terror had caused racked my body. A rift in my own bounds grew, my delusions crashing through my mind as they wrestled with it. My knees faltered, my legs going out from under me as I fell to the ground. My breathing constricted. I could feel Jacks' presence, his confusion as his power was drawn to mine.

"Del!" Graham screamed again.

The ground quaked, the boundary that separated Heart from

Nightmare quivering with the impact on its children. My vision blurred, my mind ripping apart with the further shredding of my power as terror fought for control.

Del? I heard Jacks' confusion as his mind touched mine further. It was something that shouldn't have happened through the sequestered status he was in. But it had because we were both fracturing. Delusion and Terror were meant to be close but never together.

The hold on my power slipped from my grasp, a thick tear of silver sliding down my cheek as everything I was crumbled within my mind.

CHAPTER 13
GRAHAM

Something was happening to Del. The creature was barreling down on her, and she hadn't moved. Her delusions hadn't slowed it, nor had the release of her full power. I was running to it, but my eyes were glued to her. Fear had overtaken her eyes, the silver in them stilling then growing. With each step closer the creature came, the silver grew until nothing was left of the green. She'd fallen to her knees, no life left in her as a vacant look overcame her features.

I dug my weapon into the ground and used it to propel myself onto the back of the beast, taking my other weapon and ramming it down into a soft spot the wings had covered. It reared back, the ground flying up over Del who still hadn't moved. A flow of silver was streaming from her eyes, and my heart thudded at the sight. I hadn't been so scared since the day Claire had been attacked.

I dug the weapon in further as the beast struggled. Drawing on my power, I threw my hand out and drew the rays from the sun down, casting its heat in a blast that set the beast on fire. I flung myself from its back and ran to Del, ignoring the screeches of death that were pouring from it.

"Del." I took her face in my hands. Her eyes were solid silver that leaked down her cheeks. "Del, please. You're safe. Wake up."

I shook her, but she only slumped into my arms, staring vacantly ahead. "Del, it's over. The beast is dead."

I didn't know what to do or what was wrong with her. I could barely feel her breathing. Pulling her close to me, I brushed her hair back, trying to think of what to do. The silver had taken over, and the silver was her madness, the power that lie in connection with her delusions. I'd always noticed how they flickered more intensely when her power was drawn and stilled when she let her vulnerability show. I had to draw her out, release her from the hold her power had on her, locking her in her mind. She was in a catatonic state, her insanity full-blown and out of control. But how did I fix that?

I had two sides to me, control and chaos. She had one to her, only her madness. There was a chance one side of my power could call to her. I just wasn't certain which one. She wanted my chaos, always invited it, freeing it when we were lost to each other. My chaos and her delusion were compatible but did one rule the other? I drew my chaos to the surface, noting how my body reacted, how my mind came alive. Setting it free, I let it surround us and cascade over her body.

"Wake for me, Del," I said softly, bringing my lips to hers. "Wake for me."

I felt the connection as my power searched for its other half, the delusion in her that brought me to ecstasy, the part of her that called to who I truly was. I bit down on her lip hard enough to break the skin, hoping to stir her more.

"Del," I whispered against her lips, kissing her once I'd licked the blood away.

140

I gripped her arms, knowing I was squeezing the bruises I'd left, the ones that lay below those that the vines had caused. "Del, wake up now before I turn your ass around and make it sore from more than my hand," I growled.

She inhaled sharply, her body arching against my hold and I watched the silver crawl back to her eyes, breaking into fragments that came alive behind the sage. Blinking, she brought her hand up shakily to touch my face.

"How—"

"Shhh," I said, dropping my head to hers. "You're safe now." I had sensed the fleeing of Jackson's power, like a draft across my skin, when she'd returned to me. She'd been afraid to the point that terror had touched her. The mixing of two powers that intense, brother and sister, had broken her. And Jackson and Del were extremely close. Close enough to shatter their kingdom if the two were damaged. I wondered if it had affected Jackson as well and if Claire was on the other side trying to break through to him as I had been to Del.

"You brought me back," she said with a tremor in her voice.

"I told you, I promised Theo and Jackson I would keep you protected. I'm not about to piss them off any more than they already will be when they find out I touched you."

She smiled, and it was glorious, but then it faded too quickly. "What happened, Del?"

She shivered, her eyes looking away. "I was weak. I...I couldn't defeat it. I tried, but my power bounced right off it, and—"

"And you were terrified. Letting Jackson's power invade you."

"Yes. I've never experienced terror, he's too close to me."

"But you let pain in?" I was so confused.

"Theo's power is different. Jacks rules our kingdom, and because of that, he rules delusion and pain. Even before he ruled the kingdom, he ruled us. Theo is older, more distant from my power, so when pain touches me, I don't feel him within it or my connection to our kingdom. It's only pleasure that pain brings, likely because I do have a weak tie to it through my blood. Terror is different."

"Because it's too close to you, Jackson is too close to you."

"Yes, Jacks and I are only a year apart in age. Our powers are sourced from the same place, they intersect on many levels because of that. So when terror overcame my power, the two began to battle within my mind, and I think in his. The delusion incites terror, and terror begets delusion, so my mind collapsed. But you brought me back. How?"

"I don't really know. I just sent you my chaos, knowing you loved it, and I gave you a bit of pain, and a few threats."

"Mmm, distracting my mind's grip on the terror and offering pleasure in its place. I do remember a threat of you giving my ass pain that wasn't from your hand."

The flicker of desire in her eyes was enough to make me forget the fear I'd had.

"So I did."

"Want to try me out?" she asked in a sultry voice.

"Hmm, it's tempting because I really do like that ass. However, there's a strange creature behind me that did not respond to your power, and that makes me nervous. I'd prefer to get to your realm before I bend you over and have my way with you."

"Damn, that would have been a nice way to bring me completely back to par."

"Fucking you in the ass would bring you back to par?"

I saw the shiver that ran through her, the slight quake in her body.

"Damn right it would, and if you keep talking like that, I'm going to be too wet to walk."

"Shit, Del. You make things hard, don't you?"

Her hand reached down and stroked the firmness that lay in my pants. "It would appear I make them very hard."

I shoved her hand away and brought her against me, kissing her. I wanted to take her with a desperation, but I'd almost lost her and who knew if there were more of those things out there vying to take her from me. I drew back and lifted her body from my arms. Standing, I pulled her up with me.

She wobbled a little, and I threw her a look.

"You have that effect on me," she said. "That's not from the creature, that's all you, Turning." Damn, I loved it when she called me by my power, The way she said it was always so erotic. "Watching you battle that thing had me so wet. By the Creator, you're sexy when you fight."

"Really?" I asked, giving her a cocky grin. "I'd be happy to battle a few more things if it has that effect on you."

"That's dangerous."

"I like danger."

She laughed, but I saw the slight shimmer of her true self slip in, the vulnerability that she'd almost been lost, a prisoner of her own mind in the same way she infected mortals. I pulled her close, holding her tight, ignoring how fantastic her body felt against mine, and kept her in a protective hug. She melted into me, and we stayed that way for a few minutes until she finally pushed me away.

"Stop that, you'll give me a bad reputation."

"I thought you already had a bad reputation. Aren't you the resident crazy goddess?"

She stuck her tongue out and twisted her fingers through her hair. Those two moves combined made my dick jump. She was too sexy for her own good.

"Keep that tongue in your mouth before I put it to use," I said, turning back to the beast and walking away from her.

"I wouldn't mind that. I bet you taste like no other god."

I looked over my shoulder at her. "Do I want to know how many gods you've gone down on? I don't want to hear about my few fuck sessions with all the times I bet you've had other gods in your pants or your mouth."

Her lips curved in a coy grin, and I knew it was true. "There may have been a few."

"A few? How many centuries are you?"

"Enough to know none of them were as good as you."

"Nice try," I said, studying the beast closer.

"I'm serious. They're all intimidated by me. No one ever took my insanity head-on like you do."

"That's because they're not real men like me. I'm the only one who knows how to please that side of you, Del."

Her eyes grew soft, her expression childlike. "Yes, you are."

"So, what is this thing and why is it in Heart's realm?" I asked, ready to move on from the subject and this place. I really didn't want to know how many men or gods she'd had. From watching her in the alley with that mortal, I could only imagine what the number was, and it stirred my jealousy.

"Not sure but look."

I turned to see another one further away. "It's dead. I didn't even notice it."

"We were too busy fighting."

"I was too busy fighting. You were too busy playing the damsel in distress."

"Really?" There was a bit of hurt in her voice. It irritated her that she'd fallen and that I'd had to pull her from the brink of death.

"Don't like being rescued?"

"No, I don't."

"Well, you'll like it later when you're thanking me with that mouth of yours."

"I thought it was my ass."

"Don't worry, I'll fuck that, too, but first I want that mouth."

Her reaction was everything I'd hoped. I truly didn't care how I got to take her, as long as I was taking her.

Grinning, I asked, "Do you need a dry pair of pants?"

She narrowed her eyes at me, her lips set in a scowl.

"You're adorable when you're angry, Del." I looked toward the other dead creature. "I'm guessing Angst and Violence ran into the other one and took it down."

"Shame it didn't eat her," she muttered before she looked at me, her eyes questioning.

"Really? You want to know if I went down on her? You are a masochist."

She stared me down.

"No, I did not. Like I said, she wasn't up to my par, so I didn't want to give her anything extra. Now Pen, that's another story."

I ducked as her delusions whipped at me. Laughing, I dragged her to me and kissed her. She fought against me, but I was stronger.

"Don't even…" I deepened my kiss to cut her off, sweeping my fingers across her breast.

"Now, stop it and lead the way to your kingdom so I can ravage you like my dick is aching to do."

I released her and walked away, leaving her with that annoyed look that made me smile. She trudged behind me quietly, but I could feel her irritation like daggers in my back.

"You're going to have to fight to get a piece of me when we get there," she grumbled.

Laughing, I replied, "I look forward to the challenge. Fighting with you is quite the turn-on. Will you continue to fight when I'm thrusting into you? Because that might make it even more exciting."

"You're demented."

"Says the goddess of delusion."

I heard the huff and couldn't resist turning back to her, letting her smack into me since her eyes had been trailing the ground instead of me.

"Are you going to stop grumbling?"

"Are you going to stop being a perv?" There was a twinkle in her eye, but I didn't give her the privilege of receiving a smile from me. Instead, I pursed my lips into a grimace and glared at her.

"I'm not a perv. It's only gross if you don't enjoy it."

"And what if I don't?"

I raised my brow at her. "I find that highly unlikely." Bringing her closer, I dug my fingers into her hip, seeing the reaction, the spark of lust that filled her eyes. "All you have to do is say the word, and I'll go gentle on you."

It was the truth. I would never hurt her if she didn't invite it, never take her if she didn't want it. That wasn't me, and it never would be. The chaos in me may have changed me when I finally accepted it, giving me that thirst for roughness, the thirst for pain, but the man I was would never allow me to take those things without permission. Even the thought sickened me.

"But I don't know the word." Her voice was seductive, causing my need for her to rise again.

I needed to let her go and turn my focus back to getting us out of there before I gave into that need again. "Do you need one?" I asked, nibbling at her neck.

"No," she answered with a deep sigh. And I knew it was the truth. She didn't need a safe word because her intensity matched mine, and she trusted me to keep her safe. Anything I did to her, she'd do right back to me, and I trusted her the same way. She could hurt me all she wanted, and I would climax each time for her, just like she would for me. It was twisted, demented even but it was who we were and why we fit so perfectly together.

I bit her, hearing the purr it caused, and forced myself to let her go. Damn, she'd made me hard again and walking was going to be difficult. I adjusted myself and turned back to the task of getting us out of this realm and this tournament.

"This is the last tournament we do, understood?" I griped.

"Why Graham, only bonded gods can avoid it or those who are promised to bond."

I glanced back at her. "Pen and Cal are bonding?"

"Guess you were her last free fuck. I hope you made it a good one." I could tell she was forcing the humor out. That it still irritated her that I'd taken Pen instead of her. But I'd given her my reason and it had been the truth. I couldn't touch her because doing so would have caused me to admit that I'd loved her all that time.

"It was, especially when my face was between her legs," I taunted, waiting for the reaction.

Her delusion stung me faster than I expected, striking my mind with a force that stopped me in my tracks before it ripped free from me. I threw her a look. Her eyes were brilliant, the green dancing with the slivers that were speeding around it.

"You're too sensitive, Del. But next time, sting harder. I invite the pain." Her jaw tightened, and I couldn't help but laugh. "As I said, next time, we sit this one out. I can ravage you plenty without all this tournament nonsense."

Her mouth opened, and I saw the understanding. Her eyes lit, the silver stilling for just a moment. Throwing her a wink, I turned back to our trek, knowing her thoughts. Knowing she was questioning me. But I was certain. She was it for me, there was no other who would ever make me feel like Del did. No other who would call to the chaos in me, nor that my chaos would heed. And I knew there was no other except me who could revel in her madness, who could own it the way I did.

Now that I'd let my walls down and admitted my feelings for her, I would never again cage them. And I would never let her go. Bonding was the ultimate step for gods and only a rare few did it, my sister and Jackson included. It was our version of marriage but one that went deeper, one that was eternal. I had no doubts. Del was mine, and I would never let her go again.

CHAPTER 14

DEL

I stared at Graham's back as he continued to walk. Bonding. The idea made my heart jump within my chest. The idea that I would be his forever, that he would never belong to another, only me, sent my delusions into a frenzy. They whipped around me in excitement.

"Catch up before I come back there and carry you again," he growled, the sound warming my heart in a way only he could.

I ran and jumped on his back again, wrapping my arms so tight around his neck that I heard his airway cut off for that moment. He ripped my hands away and turned fast, flinging me over his shoulder before I could even react. A giggle escaped me as he began walking again.

"You ever strangle me that hard again, and I'll be coming in my pants, dammit. You can't just do that while I'm walking. Being with you is torture to my dick." He continued to grouse, my smile growing with each complaint until he smacked my ass, and a gush of arousal soaked my pants.

"You're a tease, Turning," I said, knowing how he reacted each time I called him by his power.

"And you're naughty, Del," he replied, his hand drifting between my legs and rubbing against that fresh dampness. "And soaked. Shit, I can feel it through your pants. That was a mistake."

"Well, you could put me down and take advantage of that."

"No."

"Stubborn."

"Tease."

We continued to banter playfully, my body slung over his shoulder, until darkness surrounded us, and I could feel the change in power around us.

"Are we in your realm?" he asked, dropping me suddenly.

I wobbled a little after being in the air for so long, and his strong hands encased my waist to steady me. There was nothing sexual about the move this time, only tension. That tension blanketed him.

"No, not yet. The darkness isn't pervasive enough. But we're close."

I took a step further into the dark, but he grabbed me back. "Something doesn't feel right about it."

I reached out for my connection to my realm, the nightmares that it held, the layering of my brother's power with Theo's and my own. He was right, there was something off about it, something corrupt, as if it were no longer pure.

He pulled me back a step. "You feel it, don't you?"

"Yes, but I don't know what to make of it. And we need to get to the border to cross out of Heart."

He rolled his neck, his brow creased in thought. He was cute when he was like this. I couldn't help but run my hand through the tussle of his auburn hair. Snatching my hand back, he scolded me, "Not now, Del. We need to be on guard. My chaos is stirring in a strange way, and I don't like it."

I dropped my hand, trying to hide my hurt. I should have

been used to it. He'd been like that—gruff and unyielding—since I'd met him, but now that we'd taken the next step, I hadn't expected the rebuttal.

His eyes drew from the darkness and dropped to mine. They were hard, and I could see the warrior in him was on guard, the protector. "I won't risk you being harmed again, so don't touch me like that until we're out of whatever this is. Then, you can run your hand through my hair all you want." He lowered his mouth to my ear. "But I prefer when you're pulling it."

Creator, he was going to break me right there. My knees buckled, but he held me up.

"Now be on guard and ready your powers. I don't want anything touching you except me."

I clung to his arm, trying to remain upright. He had me so tantalized that I locked my thighs tight in reaction.

"None of that, Del. When I'm ready for you to come, you'll know. But keep that wetness there because I'm going to fuck you so hard later that you'll be aching for days."

The moan I'd been biting back escaped, and he chuckled as he bit my ear and walked away. "Damn, I bet you're soaked even more now," he muttered, leaving me there.

Come back with something, Del, I yelled at myself. But he'd left me aching too badly for him that my words wouldn't heed my command. The way that man unraveled me was too much.

I calmed my breathing and tried to focus on anything but the way his muscles moved when he walked. My mind recalled how they'd felt when they were ramming into me earlier. He made it hard to think, he always had.

He stopped, his muscles tensing, and the move woke me. I scooted to where he was standing.

"Do you feel it?" he asked, his power spilling out around him. It called to my own, the seduction of his stronger powers and the promise of his chaos. My delusions reacted, slipping from me. I could see the wisps of white flitting around.

But then they moved back, closer to me as if they'd touched something they didn't like. I perceived it in the air, a stirring of something that I couldn't quite pinpoint, and within it sat the power of my realm and Claire's. Nightmare and Chaos shadowing something below, Heart's realm softly humming around them.

"I do, and my delusions don't like it."

He glanced at me, no play in those brown eyes, only worry. He took my hand and moved forward. There was no other option. Nightmare was the next realm in the tournament. It always was. Every one of us knew the map, following the lead of the Elders, knowing the path had been the same through every tournament since they'd begun. Although they had changed the path already, pushing straight to Heart rather than Nature. But the instinct to go to Heart had been there. A subtle draw, not this. This was more like a blunt redirection, a force pushing us from Nightmare's border.

He kept me close, which I found adorable. His need to protect me—a goddess who had lived countless centuries more than he had—was endearing. I didn't mind. I was safe with him and knew he would never compromise the side I hid from everyone but my brothers. That he understood it and would always shield it.

Each step took us further into darkness, and I could feel the call of my realm. Home. It settled on me like a soft blanket, reassuring my delusions, strengthening my madness, my powers pushing to release at the touch. But in that comfort lie a trace of that uncertainty. A sense of that unknown that neither of us could pinpoint along with a touch of chaos. The only time I noticed nightmare and chaos mingling was when Claire and Jacks were around, or the times Graham had released his chaos when we'd had sex. His chaos was comforting, like the nightmares were, like terror and pain were when they touched the surface of my power.

Graham's grip on my hand tightened. We stayed silent, both on guard. Theo had said the Elders had added extra challenges, upping the game this time. With Jacks sitting in with them now, I wondered if he had added his own games in our realm. But even if that were the case, I shouldn't have been unsettled. I was stronger in Nightmare. Every god was stronger in their own kingdom.

After some time, we came to the border. It was pitch black, but Graham threw a trace of light out for us to see the path ahead. When we reached the thickness of Nightmare's hold, we could go no further. The air grew heavy, and we couldn't move past the border. That force I'd been sensing seemed to have transformed into something physical.

"What the hell?" Graham muttered, his hand trying to break through the thickness that lay before us. It was like a wall we couldn't pass through.

He looked at me, waiting for an explanation, but I had none. I tried to move forward, but no matter how I tried, I couldn't. Calling my delusions, I sent them free to break through, but they only bounced back at me.

"I don't understand," I said, knowing my face reflected my confusion. "Nightmare is always next. There has never been a change."

"Well, someone decided to change it. Let's see if we can get through further down."

He didn't wait for my reply, dragging me along beside him. His walk was fast and determined, but I could see the tension in his muscles which were ready to strike. His hand was on his weapon, his power drawn.

"None of this feels right," he mumbled, walking us further

153

on. He stopped every so often groping for an entrance but not finding any.

Pulling his hand back after we'd walked for some time, I said, "Graham, stop."

"Keep moving, Del. I'm not stopping here. It doesn't feel right."

I dug my heels in the ground and yanked him back. "They won't let us through, Graham. I think we need to go through Chaos first. And…I need to move away from the border."

His eyes evaluated me. "What's wrong?"

I didn't know how to explain it, but the more we walked along the border, the further south we went, the more frantic my power had become. It was moving through my mind like a swarm of bees. The sensation was so intense that I knew I could go no further.

He moved closer, his finger going to the corner of my eye, concern deepening in his expression. "What is it?"

I searched his eyes, wondering why his voice held such worry.

"Dammit, Del. What's wrong? Your slivers are out of control, almost chaotic."

So it was showing and, of course, he would notice.

"I don't know. It's that same reaction I had earlier, but now my power is screaming, rattling around my head like a nest of hornets."

He scrunched his eyes, and I could see him thinking it through, trying to find the reasoning behind it but finding none. "That's it. We walk to Claire's realm, but we backtrack away from the border."

"That will take us hours. We'll—"

"I don't care. I couldn't give two fucks about this tournament. The only reason I'm doing it is because I'm with you, and I promised your brothers I'd watch you. I would have conveniently hidden in the mortal world to avoid this nonsense otherwise."

I tipped my head. "And risk the wrath of the Elders?"

"Fuck the Elders. I've never been part of this shit, I don't need it in my life now."

I couldn't help my smile. Creator, how I loved this man. "You sound like you've had a touch of me," I teased.

"I have, and I'll be touching you again once we're out of this disturbing shit."

"I don't remember you being this gruff when we first met," I observed while we walked away from the border.

"I wasn't. Well, I suppose it was there, under the surface. I never accepted my powers fully when I was in the mortal world. I couldn't, it would have revealed me and Claire." He dragged me along, not bothering to look at me while he spoke. "I didn't change until I accepted it. The chaos that lies below my control over the dawn and dusk provokes my aggressive side, and when I'm aggressive, I feel—"

"Content," I finished for him, understanding what he experienced on a level I knew only he and I would.

He looked over at me, searching my eyes. "Yeah."

I squeezed his hand. "I'm glad you accepted it," I said quietly, and he squeezed my hand back.

We walked on, the darkness still upon us, but the heaviness lifting, my power calming.

"It's dark, we should stop," he said, turning me to him and holding my head as he tipped it up to observe my eyes.

"I feel calmer," I said, hoping we could stop. I was tired, ready for rest, ready for him.

"Good."

He looked around, walking over to a tree that had fallen and rested upon another at a slanted angle. After pushing on it quite roughly, he turned to me and removed his shirt. My heart beat out of control, my delusions flickering in a frenzy.

He gestured to me with a finger, and I raised a brow at him.

"I think we promised each other some pleasure and…a whole lot of pain," he said.

My legs twitched, my chest heaving with the breath he'd stolen from me. "Did we?"

"Mmm, yeah. Something to do with your mouth and your ass."

"Creator." I sighed at the thought. My hands had grown clammy, my pants soaked.

"You going to make me carry you over here?" he asked, unbuttoning the top button of his pants.

This man was going to be the death of me. My eyes perused his chest, watching as he unhooked the next button. I couldn't help the way my mouth had started salivating. I wanted to taste him like I wanted to torment mortals. The thought sent my delusions slamming through my mind.

Walking to him, I lifted my shirt, freeing my breasts and watching how the hunger in his eyes grew as they devoured them. I moved his hand, running both my hands up his chest, reveling in the firmness of his muscles. He palmed my breast, cupping it before sliding his fingers along my nipple. A moan slipped from my lips, and I pushed my mouth to his, kissing him with an insatiable need that was burning through me. His fingers weaved through my hair then gripped my neck, shoving my mouth harder against his. The need that was there sent a flood of warmth through my body, and wetness growing between my legs.

"Del," he groaned against my mouth. My hand worked the rest of his buttons open, then moved in to feel him. I grasped his thickness, stroking my hand along it and craving it, but he distracted me. His hand slipped down my pants, dipping into the moisture I knew had puddled there. I tightened my grip around his length, and a grunt escaped him that tore at the depths of my need for him. As I pushed at his pants, he shoved mine down, slamming my body so hard against the tree that my lips were forced from his by the cry that clawed from my throat.

His hands were all over me at once, my body ablaze. It was so bad I couldn't move from his touch. My body was riveted by the sensations that were assaulting me. I tipped my head back, biting my lip against the scream that was welling inside of me, begging to tear through me. I was lost in his touches, the squeeze of his hand, the pinch of my skin between his fingers, the bite of his teeth around my nipples. All of it caused my delusions to burst from me in a fury of power that shook the ground around us as it coaxed his chaos out to dance with it.

My scream broke free, and my climax ripped through me, breaking me, shattering me from the inside out. All I could do was hold his arms as I lost all control, my body his to own, to use and take as he wanted. His hand grasped the back of my neck, forcing my lips to his, my scream stifled by his kiss. My body shook uncontrollably in his grip as he lifted me. All thoughts of tasting him fled my mind when he sank deep into me, waking my body again with the fullness of him. Each thrust sent the bark of the tree further into my skin, opening the wounds from the prior night, the wounds my bound immortality couldn't repair. They were marks of our love, of our passion that I would carry until we finished the tournament that had brought us to this point.

The pain blended with the pleasure, the rhythm of his move-ments, and the weight of his body as it pressed into mine. The way he kissed me as if he would never have enough of me, drowned me. Our power encased us, a blend of madness and chaos that sent shivers along my skin further hurtling me toward a second climax. I clung to him, my nails ripping through his skin. My other hand pulled his hair so hard it tore but his hand was deeply wound in my own hair, doing the same. My release slammed through me with such force that I shook violently in his arms. My cry against his lips met the groan that poured forth from his mouth as his own release forced its way through his body.

Electric currents flashed in waves within my body, the madness I lived in so stimulated that it scraped at my mind. As he pushed the last of his essence into me, my head fell to his chest. I could barely move, barely think, barely breathe. He backed away from the tree, keeping me in his arms, his hands holding my ass. My legs were clinging to him so tight he could have removed his hands and I would have remained there. Nothing was moving me from his arms. Nothing would ever take him from me because I would never let him go.

He kissed my neck and lowered me to the ground, a soft blanket pampering my back.

"You going to remove your legs, Del?" he asked, his voice raspy. It was a sexy sound and stirred my need for him again.

"No, I don't think so."

He laughed against my neck, licking his way to my lips and kissing me softer.

"Why not?" he asked through his kiss.

"Because I don't want to let you go," I replied, my voice barely a whisper.

He nuzzled my nose then drew back to look at me. "You never have to let me go." I couldn't help my smile, loving how it lit his eyes, the gold in them sparkling. "You okay?" he asked.

I squinted my eyes at him. "Why?"

"Because your back is raw and bleeding."

"Is it? I didn't notice."

I hadn't. The pain had only sent me over the cliff of ecstasy with his body. He pried my legs from him and I gave him a pouty lip.

Laughing, he bent down and nibbled my lip. "Turn over," he said.

"How many times do I need to tell you I don't take commands."

Growling, he grabbed my legs and flipped me, forcing my body down. I gave him a purr and he shivered.

"Is this where you take my ass?" I asked, tilting my ass to him. He shoved it back, my pelvis hitting the ground with a flash of pain that had me wet again. "Don't tease, Turning."

His hand caressed my ass before he pulled the legs of my pants down the rest of the way. Slowly, inch by inch, his fingers stroked along my skin as he removed each side. I hadn't even noticed they were still on, ripped straight between the two legs with his aggressive need to take me. The thought made me shudder. His hands swept their way back up my legs, squeezing them as they came closer to my waiting warmth. He dipped his fingers into my wetness, stroking along it, teasing right on the outside then sliding to my clit, brushing it firmly before pinching it so that I let another cry loose.

His hands moved over my ass, his thumb rubbing my wetness along my seam, sending a river of moisture to me. My body shook in anticipation. But he moved his hands further up, gently caressing my back, his fingers tiptoeing around each cut, each scrape that layered it. He hovered above me, his hands pressing into my arms after moving my hair to the side.

"I don't want to continue hurting you like this, Del. I can't," he whispered against my ear. "The kind of pain I want to bring you doesn't look like that. You need to heal."

"But it feels good," I admitted, wondering if I'd read him wrong. No one ever understood the depth of hurt I could take, my madness wanting it, my mind needing it because it woke me from the madness for just those brief moments, taking me above it so I could see clearly until I was drowning in the ecstasy of the freedom it provided. It was erotic as the madness, the insanity, danced in the knowledge that pain was my medicine, my sanity. The tightrope I walked in those moments sent me to the heights of orgasm. It was a rush I could never explain, and I had thought he understood when he'd confessed to me about his chaos.

A sadness filled me until he brushed his thumb along my cheek, sliding it over my lips so that it sank into my mouth. The taste of my arousal met my tongue, the rumble from his chest deep and sensual. I hadn't been wrong. He reveled in it just as I did. He moved quickly, picking my hips up and holding them so tight the feel was excruciatingly wonderful. I started to pick my head up, but he slammed my shoulders back down. His hand wrapped around my neck, the pressure sending rivets of tingles pulsing in me.

Leaning against me, he whispered, "I think I promised to fuck you so hard you'd be aching for days."

I sighed, his firmness sliding along my wetness, bumping against my clit so that I was writhing against it. "I don't think so. I'm not ready for you to come, Del. I want to hear you scream first."

"By the Creator, please make me," I moaned.

He gripped my neck tighter, my breath stolen for a matter of seconds before he released it and lifted himself. His finger ran along my ass again, playing until it sank deep into me, his length pushing further against my clit as my arousal seeped around him. My body was ablaze with anticipation, knowing how he liked it, knowing he was going to own every part of me. I gripped the blanket in anticipation as he positioned himself, sliding his fingers deep into my wetness first then plunging his length into my ass with a force that shattered me. My scream cut the silence, raw and sensual. He tore into me with the aggression I knew he reserved for only me, one that no one had ever seen or experienced but me.

"Harder," I cried, and his growl was feral as he pounded into me.

The mix of agony and pleasure was like seduction to my power, and it flared, my delusions toppling the fallen tree and only further enticing his chaos. The result was a grip so tight on my waist that I could have sworn something snapped. I gritted my teeth as my climax pushed for release, climbing with each penetrating drive until it hit me with the same intensity as his thrusts. My scream came from a place I'd never accessed, and I pushed against him until he drew out and slammed into my clenching muscles, stimulating what was still spasming. A second orgasm built before the first could even calm, and I came again, my body drifting downward with the ecstasy that was overwhelming it. He held me by my waist, continuing to pummel me, going so deep that I could barely breathe. My body was quivering in a way it never had, and I thanked the Creator my head was still barred against the blanket for my arms would never have kept me upright.

As it stood, my legs were shaking so badly I didn't think they'd last much longer. As if he knew, he shoved me down, grabbing my legs and flipping me before entering me again brutally. His chest came down against mine in one rough move. I grabbed him by the nape of his neck and lifted my head to meet his lips, my fingernails sinking deep and breaking his skin. Biting his lip hard, I stifled his groan with another kiss as he continued to ravage me.

He took me by the wrists, forcing my arms above my head, his body banging against mine with a passion that left me clamoring for release again. It was climbing, the intensity of his eyes on mine doing nothing to stop it. I'd never wanted a man to ravage me as much as I wanted him to. His jaw was clenched, and I could see he was fighting his own urge to climax. But I wanted him to break. I'd broken twice already.

When he dropped his head to my breasts, biting at them, the sensation was overwhelming. As he went to rise, I arched my back, forcing my breast to remain in his mouth. He chuckled against my skin before nipping at my nipple, pulling it between his teeth in a way that drew me closer. My body was like a raging storm, waves pounding at a cliff that was beginning to crumble.

"Come with me, Graham," I begged him, drawing my legs further up and contracting them around his body, knowing I was bringing him pain. The grunt he emitted sent the waves spilling through me, my climax crashing over me. His thrusts grew more frantic, and he shattered, his head pressing into my chest and stifling the guttural groan that rippled across my skin. I relaxed my legs, my body overcome with an onslaught of pleasure, and wrapped them around his back. He breathed raggedly against me, filling me with a few final thrusts, resting his head there until he finally released my wrists. In my bliss I'd forgotten he had them, my body had convulsed against his hold as he'd held my arms in place.

"Fuck, Del. You are something."

"I could say the same for you, Turning."

His chest rumbled. "I love it when you call me that."

"I know, and it's sexy the way you respond to it."

He lifted his head, pushing himself from my body and hovering over me. His lips slid across mine and I lost myself to the sensuality, the softness of it. Pushing my leg from around him, he let his hand softly caress it, skimming along its length then up my body. Rolling from me, he turned me into him, his fingers sliding across my breast. I looked into his eyes, watching how the gold around them shimmered.

"I love you," I said, running my hand along his jaw.

"Do you? Even after that?"

"Seriously? You can have my ass anytime you want because that was amazing."

His eyes flashed with desire. "I may just take you up on that. I am quite partial to that beautiful ass of yours." He slid his hand down my body and between my legs, sinking his fingers into me. "Although there is nothing like sinking into this goodness."

"You keep those fingers there, and I guarantee there will be more of that goodness than you know what to do with."

He licked his lips, a devious grin forming. "I know exactly what to do with that."

A flutter ran through my stomach as his fingers swept across my clit. I couldn't help the tremble his touch caused.

"Are you going to come for me again, Del?" he asked, his eyes mischievous.

"I do believe I will if those fingers don't stay still."

He stopped his movement but pressed his thumb against my sensitive nub. With the slightest of movements, he teased it. My breath hitched. Each tiny twitch he made was like a strike of lighting.

"What were you saying about staying still?" he asked.

I couldn't answer, my body ablaze once again. Dipping his head, he sucked my nipple into his mouth. He let it sit there against his tongue, and with each minuscule move of his thumb, his tongue twitched. My body shook, aroused to the point that I thought I would fall apart with madness. My delusions were flittering through my head, unsure if they wanted to escape because there was no force pushing them to release. The coaxing of my climax was too subtle, too gentle. The tremors increased, my body on fire in a way it never had been.

"Should I move," he muttered against my breast, his breath cooling the wetness along my skin from his mouth. I lurched, my release so close that my muscles were quaking. In one move, he broke me. The flick of his tongue to my nipple combined with the flick of his thumb against my clit, and I fell apart. My body shook so hard that he had to hold me. My cry was a multitude of sounds that I was unable to stop, an epiphany of ecstasy that gutted me with the sheer force of it.

"I love it when you come," he mumbled in my ear. All I could do was quiver in response and as he slipped between my legs and penetrated me again I knew I would never return from the abyss I'd entered, nor did I ever want to.

CHAPTER 15

GRAHAM

Del was asleep in my arms, snuggled as tight as she could against my body. I watched the rise and fall of her chest like I'd been doing most of the night, still in a daze that she was really mine. I'd taken her so many times before we'd both collapsed that my body had been exhausted. My mind, however, raced. I lay there, letting the night pass by. Thoughts of Del filled my mind when it wasn't on the tournament. She'd matched every demand my body had of her, and the image of her ass as she'd let me own it was enough to tempt me to wake her and fuck her again.

I'd only had a few women that way, trying it with Angie once when we'd both been drunk. It had been erotic, but she'd never let me do it again. It wasn't her. She was all softness, and that was a part of me she didn't know, one the alcohol had tempted. But with Del...there was rarely softness. That softness I knew I would treasure each time it was present, but I would ravage every bit of her rough side. The side that let me have her like I craved, the way other women wouldn't because there was no other woman who matched me, who called to me like she did.

I looked at her, taking in the beauty of her, the perfection of her. Her mouth was slightly opened, those lush lips forming an inviting pout that was just asking to be kissed. I had to look away, my dick coming back to life and twitching to feel those lips around it.

Shit I needed to stop, or I would have to wake her.

I focused instead on the two things that were still nagging at me. The strange beast and the unsettled aura around the border of the nightmare realm. My instinct was screaming, the chaos in me stirred. Although it always stirred around Del, her presence waking it from where I chose to let it sleep. I was my mother's son, not my father's. That's what I'd always told myself, what I remembered Del telling me the first time we met. The first time I'd seen her, knowing exactly who she was and stunned by how that chaos moved within me where I'd never felt it before. She'd hooked me that day and had made no qualms about stating that her eyes were on me.

I smiled at the thought. She'd claimed me then. My heart had belonged to another, but Del had put her stake on it, taking her time to wait until it was ready for her. Until I was ready for her. Had she seen the chaos in me then or had Claire's connection to our father's power overshadowed it?

No, she'd seen it. I had no doubt. She'd sensed it there. She'd owned me that day and continued to own me until there was no denying it. I tightened my hold on her, that instinct nudging me again. That worry returned that I didn't want to continue this journey, that I wanted to stay here with her in my arms, safe and protected. I hated the fact that her immortality had been locked as all of ours had been. Hated that she could be hurt and something beyond this border awaited us that I didn't understand.

The threat wasn't the tournament. Part of me sensed that it was something more. There was a sense of foreboding that I couldn't shake. That was my mother's power, the turning in me, the stability and control that ruled most of me and allowed me sway over the cycles of the day and night. It was strong in me because I was my mother's son. I was ready to step into her shadow, to take my rightful rule on the cycles, to let Pen go and return to her original duties of ushering the stars to the sky. She was Night's daughter and had stepped into this role only after my mother's death had left it open, but the power was mine.

My mind continued to dwell on the strange blend of chaos and nightmare that had seemed corrupt the closer we'd come to the border until I felt the pull of the coming dawn.

Gently, I removed my arm from under Del and moved from beside her. She grumbled a little in her sleep, making me smile. I pulled the blanket up over her body and after putting my pants on, walked to scout our surroundings. I didn't want to move too far, but I did want to find someplace to rinse off. Sustenance wasn't an issue. We could make our own food and water, we just hadn't been hungry for anything but each other. I could, however, use a good rinse, as could she after all we'd done the prior night.

Looking to the south, I wondered how far we were to the border of Chaos. My link to it wasn't strong enough to tell me. While I didn't want to see what awaited us, I did want to get this damned tournament over with so I could start my life with Del. As I wandered back to her, I thought about a life with her, and how we would work it out. She needed Nightmare as I needed my kingdom and we'd need to spend time in each realm, just as Jackson and Claire did. The balance needed to remain in place.

I stooped over her, moving the blanket down to free those beautiful breasts. Letting my finger brush over one, I lingered on her nipple, watching as it rose to meet my touch.

"Mmm, you should stop that before I make you please me again," she murmured, her eyes blinking open slowly. The green in them was hazy with the silver, the slivers not defined.

"Make me? Now I know you don't think I yield to your commands, Del."

Her lips curved deliciously. "No, we don't do commands, do we?"

"No, I don't need them."

I saw the shiver that ran through her, leaving a light coating of goosebumps on her skin. Rising, I scooped her naked body into my arms, smiling at the squeal she emitted.

"I could have told you to get up, but, like I said, I don't do commands."

Her giggle lit my heart, and I tightened my hold on her as I walked her back to the small stream I'd found that fed into a quiet pond. The sun was just beginning its ascent, and streams of pink lit the light haze of fog that sat over the water. I set Del down, but she didn't remove her arms from my neck. Instead, she leaned into me and kissed me. The feel of her breasts against my skin was enticing, but I forced my hands down, sliding them over the bruises that had formed on her wrists. Damn, I'd done that last night, and I hated that I'd hurt her that bad. If her immortality had been present, she'd have healed within seconds but not here, and that was killing me. She invited the pain as did I, but the evidence of our roughness still hurt me.

"You need to get some water on your back, Del. I'm afraid it will become infected if you don't."

She chewed her lip. "Is that a command?"

"No, it's a request because I don't want to explain to your brothers how your back became a puss-infected mess. Besides, you're sexy but that might just mar that look enough to turn me off."

She hit me, her slap to my chest a pleasant sting.

"Don't worry, though. It would take a lot for me to turn you down."

A smile lit her eyes before she skipped off to the water, her ass swaying with the motion. My mind went back to the prior night, my dick twitching at the thought. She turned, sinking her breasts into the water. They bounced just above, teasing me. Taking my pants off, I watched the way her eyes perused me as I walked in.

"You know, the last time I was naked in the water, you resisted me," she said, her smile mischievous.

"So I did, but in my mind, I was fucking the shit out of that amazing body of yours."

"Were you?"

I'd entered the water away from her purposely, wading in just enough to splash some water on me and rinse off the grime of the past days and our prior activities.

"Damn right I was. I jerked off that morning before I found you, the image of those tits bouncing in my mind with each stroke I made."

Her eyes blazed, and I knew I had her. I finished rinsing off, stepping back enough that my very prominent hard-on was visible.

"Is that for me?" she asked, licking her lips.

My dick lurched, and I brought my hand to it, stroking it. Her eyes lit at the action.

"I do believe you owe me that mouth, Del," I said, stroking more firmly, imagining that mouth sinking around me.

"So I do." She rose from the water, droplets running down her breasts as she strode to me. I salivated in an instinctual way, wanting to run my tongue over them and catch each one. With every stroke and image, my need grew. What she did to me with just a few moves of her body was lethal.

Her hand encased mine, moving with it, her eyes watching mine intently before she dropped to her knees. I brought my finger out to trace a drop of water that was making its way down her breast, taking her nipple between my fingers and rubbing it.

"I do believe you're turning me into a breast man," I said as I pinched just to the point of pain.

Her eyes shimmered, the slivers bouncing playfully before she pushed my hand away from my dick and took control.

My groan was deep, reverberating through my chest. Her strokes were firm and silky at once, and when her tongue teased along my tip, I almost lost it. She traced along my shaft, following the route of her hand then ascended so erotically that it was hard to keep my knees from shaking. When she reached my head again, she swirled her tongue around it, taking time to lick the precum that she'd elicited from me. Descending on me in one swift move, she took my length in. My grunt was uncontrollable. She was good, so good that I knew I wouldn't be able to contain myself for long. She took me like she was claiming me, marking me so that I'd never want another woman's mouth around me. But fuck, who would after experiencing this? Every inch of me slid into her throat without a complaint and thankfully with no gags. Shit, if she'd gagged it would have been the end of me. I was having enough trouble holding on as it was.

I dug my fingers into her hair and pulled, hearing her moan and seeing the quake that ran through her body. I wondered if she was close to breaking as well. The thought of her turned on so intensely by this act was too much, and my release grew closer. I stilled her head and took over, unable to help myself, and fucked her mouth like I'd always wanted to. She gripped my legs to steady her body which only pushed me closer. Her nails dug into my skin bringing me a painful sensation that sent me further toward the need for release. The cry that fled her mouth when she came broke me, and I shoved myself deeper down her throat, spilling into it. I couldn't stop, my body so tense that I knew I was pulling her hair too hard, but my climax rocked me.

Finally able to grasp control again, I loosened my hand. I thought she'd pull away quickly and worried I'd been too hard, too rough. It was so difficult to tell where the line was with her —if there even was one. But she brought her hand up and held me, slowly removing her mouth. Her tongue slid along my shaft with her lips then swirled over my tip as she sucked the remaining drops of me up.

"Fuck," I swore, bringing my hand to run through her hair. She looked up at me, her eyes brilliant in the morning sun, the silver slivers so thick they almost covered the green completely. Her tongue came out and swept around my tip once more before she slid her body along mine, her breasts encasing my recovering dick with their suppleness then coursing up to press against my chest. Her eyes never left mine, adding a level to our intimacy that reached deep into my soul.

"That was intense," was all I could manage. My legs were shaking so hard I didn't know if I could walk let alone continue to stand.

"I'm a cock girl, myself," she said with the tease of a smile before sauntering away, leaving me to fight the need to crumble from her blow job and her words.

She was something else. My eyes followed her body, unable to do anything but settle on those hips as they swished back and forth with her steps. She threw a look back at me. "Coming...again?"

"Not yet, but I will be," I replied, giving her a wicked grin and knowing I'd be ready to ravage her before I stepped from the water.

She sat facing the pond in a patch of high grass and propped herself on her elbows. I followed the movement of her legs as she drew her knees up and spread her legs, showing me every inch of just how glorious she was. Damn, I wanted to take her like that, to slam into her and hear the pounding of our bodies, but I worried about the bruises, the cuts on her back. Worried about truly hurting her.

"I'm a goddess, Graham, I won't break," she said as if she'd heard my thought. Her voice was a thing of seduction that made her ever harder to resist.

I didn't move, waging an internal battle, the conscious part of me winning. I walked from the pond, seeing her eyes greedily fall on the hard-on I couldn't stop. Standing over her, I fought the urge, every part of me screaming to take her I wanted her so badly.

"You will here," I said, turning from her and grabbing my pants angrily. I hated myself for walking away from her, but I had no choice. I couldn't damage her any more than I had.

"You're serious?"

"Yes, now get dressed, and no, that is not a command."

"You're turning me down after I did that?" I kept my back to her, knowing if I looked over, I'd lose my battle.

"Guess you were just too good with that mouth," I said, walking away.

"But, Graham, I'm so ready. I need to come, please."

"Ha! You just came magnificently with your mouth around me, which is a feat in itself since you didn't spill a drop." I couldn't help glancing back at her. The pout on her lips was perfect and tempting. The need to drop over her and take her bottom lip between my teeth was difficult to ignore. "I think you'll survive."

I walked back to where we'd slept, hearing her stomp behind me.

"Does Delusion throw temper tantrums?" I teased.

"You can't imagine," she fumed.

Oh, I could, and I avoided watching, knowing those perky tits would be bouncing in a way that would have me breaking in no time.

She snatched my hand and yanked me around with more strength than I'd given her credit for.

"No one turns Delusion down."

"Don't talk about yourself in the third person, it's weird." I took a handful of her hair and jerked her head back, her body arching into mine.

That was a mistake, I thought as her breasts pushed against my chest.

"And don't try to overpower me. You'll lose each time."

Her chest heaved, and those damned slivers flickered in her eyes. "Show me," she purred.

"Get dressed, and I'll show you later when we're out of this blasted place and back to where you heal quickly." Shoving her away, I continued, "I won't hurt you anymore here, Del."

"Then bend me over—"

"Without bruising those hips or ripping your hair? I don't think so. I'm not risking breaking something because you want me to hurt you."

Her bottom lip protruded out in another beautiful pout, and I pulled her to me, pushing my fullness against her before running my hand along her curves. Giving into temptation, I bit that lip before I kissed her, my body aching to just take her like she wanted. I'd spent years resisting her, but I wasn't certain I could now that I'd tasted her. "Put some clothes on, now," I said against her mouth before I shoved her away.

The glare she gave me was lethal, and I knew it would have stung if she'd set her power free, but she refrained. Instead, she stomped past me and snatched her shirt. She stared at it for a moment before tossing it aside.

"I'm not fucking you, Del. Stop trying to seduce me."

Shooting me a look, she used her magic to create a new shirt, pulling it over her head and drawing her long locks out from under it.

"Leather?" I asked. "I thought you didn't need that now."

She pulled on a new pair of pants she created—light tan and

almost see through enough to confirm she was a natural blonde. These pants were even tighter than the last ones, curving around her ass to show the perfect definition. They were painfully tight as were my own with my length pressing toward her.

Turning to me, she replied, "We're going into Chaos, and I don't know what's there. Claire's new, and with her and Jacks together, they likely whipped something wicked up. Plus, I like the feel of leather on my skin."

Her hand drifted along the emphasized cleavage from the leather shirt, lingering on the swell of her breasts before it moved to her bare stomach. She was killing me, and she knew it. The pants hugged her hips, dipping exceedingly low, showing most of her torso, the luscious ivory skin there for me to lust for.

"When you tie me up, will you use leather or silk?" she asked in a voice that commanded my dick to jerk in need for her.

"Both. The leather for your wrists, the silk for your eyes," I played back, brushing past her, hoping she didn't notice how badly she'd turned me on. The thought of tying her up was tempting, especially after the incident with the vines, and I could picture the different ways I'd take her like that.

I glanced over at her as she walked silently beside me. She was irritated, I could see her delusions fluttering around her head like a white halo of snakes. To others, it would have been disturbing, but I knew the touch of those delusions, and to me, they were seductive. My eyes traced her arms, seeing the bruising from my grips, the purple around her neck from when I'd held her throat. It made my gut wrench, and it angered me. That wasn't the way to treat a woman, I knew that, I knew better. I also knew that each one of those marks had elicited a cry of pleasure. They'd been wanted, invited.

I rubbed my hand across my face, wishing she had her immortality again, wishing away the reminders of my chaos.

"What's your safe word, Del?" I asked, knowing I needed a

line drawn, needed to know when my chaos drove me too hard. Whether she thought I did or not.

"I don't need one," she said, repeating the words I'd said earlier about commands.

I took her arm and spun her toward me. "I need one. I need to know if I'm too rough—if I'm hurting you more than I should." More than I should? I shouldn't be hurting her at all.

Her smile touched the corner of her eyes in a soft way. "I told you how the pain makes me feel, what it does to me. It's my clarity, Graham, and you're the only one I trust to give it to me." She traced my jaw with her thumb. "I don't need a safe word, especially not with you. You understand me well enough to know when it's too much. You're already doing that."

She gave me a small kiss then turned and danced away, her moment of softness overtaken by her madness to compensate. "Why do you suppose Claire is so different from you?" she asked randomly.

"What do you mean?" I chose to move on, knowing her mind had left the conversation. If she didn't want a word, then she didn't have to have one. And perhaps she was right, I already knew her limit, knew it better than she did. I'd refused her attempts, afraid of doing more damage to her already battered body.

"Well, chaos rules her completely, but she doesn't have that brutal side of her like you do."

That was a thought I didn't want to imagine for my sister. But I knew Del was right. If anything, Claire was submissive, something I could tell by the way Jackson commanded her and from Del's comments. Claire was a force to be reckoned with but apparently not in the bedroom where Jackson called the shots. I shook my head, trying to free myself from those images quickly.

"I don't know. Maybe because I'm more of a mix of our parents than she is. I hold a dichotomy within me."

"Mmm, right, the control of Turning and the disorder of Chaos. Your rule of the cycles, the orderliness, the sheer power of running the world's rhythm takes aggression. It's something subtle and not noticeable but extremely powerful." She glanced at me. "I think they've underestimated you even more than they have me."

"So, it's not my chaos but the other side of me?"

"No," she said, that sly smile forming. "I feel your chaos all over me when you're asserting your dominance. The chaos fuels that aggression and sets it free when you're with the right person, otherwise your other powers keep it in check." She turned, walking backwards as she continued. "You tried to set it free with Violence." Her teeth clenched when she said the name. "But since it wasn't reciprocal, your other side forced the chaos back in its space. But with me—"

"With you, it runs free."

"Because I want it to run free, I want it to play with my delusions while your aggression runs unchecked because your chaos is unchecked."

"Damn, I sound as messed up as you," I told her.

"Does that mean you'll fuck me now?" Her eyes twinkled, and I couldn't help but chuckle.

"No, it does not." That lip pouted again, calling for me to bite it. "Put that lip away before I make it bleed."

She shuddered in a very enticing way, and I fought the temptation to pull her to me and kiss her. Instead, I brushed past her, ignoring the spark as our skin touched. She walked quietly next to me for a while.

"So...do you really want to bond with me when we're through with this?" Her voice was low, but I could detect the vulnerability.

Stopping, I did pull her to me this time, my eyes dropping to watch the way her breasts squished over her shirt when they pressed against me.

"Do you?" I asked her, holding her gaze, noticing how her slivers had stilled.

She parted her lips, and I had the urge to run my mouth along them but stopped myself.

"Yes," she replied, her breathing strained.

"Why?" I knew the answer. I knew why she would. It was the same reason I'd told her that's what I would do.

She didn't hesitate. "Because no one will ever come close to making me feel the way you make me feel, to doing the things you do to my body, to my delusions." She leaned up and nibbled my lip. "Because you own me, and I don't want to be owned by anyone else but you, ever. I've been yours since the day I first saw you."

Unable to resist, I slid my tongue along her lips. They parted, my lips meeting hers in a needy yet sensual kiss that stirred the deepest part of my being. It wasn't aggressive or power driven; it was us, the raw vulnerable side of both of us. Given to each other in trust, in faith that we would protect each other, that we would keep that side of us safe.

"I love you, Turning," she said, and my heart beat faster. I needed to stop kissing her, stop this talk and focus, or I'd go against my judgment and make love to her.

"Don't call me that when I can't fuck you, Del."

She let out a purr that stoked my desire for her. "You're the only one saying you can't fuck me."

"I can't, and even if I could, this is one of those moments where I'd make love to you. Slow and soft."

She pulled at my shirt. "Then make love to me. I want you, Graham."

"Shit, Del. You make this so hard."

Her hand dropped to encase my length. "It's very hard, so

why don't you let me relieve that?" Her lips mashed against mine, her kiss more aggressive.

"That's not making love, Del."

"No, I think I just want to be fucked."

The growl came from deep in my core, tearing through me, uninhibited and feral. I jerked her closer, gripping her hip so tight that her breath hitched, and I saw the flickers of silver that slashed across her eyes like whips of light. She kissed me again as I squeezed more, her quiet cry slipping between our lips. All resolve not to touch her fled, my need for her too great until I moved my hand up her back, grazing the raw cuts and scratches, touching the tiny shards of crystal that still sat in some spots. She was right, I knew when she needed a safe word, better than she did because she would have reveled in the pain as I added more bruises and pounded her back into the ground with each thrust. I could have taken her from behind, but the bruises would still have come.

I forced her from me, trying to catch my breath and calm my throbbing dick. She tried pushing back to me, but I held firm.

"No, Del. I won't. I can't risk it."

Her eyes gleamed with her irritation, and she pulled her shirt over her head, freeing her breasts. "You will fuck me, Turning."

Damn her. This is how she'd broken my resolve in the first place. Well, two could play at this game, and I wasn't about to let her win.

I grabbed her wrists, likely too hard, but at least I wasn't hurting any other part of her. The flash of lust in her eyes let me know she liked the move.

"You are a pest, and you're starting to piss me off."

"Good," she said, trying to kiss me. I jerked her wrists, moving her back from me.

"You want pleasure, Del? You want me to make you come?"

"Yes, but I want you inside of me, deep inside of me."

"No," I said firmly. Yanking her closer, I squeezed her breast, kneading the soft skin and sweeping my thumb across her nipple. She tried to press against me, but I kept her in place, holding her wrists firmly behind her back. I pushed her hands to her ass, shoving her pelvis to mine, letting her feel my very distinct erection as I continued to play with her breasts. Never dropping my eyes from her, I pinched her nipple, rolling it between my fingers. Her parting lips accompanied a low moan, and my dick ached.

"Take me, Graham, please," she said breathlessly, her voice shaking.

I ignored her request, and she ground into me with a movement that only further tormented me. As punishment, I twisted her nipple more, seeing the resulting expression of pleasure on her face. Sighing deeply, she increased her grinding, her eyes still locked to mine. A flush grew on her cheeks, and I knew she was close. I could feel the quiver of her body in my hands. Her head dipped back, and I took the opportunity to drop my mouth to her other breast, sucking the tender skin in and rolling my tongue around it until her body was trembling.

I needed to be careful. I was playing with her, but if I pushed too hard, I'd end up so turned on that I wouldn't be able to stop. But I wanted to punish her for pestering me, for not letting me be, like I'd asked. Just as I felt her cresting, I made the asshole move of shoving her body away.

The cry that came at me was desperate and confused.

"I told you no pleasure, Del." I left her there, her legs crossed as she fought to hold on to the climax that had been rising. "Now stop being a cock tease and put your shirt back on."

Adjusting myself, I didn't look back. We needed to get into the next kingdom and see what awaited us. Needed to stop playing games. The sting of her power hit me unexpectedly, and I stumbled slightly.

I turned sharply, complaining, "I think you broke skin on that one."

Another delusion struck me hard at the same moment that one wrapped around my ankle. The combination sent me falling backwards, the impact knocking my breath from me. She shimmied out of her pants as I tried to pull myself up. Ropes of her magic grabbed my arms and held me down while she walked to me. I couldn't help but be impressed and seriously excited. She was gorgeous in a mad, frightening way that called to my chaos. Her hair was billowing around her, the insanity turning it white in certain locks. Her eyes were terrifying, the silver and green fighting for dominance in a symphony of color.

She dropped over me, and I couldn't contain the smile. "Why, Del, are you playing aggressor with me?"

Her eyes narrowed and she ripped my shirt from me in a move that had my dick pressing so hard against my pants that it may have bruised. No woman had ever tantalized me the way she was.

"You are going to finish what you started," she growled at me, and the hunger for her grew with the sound.

"And you're going to make me?"

She rammed her mouth onto mine, her kiss demanding and powerful. Digging her nails into my arms, she bit my lip so hard my body lurched into hers.

"Mmm, I like this side of you, Del. Now let my arms go—"

"No." She reached down and tore my pants open, my happy length springing free. Damned traitor, there was no way I was getting it to listen to me now. And as she sank over it, her arousal soaking it, I didn't think I wanted it to listen to me.

"Damn, you're playing dirty," I teased.

"Only because you played dirty." She rose and fell on me in a rhythm that was too erotic not to enjoy.

"Let my arms go, Del."

"No, I'm going to satisfy myself, and maybe I'll consider letting you join me."

I laughed. "There's no way you're stopping my dick from coming like this. Now let my arms go so I can fuck you properly."

Her eyes lit, and a flood of moisture hit my length. "I thought you said you wouldn't take me."

"You're making it too difficult to do that and from the looks of it, *you're* taking me."

She rose, lifting herself just so my tip stayed nestled inside of her. I wrestled to free my arms, wanting to shove her back down but to no avail. "Dammit, Del, drop your ass back down and let my arms go."

"No," she said. "No one teases Delusion. Not even you, Turning."

She slid further so that I slipped from her, and I arched my back trying to reach her. Lifting herself, she let her breast drift over my mouth. The damned thing was too tempting not to catch, and I pulled her nipple in, playing with it. She pushed further into me, so I took more of it in my mouth, sucking and licking until she was moaning loudly. As she pulled away, I caught her nipple in my teeth, letting them drag over it until it popped free.

She lowered her head on my chest, and I could feel the shake in her body. Slipping over me again, she moved so that I sat pressed against her clit. She was soaked, and I twitched in anticipation. But she didn't envelope me like I thought she would, like I wanted her to. Instead, she moved so that she was sliding back and forth over me, using me to finish herself off while seriously torturing me.

The laugh that escaped me was laced with humor and irritation. "You are something, Del," I said, gritting against the pleasure and the ache of not being inside of her. She still felt so good that there was a high probability of climaxing and spilling all over her.

"You said you didn't want to hurt me, so I had to take things into my own hands." Her voice was shaky, and I could tell she was close.

"Free me, Del, and let me help you."

She was grinding against me now, moving her clit against my dick in a way that threatened to break me. Each move rubbed her breasts over my chest, my hands fighting to get to them. A moan fell from her lips, and she sat up, continuing her motion as she looked into my eyes. I saw the madness there, the insanity that ruled her, and I fell deeper for her. She was moving her hands over her breasts in an erotic way, her fingers tugging at her nipples. The muscles in her stomach quivered, and I wanted so badly to free my hands and hold her.

"Free me, Del, please," I begged, needing to touch her, to feel her tighten around me as I plunged into her.

She threw her head back as she fell apart, her hold on me slipping. Grabbing her hips, I held her as she trembled, lifting her quickly and thrusting into her. Another cry escaped her, meeting my own. Her body was shaking, but I didn't let go of her waist, driving into her as her muscles bared down around me. The torment she'd given me left me no chance of doing anything but crashing with her as my climax ripped through me. My cry tore from the depths of me, and I continued to thrust into her until there was nothing left of me to give her.

She fell against my chest, her breaths heavy, small quivers still running through her. Relaxing the hold I had on her waist, I moved my hand to thread my fingers around her neck, forcing her head up to look at me.

"That was wicked," I said, tightening my fingers and seeing the flare of pleasure in her eyes.

"I am wicked. I thought you knew that. I'm not one to be toyed with, Graham."

"I beg to differ. You are fantastic to toy with." Her smile was one that I knew she reserved just for me, soft and innocent.

She searched my eyes, and I wondered what she was looking for.

"Tell me you love me," she said quietly.

"Doubting me after that?" I teased.

Her giggle was adorable. "Tell me."

Squeezing her neck more, I replied, "I thought we had that command conversation."

Her sigh was enough to make me hard again, and I knew I needed to remove her body from mine quickly, or we'd be here the rest of the day.

"I love you, Dellamine, goddess of delusion. I will always love you, and each day, I love you more."

The green of her eyes overtook the silver, the innocent small child inside of her surfacing at my words. I'd never realized how complex she was, how many facets to her there were. Relaxing my grip, I brought her mouth to mine and kissed her, gentle and full of the love I had for her. It was a kiss she returned in kind, her emotions for me layering it.

"I could kiss you all day, but we really should get moving again," I mumbled as I drew my lips from hers. "Besides, if you continue to kiss me like that with this tempting body on mine, I will be forced to make love to you."

"I wouldn't be opposed to that."

"I bet you wouldn't." I let her go and smacked her ass, the sound echoing in the hush around us.

"Continue to smack my ass like that and I'll tie you back up again."

"I prefer to be the aggressor in this relationship...but I do like it when you're riled up. Now get the hell off me and get dressed."

"Mmm, another command. I think I'll punish you each time you try to command me." She gyrated, and I reacted instantly, her words not helping the response.

Glaring at her, I said, "Now, Del. That's enough. I want out of this damned tournament. Plus my instinct is screaming that we need to be on alert. I can't protect you if you have my dick in a frenzy."

She kissed my nose and rose from me. "I think I just proved that I don't need protecting." Her eyes fell to my re-emerging erection. "You, on the other hand, may need protection from me."

"I can't help what my dick does around you. It has a mind of its own, and you control it. Looking at that naked body of yours doesn't help."

I brought myself up, watching her clean up and dress. Throwing my ripped shirt at me, she said, "Get dressed and cover that thing up before I decide I'm hungry again." Her tongue slid deviously over her lips, and I fell back, groaning at the thought.

This time it was her laugh that filled the air as she walked away, having broken me yet again and enjoying every minute of it.

CHAPTER 16

DEL

I couldn't look back at Graham. That amazing length was bobbing there, calling to be licked and played with. I'd tasted him earlier, and it had spoiled me. I would take every chance I could to have him in my mouth again. I heard him grousing about how I'd ripped his shirt, but I could hear the humor in his voice. I'd been fired up. No one turned me down, and he was mine, he wasn't allowed to turn me down. Yet he had for years, tormenting me every time he'd been around. Each time left my mind filled with all the ways I'd wanted him to touch me.

I didn't expect him to turn me down now that he finally had me. Stubborn god. And then he teased me, leaving me on the brink of my climax as it battered for release. There was no way I wasn't getting what I wanted, and he was what I wanted. I'd needed desperately to have him inside of me, but since he'd tormented me, I needed to reciprocate. Torturing him had been phenomenal. I'd seen the strain in him, the tension, and the need, heard the desperation in his voice as he'd pleaded to let him touch me. I'd broken him, but then, I'd broken first.

The smack of his hand against my ass again woke me from

my thoughts. "Get those dirty thoughts out of your head and keep moving."

"I don't have dirty thoughts in my head," I argued, hearing the lie in my words.

"I know you too well, Del. You don't think I've learned to spot when you're thinking about sex with me?"

I looked sharply at him, my mouth agape.

"You're easy for me to read, sweetheart. Those slivers give you away, and right now, your mind is lost in what we just did, or maybe it's imagining that talented mouth wrapped around my dick again."

I slapped his arm, hearing the sting my hand had caused.

"Don't tease me, Del. You just reminded me that you can ride me without doing any damage to your back. And I'm always up to having you ride me with those sexy legs doing the work and those tits bouncing around for me to watch."

I threw him a lopsided grin, the thought sending warmth between my legs as my pants grew wet again. Damn, this man was like a candy I couldn't get enough of. "Don't tempt me or I might just walk the rest of the way with my breasts free just to watch what it does to you."

"Shit, you're a vixen."

"Mmm, yes, I am."

We teased each other as we walked on. It was a natural state for us, we'd been doing this for years on a less dirty, more discreet level. The change in our relationship had elevated the banter, making it difficult for me not to act on the teasing. The arousal grew with each comment.

We'd walked a few hours when he suddenly stopped.

"We're close to Chaos. Can you feel it?"

I closed my eyes and set my powers free, seeking out what he had detected. They drifted past the chaos within him and out toward the strange blend of my realm and Claire's, morphed into Heart's.

"Yes," I replied, opening my eyes.

He was studying me, his eyes serious. The gold rimming them was blurred further into his iris, giving them a strange appearance that disturbed a part of me which recognized that it wasn't right. I was about to mention something about it when he brought his finger to the corner of mine.

"Your silver is blurred, leaking into the green," he said softly. "And the gold rim is…it's blurry, too. Like it's bleeding into the silver."

I creased my brow, wondering why both of us would be experiencing the same thing. "So is yours," I said, hearing the tremble in my voice.

My delusions flickered around us in a frenzy that tipped toward manic.

"What would cause that?" he asked, a scowl forming to cover what I could sense was fear.

"I don't know. I've never seen it before."

He dropped his finger and looked around. "The darkness is returning but night's falling, so I can't tell how far we are from the border."

"I can. My delusions can feel it."

He nodded. "Del, where are the other teams? Why haven't we seen them?"

"We saw Theo and Persa and then Violence and Angst."

"A day ago. And no other teams but them."

"That's not abnormal. We took our time," I said slyly, letting my fingers run along his chest. "Usually, the first few kingdoms are nothing but focus on the trials. Heart is a slight break, but it's typically later in the tournament. Death and Nightmare are two of the hardest, and we don't usually let ourselves have fun until we at least pass through Nightmare. The other kingdoms are smaller, and there are more creatures we can ensnare and manipulate into taking us to the next realms."

"What do you mean Heart is later?"

"It's usually Death, Nature, then Chaos, Heart, and Nightmare before we move to the other kingdoms. For some reason, they routed us to Heart after Death."

His scowl remained.

"It's fine, Graham. The Elders have changed the course, it's not the first time although it hasn't happened in a very long time." Still no change in his demeanor. "This is normal. I wouldn't have expected to even see Violence and Angst. I was surprised when we did. They purposely put themselves in our path."

"I don't care. Stay alert. We continue until we get into Chaos, then we stop for the night."

I could see that he'd drawn his power, the control, the fierceness of his orderly power pushing the chaos that wanted me below the surface. His only thought was protecting me and getting us through whatever the next kingdom had in store. And moving beyond whatever this disturbing force was that hung in the air.

Knowing I wasn't going to sway him, I sighed, saying, "Okay."

He took my hand, and we walked in silence, the fun set aside for now. His muscles were tense, but my delusions were on edge as well. They were bashing around my head in a panic that increased the closer we drew to Chaos.

Night had fallen, and a spark of light he'd created led our path. We saw no creatures, nothing that stopped us from moving quickly to the border, except the steadily increasing feeling that something was off. As we reached the border, Graham stopped and turned to me.

The gold in his eyes had bled to his pupil and it sparkled in the low light. His brow was creased, and I could see the worry etched on his face. "There's no green left in your eyes, Del. Only gold and silver. It's…disturbing."

"I am disturbing, Graham," I tried to joke, but it came out hollow.

His eyes narrowed, and he brought his hand around my neck, pulling me closer to him. "I want you behind me. If we step through to Chaos, and anything is off, you run. Understand?"

"Graham, it's Claire's kingdom. Home of your father—"

"That doesn't feel like home, and it doesn't feel like the chaos I know or that clings to my sister. Are you sure there isn't any other way to get through this tournament?"

I shook my head. His worry had my delusions frantic. "We have to follow the path the Elders laid for us."

He drew my lips to his, kissing me hard, and I clung to his shirt. "Can't we just go back into Heart and spend the days devouring each other? Eventually, they'll come looking for us."

He smiled against my lips, and I kissed him more before he drew away.

"No. Whatever this is, we face it. You said yourself, this is Claire's first time creating challenges, maybe she and Jackson got too creative. They are pretty unhinged together."

"So are we."

"That we are," he said, kissing me once more before moving me behind him. I wanted to grab his ass and tempt him to take me, but I didn't think he'd budge. He wanted us past whatever lay before us, and I wasn't going to sway his determination.

Squeezing my hand, he stepped forward. I followed, my own tension high as my power battered me in a strange way. The moment we stepped into the realm, my power screamed at me as if something had locked it inside of me, and I shook my head to steady it. Graham's grip on my hand was so hard that a bone snapped. I gritted my teeth against the pain that wasn't pleasure induced this time. My delusions were roaring in my head so badly that I doubled over.

"Back up now, Del. We need to get out. This isn't right. It's not Chaos." He pushed me back with his body, but I hit something solid. There was no going back.

"No, it's not Chaos." The voice I heard was familiar, one I'd known all my life but one the Elders had silenced. "It's Discord."

Discord stepped in front of us, his aura glowing with his power. Graham dropped my hand and drew his own power. I knew he'd summoned it, but his power didn't heed his call, nothing happened. I called my delusions only now noticing they were silent. My mind was clear, empty of the insanity that comforted it, empty of anything but clarity. My power had been stripped, replaced with sanity.

CHAPTER 17

GRAHAM

There was no way to get Del to safety. Not with Discord standing before us. I stared the god down, my hatred of him burning through me. My power wouldn't heed my command and the thought startled me. Del tried to draw hers, but nothing happened. I couldn't detect anything from her; even her delusions were silent. They weren't there below the surface, seducing me like they normally were. We were both powerless.

I dropped her hand and moved in front of her, knowing I needed to keep her safe, no matter what. Magic may not have been at my call, but I had physical force. I pulled my weapons and rushed him, nothing in my mind but vengeance for the man who'd stolen everything from my childhood.

"Nice try, son of Chaos," he said as his power slammed into my body, leaving it shaken and neurotic. Something similar to Del's delusions slithered through my head, but it lacked the seduction. Instead, it carried voices and darkness that berated my mind. My hands dropped to my side, the weapons retracting as Del's cry sliced through the discord. "But you are not your father."

I fought the hold of his power but without my own to combat it, I was weak against it.

"And Delusion, one of my favorite nieces, so close to my heart…until your brother fucked things up." His words fell from his mouth like a snarl, the venom in them palpable.

"How did you escape banishment, Uncle?" she asked, her tone acidic like the word had caused a distaste in her mouth.

Everything about him left a distaste, a foul, corrupt one that I needed to purge but couldn't. His discord continued to slither through me, coating my mind like sticky webbing.

"None of your sick minded business." He brought his hand out and dragged her to him with his power. His hand came to her neck, and I pushed against his power. The effort was draining, the weight of his discord too heavy to free myself completely from it. I unfurled enough to move my limbs and rush him. My move knocked Del free, and I was able to land a hard punch on Discord's chin before he gripped me with his magic again.

"I think I'll have some fun before we get to business," he said, his eyes alight with humor that had no place in this situation. "I have the others. There is no way out of this realm, no way to get your powers back. Stay alive and find me at my castle. Don't tarry or I'll start killing your cousins one by one, starting with that annoyance Pain and working my way through. You two are the only ones I need so don't get killed by anything on your way there."

He shifted away.

"No!" Del cried, rushing to where he'd been.

I rose, dusting myself off and glancing around at the darkness that surrounded us before I turned back to Del. Her eyes met mine, a crystal green, no slivers to be found, no silver, not even any gold around their rim. Powerless, mortal green eyes that gutted me at the reality they held—she was vulnerable, and I had no way to protect her.

"What do we do?" she asked. "They have the others. Theo—"

I moved to her, brushing her hair back with my hands and holding her face. "Shhh. We'll get to them. We'll find our way…" But I didn't know where to go. We couldn't return to the Elders without finishing the tournament. They had no idea Discord was here or that he'd changed their tournament. I doubted there was a way out of the kingdom. We hadn't been able to step back into Heart. And even if we could, Discord had threatened to kill the others. That's why we hadn't seen anyone, they'd stepped into his trap, all of them likely powerless like us. "I find my way to the castle, and I face him."

"You? He said us."

"There's no way I'm letting you anywhere near him again." And I meant it. I wasn't risking losing her to that lunatic. I'd lost my parents to him, almost lost Claire. He wasn't taking Del from me.

Bringing her hand to my cheek, she let her fingers gently drift over it. "You can't keep me safe, Graham. He has Theo and the others. He wants both of us to go, or he'll kill Theo. I can't let that happen. We both go."

I studied her, fascinated by how clear her eyes were but missing her slivers terribly. She was so calm, so unlike herself that it unnerved me.

"He took your insanity," I said as the realization set in. He'd stolen the part of her that I loved the most, the unpredictable, childlike madness she carried.

She nodded, her confidence faltering. I could see it in the downturn of her lips, the slight slump of her shoulders. "My mind is clear," she said in a hushed tone, dropping her eyes before bringing them back to mine. The vulnerability I saw there gripped me. "Do you still love me without my delusions?"

"Are you serious?" She continued to stare into my eyes,

waiting for my answer. I couldn't believe she'd think such a thing. "I will never stop loving you, Del. Delusions, or no delusions. I'd miss them, but it wouldn't keep me from loving you."

Her smile formed quickly then dropped again as her brow creased. "Without my delusions, I don't know if I would crave the pain." She looked so sad that I couldn't help but laugh. She furrowed her brow more. "I'm serious, Graham."

Kissing her forehead, I said, "Without my chaos, I suppose I wouldn't be giving so much pain. Looks like we're stuck with soft and slow." I pulled her against my body. "I'll take your delectable body any way I can have it, Del. If that means I gently make love to you each time, then so be it."

"Really?"

"Really." I kissed her, aware of the difference, the woman behind the insanity, behind the child who had fled with that madness. This was who she would have been if her power hadn't ravaged her mind, morphing her to be the woman I loved. I hadn't lied, I'd still love her to the ends of the world, but I'd miss the delusions if she were rendered powerless forever. Would miss the wildness of her, the playfulness that called to my chaos. The chaos I no longer held.

Dropping my forehead to hers, I sighed, knowing we had no choice. We needed to find Discord, or she would lose Theo. I had no doubt that he'd kill her brother and that Theo would be the first to die. "I don't want you anywhere near Discord," I said, hearing the weakness in my voice.

"You don't have a choice. He wants us both there, and I won't leave Theo or the others to face his anger if you leave me behind."

"Fine. Now how do we get there?"

She chewed her lip. "I have no idea. Without my power or yours, there's no way to sense it."

"Then we start walking. I think Discord is only having fun.

Nothing he throws at us out here will be unmanageable. If he needs us so badly, he won't leave us out here long, and he won't let either of us die."

"He may let us get injured," she said, and it caused a knot in my chest at the thought of her hurt.

"True" I grabbed her shoulders, my words and my expression stern. "Stay by my side and stay on guard. If you see anything move, you tell me immediately."

"Right."

I moved hastily, keeping her close. All the while, I replayed the scene with Discord over in my head. I couldn't figure out what he wanted with any of us, particularly me and Del. He could have taken us prisoner like he said he'd done to the others, but he'd left us out here to find our way. Like he was testing us...or torturing us. The threat of us not moving, not following his instruction was Theo's life. It seemed impossible that I was worried about Theo, an immortal god who brought pain to mortal life. But that's exactly what I was doing because if my power had been stripped from me, so had his. And none of us had our immortality.

So what connected the three of us? Discord could easily have threatened us with killing any of the others, although Theo was closest to Del, and he knew she'd never let him die. He didn't know that I wouldn't, however. There was no way he knew about me and Del and the fact that I would risk my life to keep her safe as well as both of her brothers. Letting Theo die would destroy her, and I would never let that happen.

There was a reason he'd chosen Theo, other than his tie to Del. The other gods never thought of Del as a strong goddess. I was certain Discord underestimated her abilities just as the other gods all did. So who else would suffer with Theo's death? Jackson. And Jackson was the one who had called Discord out, revealed his crimes to the Elders. Jackson stood to lose the most if Theo or Del were lost. No one else knew her death would destroy me, except Del.

This wasn't about me, though. At least not yet. Whatever he was up to, his target was Jackson. I was certain of it. And hurting Jackson meant hurting Claire and Del. Neither of which I would let happen. I fisted my hand tightly at the thought.

"Graham?" Del's soft voice brought me from my thoughts.

I glanced at her. Her green eyes were evaluating me, and I missed the silver of her madness as soon as I met them.

"Just lost in thought."

"He wants revenge. Revenge against Jacks," she said, voicing my thoughts.

"I think so. But why go about it this way? Why here in Claire's kingdom?"

She opened her mouth to reply, but something dropped from above us, hitting her shoulder before it hit the ground. Following its path, I spotted a thick black snake slithering away. Del screamed and scrambled closer to me, pushing her back against me so hard the movement almost knocked me over.

"It's just a snake," I teased her, shaking my head and giving her hip a squeeze.

"I loathe snakes," she hissed, a sound I found quite funny given the snake's appearance.

"You're a child of the Nightmare Kingdom, and you hate snakes? How is that possible with all the terrifying creatures that live in your realm?"

"I'm not a child of Nature's kingdom, I don't have to love all the creatures in our realm. There are quite a few that gross me out and snakes are among them."

I laughed, giving her a peck on her neck, grateful for the momentary reprieve from the reality that surrounded us. "Where did it come from, anyway?" I asked, looking up and regretting the act as soon as I saw the multitude of snakes hanging in the trees above us. "Shit."

Del followed my gaze before I could stop her. I slammed my hand over her mouth, stifling the scream I knew was coming. She glared at me, but the shake of her body gave away her true condition. If we weren't surrounded by snakes, I would have teased her more.

Letting my hand go, I placed a finger on my lips so she understood we should remain quiet. I took her hand and ever so slowly began to walk, praying the snake-infested trees didn't encompass the entire realm. I briefly wondered what poor Claire would think of what Discord had done to her realm. She hated snakes as much as Del did. She'd be horrified, although I had a feeling Jackson would find her reaction as humorous as I found Del's. The idea of any goddess afraid of something so small was ironic.

Another snake hit the ground to our left, and Del squeezed my hand in a death grip.

"You keep squeezing like that, and I'll fuck you right here with the snakes watching," I said in a hushed voice.

Her head whipped back toward me, a scowl etched on her face. Damn, even the threat of sex wasn't enough to calm her. I was thankful she didn't have her power, or her delusions would be stirring everything in the vicinity. Our power. That was why she was extra nervous, we were both powerless and mortal. I peeked back up at the trees, just in time to see several more snakes dropping.

Yanking Del back a step, I encircled her waist and brought my other hand up to silence her again. The snakes slithered around in a small pile, not scattering like the others had done. I heard the distinct sound of reptilian bodies hitting the ground behind us and cringed. There was no way we were getting out of this without a fight. The pile in front of us grew, and the quaking of Del's body increased. In any other circumstance, that reaction would have had my dick hard, but this was not one of those situations.

The twisting in the pile increased, the snakes seeming to multiply, growing until it was blocking our path completely. No snakes had joined the pile, yet it continued to multiply. The sounds of snakes dropping behind me hadn't stopped, and several fell directly above us, flopping onto Del's head.

As her screams cut the silence, she jumped into my arms. The pile stopped churning, morphing to form one very large snake and I was thankful she was looking the other way.

"Shit, that's not good," I muttered. Glancing around us, I found no way out. While the one large snake lay in front of us, the ground was littered with snakes twisting and writhing in every other direction. We were surrounded.

Del had buried her head into my shoulder, her hands gripped around my neck so tight I could barely breathe.

"You need to stop strangling me, or that same threat stands. I don't give a damn if these snakes watch as I fuck you."

"That's not funny, Graham."

"It's very funny, sweetheart. Now I'm going to let you down before that big one decides to have us for dinner."

The snake had grown another foot, and its head was rising, a long, forked tongue flicking in between the very sharp fangs it had sprouted.

"Discord's an asshole," she mumbled as I dropped her legs. Her arms were still cinched around my neck, and I pried them from me.

"You're just realizing that?"

Slowly, I pulled my weapons out, enlarging them with a quick snap and hoping the movement didn't startle any of the snakes. My weapons looked like nothing more than metal rods, but when activated, they became spears that would gut even the largest of predators.

I handed her one of the weapons which she stared at as if it were one of the snakes. "You're going to take one of these, Del, and we're going to skin ourselves some snakes."

"I can't fight with this!"

"You can and you will. This is just Discord's magic, that's all it is."

"Those are snakes, Graham." I couldn't help but chuckle at the hiss this time. "You're laughing?" she snapped.

"Damn right, I am. Now get behind me and start fighting those little guys while I take this big bitch before she leaves a mark on that pretty skin of yours. I'm the only one allowed to leave marks on you."

She couldn't hide the smile, even if it was a shaky one. I slid her behind me, hearing the scream she tried to keep muffled and feeling her trembling increase.

"And stop that shaking, I'm the only one who gets to make you shake as well. These are snakes, Del, and they're only a product of Discord. They're probably not even real."

One landed on my arm, and I shook it off. "I take that back, they feel quite real."

"Told you so. Just because they're a product of Discord doesn't mean they won't bite. Everything in my kingdom will rip you to shreds, even though it's all a product of Jacks."

"Point taken."

The giant snake uncoiled, rising so that it was towering above me, venom dripping from its fangs. I was thankful I'd turned Del around. If she'd seen it, she likely would have passed out.

"Fuck," I muttered, taking a defensive pose and watching as it pulled its head back, readying itself to strike.

Del moved behind me, and I heard the weapon's movement

against the air, too attuned to it not to notice. From the sound of it, she was holding her own. The snake before me struck, its neck moving quickly, and I barely had time to react. My weapon caught it just as its jaw opened, ready to sink into my flesh, but it became stuck vertically, wedged in between its fangs.

"Dammit, that's not good," I complained, pulling at my weapon as the snake jerked back, trying to free the spear lodged in its jaw. Each whip of its head yanked my body from side to side until I was holding onto the weapon with both hands, my body tossed around like a rag doll.

I didn't know what was happening to Del. All I knew was that if I released my grip, I was dead. Either the force would slam my head into a tree or into a pile of venomous snakes waiting for their next meal. Neither option was one I liked. Instinct took over, and I tried to maneuver my feet closer to the snake since they were flinging chaotically behind me as the thing whipped me back and forth. Curling myself into a ball, I aimed my feet toward the space between the snake's fangs, below where my hands were clinging to the weapon. At first, they slipped at contact, the consistency of the snake's skin giving no hold. After a few attempts, I wedged them against it tight, pushing with all my strength while continuing to grip my spear.

The snake's movements became more frantic, my weapon dragging through its mouth, tearing its flesh with each inch I drew it closer to me. I pushed with my feet, gritting my teeth so hard my jaw was aching. My shoulders were tense, my muscles engaged to the point that pain was shooting through them. As the spear drew closer to me, blood and venom pelted me. I was thankful the venom wasn't a surface contact poison, or I would have died minutes before.

With a violent tug, I yanked the weapon free only to realize my mistake as I fell into a pile of snakes, rolling across them with the velocity of my last tug. When my body stilled, I lay there dazed. My adversary, with blood gushing from its mouth, was pissed, and it slithered over to me before I could bring myself up. It reared to strike, and I brought my arms up to shield myself. The strike never came. Instead, I felt the breeze of a weapon and heard the slick slice of it severing membranes followed by a loud thud.

Dropping my arms, I spied Del standing over me. She wore a huge smile and appeared breathless, something that shouldn't have turned me on given the situation but did anyway.

"You know, Turning, if I have to save your ass every time we're in one of these dire situations, you're going to owe me."

I brought myself up to a sitting position, seeing the countless bodies of reptiles that layered the ground, including the ones I'd rolled into.

"You did all this?"

"Damn right I did. I told you I hate snakes." She spun the weapon around in her hand before handing it back to me. "I didn't know you were going to take the easy route and make me kill them all."

She put her hand out and I took it, letting her help me to my feet. "You're quite sexy in this warrior state you've got going on right now," I said, pulling her to me.

She walked her fingers down my chest, her green eyes bright yet still sliver-less. "No matter how sexy I am, you are not taking me here so get that thought out of your mind. Besides we have to get to Discord before he hurts Theo and the others."

The direness of our situation came crashing back down, my smile faltering.

"But don't think I won't have you make this up to me later."

"I think that can be arranged. I do love watching you climax."

Her eyes twinkled and she gave me a quick kiss on the cheek. She skipped through the plethora of snake bodies, saying,

"Mmm, I think I'll have you put your tongue to use first, then your fingers, then well, I'll let you know."

Shaking my head, I followed my deranged goddess. Even without her madness present, that small child in her was still there to keep her playful.

"What about my tongue and my fingers at once?" I asked, my eyes settling on the sway of her hips.

I saw the small stutter in her skip. Discord may have put a wrench in my plans to get this damned tournament finished, but my girl still reacted to the very thought of what I would do to her when we made it home.

Grabbing her waist, I halted her skipping, forcing her to walk with me. I nuzzled her neck whispering, "I wouldn't mind sinking my finger into that pretty ass of yours again either before I sink my dick into it."

The hitch of her breath was almost enough to make me forget that the fate of the gods rested on our shoulders. It was a terrifying place to be, but Del was a nice distraction.

She nudged me with her shoulder. "Don't talk dirty to me, Turning. I don't want that temptation when Theo could be in trouble."

"I know, but it's still tempting." I smacked her ass, loving how she hopped forward with the impact of my hand.

She shot me a look, trying to be serious.

"It's too hard to resist, Del." I glanced around, attempting to focus and take my mind off the visual of her ass. I shouldn't have played, I was stuck in this nightmare with a raging hard-on and a gorgeous goddess who was in no position to relieve it. Rolling my neck and adjusting myself, I asked, "Do you have any idea how far the castle is from here?"

"No," she replied with a shake of her head. "And you deserve that uncomfortable lump in your pants."

Pursing my lips, I narrowed my eyes at her. "Don't make me bend you over right here."

"Don't make me explain to Theo why we were late saving him."

My laugh was a loud one that brought some relief to the tension that sat in both my neck and my dick. I wondered if I was the only one demented enough to be turned on when death faced everyone I cared about.

"We're only at the edge of the kingdom," Del continued. "The castle sits in the center. Discord knew what he was doing by making us walk."

"Buying time and torturing us."

"You're torturing yourself, Graham." She gave me a playful look.

"The snakes weren't torture?" I couldn't help snapping, not liking how she'd called me out for my poorly timed erection.

She shuddered and I smirked, enjoying the reaction.

"Good point. So what do you think he has planned next?"

"Other than wearing us down with a treacherous walk?" I pointed to the forest that stood before us, one that was cast in shadows and webs. The shadows stretched as if reaching for us. "You don't have a thing about spiders do you?"

"Nah, those I like."

"She likes spiders but not snakes," I muttered, eyeing the forest. We'd just left a span of trees, but they seemed trivial compared to this foreboding cluster. "That isn't really part of Claire's realm, right? There's no way my sister would put a spider infested forest in her kingdom."

"It seems more like something you'd find in my kingdom but that's Discord's gem, not Claire's. Whatever she had there before, he corrupted it with his power and this was the result. You can tell by the way there's no pattern to any of it, the webs aren't strung from tree to tree or limb to limb, they're hanging haphazardly. The trees themselves vary in size and width, the discord impacting even their growth. I'd hazard a guess to say the spiders will be a beautifully twisted mess, and they won't be the only thing alive in there."

"Great. So we don't know what else we'll find in there beside spiders?"

Del didn't have time to answer me. A violent gust of wind ripped past us, and I could feel the discord within it. The wind was fragmented like there were arms of power within it. A distinctly forceful gust hit Del and sent her flying from my side.

"Shit! Del!" I yelled, running as it whipped her around like she was nothing more than a leaf caught in its flow. She fell to the ground, the wind dragging her along and slamming her into a tree.

Another gust snatched me from my feet as I ran to her, and I was soon airborne. There was no way to stop my body from moving with it, and the force of the wind flung me sharply against the ground. I tried to snatch what I could to anchor myself but was unsuccessful. Unable to see anything but the debris that was soaring around me and burning my eyes, I didn't know how far the wind had taken me from Del.

A tree scraped my arm, and my flesh shredded against its bark, the pain sending a jolt of adrenaline through me. I worked one of my weapons free and held tight. As my body crashed into the ground again, I dug the weapon in deep, thankful that the soil was damp enough for it to take hold. I snapped it, feeling it extend further, and held on as tight as I could, digging my feet into the ground for support. The wind stung as it fought to take me from my planted position, and just as my grip began to slip, it dissipated. My body lurched forward with my intense hold, and I fell to my knees, still clutching the weapon in my death grip.

It took me a moment to catch my breath before I shakily brought myself back up. Pulling my weapon from the ground, I sent a thank you to my dead uncle who had insisted I stay constantly vigilant with my training. Something I did to this day, my muscles prime for any unexpected threat or fight.

"Del!" I screamed, running through the trees and frantically searching for her.

My heart hammered, my mind filling with all sorts of horrifying scenarios. I didn't know if she was dead, or if she'd been mortally injured. The fears were too numerous to count, and the unknown broke me until I saw her.

Relief flooded me. She was limping and rubbing her head. Her arm looked like whatever impact she'd sustained had caused it to dislocate, but she was alive. She gave me a smile, and I started to run to her, wanting nothing more than to hold her, to feel the life in her.

Discord's laugh filled my ears, and suddenly, he was standing between us.

"You two are no fun," he said as I came to a halt, Del doing the same on the opposite side of him.

I didn't want her anywhere close to him and definitely didn't like the fact that she was so far from me. Too far for me to protect.

"I think we'll take this game up a notch and make it more exciting. My turn to play."

The world swayed as he shifted us to another part of the kingdom, tossing me to the ground next to Del. The stone floor was a shocking blow to my already battered body, but still, I scrambled to my feet, putting Del behind me. We were in what looked like a dungeon, but the lights were dim, and it was hard to see too far beyond our vicinity.

"Del!" I heard Theo call.

I turned to see him pounding on some kind of invisible shield. No bars lined it, and I could see no magic to it, but then again, I had no power, so it was hard to tell.

"You touch her, and I'll kill you!" Theo screamed, bringing his fists to the shield.

"You'll do no such thing, Nephew, because you are powerless. As are all of you now."

That's when I noticed the others were all with Theo, all rounded up and imprisoned, powerless. The gold in their eyes had bled. I could see no gold in any of them, and the sight was stunning. They looked mortal.

Holy shit, my mind screamed. He'd somehow brought every second-generation god in the tournament to their knees. No power, no immortality.

"What are you doing here, Discord?" Del asked, her voice calm and serious. I turned back to her, noticing then the clear green of her eyes again. She'd moved beside me, strong and confident. She was so sane that it messed with my mind. Seeing her stable wasn't something I was accustomed to, and once again, I missed the instability of her. I wasn't certain how I felt with her in this state, without the madness I adored in her.

"What am I doing here? Look around you! I am taking back what was mine. What my family stole from me." He drew closer to her, but I stepped in front of him. Glaring at me, he snarled, "What your sister and her brother stole from me."

"No one stole anything from you. You betrayed us," I snarled back.

"You're recreating your realm," Del said, as if our conversation wasn't happening. "That's why Graham's chaos was off, why Claire looked so out of sorts."

She put her hand out, letting it drift through something that floated in front of her. "Chaos. That's what it was, Graham, why both of us were unsettled before we stepped into the realm."

She was right. I saw it now, pieces of the realm floating around us as the original realm rebuilt itself with Discord's power. That was the debris that had pelted me in the whirlwind.

Chaos scattered with no form, no structure to it. The implication was terrifying. Without control, chaos was a threat to the mortal world and would tear it apart. But that wasn't as terrifying as what it would do to the realms of the gods.

"It's a shame you're not this sane on a daily basis, Dellamine. It's quite attractive compared to that insanity you carry."

"Fuck off, Discord."

That's my girl.

"What do you want?" I asked him, trying to draw his attention from her. I knew he wanted revenge on Jackson, but there was something more. However he'd found a way to return, he'd done so with a purpose. Otherwise, there would be no reason for him to go to all this trouble. He could easily have faced Jackson head on, catching him unawares and attacking.

"He wants to take over the realms!" Theo yelled. The others started shouting at us but with all of them yelling over each other, it was hard to grasp what they were saying.

"Shut up!" Discord screamed, the ground shaking with his power.

He snapped his head around and reached for Del, but I stopped him, grabbing his arm and feeling a bone break. He didn't flinch, his immortality healing him within seconds. His laugh was the only reaction as his power rushed me, throwing me across the ground. I landed with a thud that knocked the breath from me. His power encased my mind, ravaging my clarity in a way similar to Del's delusions but without the delicacy of them. There was only a cacophony of noise and pain that lacerated my mind.

He grabbed Del by the neck and pulled her close. Fear tore through my heart, spurring me to fight harder against the discord that was pounding in my head.

"Let her go!" I yelled, my teeth gritted with the effort it had taken to say the words. Theo's shouts and even those of the other gods resounded around us.

Del looked at Discord with defiance in her lucid eyes as he studied her. "So many bruises," he muttered, picking her arm up with his other hand. "And not all of them from creatures or my power." He glanced back at me. "Well, well. Has Delusion finally met her match? Isn't that perfect? It makes this even easier than I'd expected. I have no reason to threaten Theo. You've given me something more motivating. It seems I have something you want, Graham, and you have something you are going to bring me."

"I'm not giving you anything, and you're going to get your hands off of her before I rip your limbs off."

His laugh filled the space, and Del struggled as his grip tightened around her throat. The same throat I'd brought her to rapture holding. I wanted to rip his hands off at the sight. He twisted her around and brought his chest to her back, whispering, "Do you like it rough, Dellamine? Does this turn you on?"

She kept her eyes on me, and in them, I found no fear, only determination. "Not from you," she bit back. My smile broke through my discomfort.

"Well, how about this then?" He yanked her arm, forcing it back into its socket, and I saw the flare of pain in her eyes, one that wasn't laced with desire as my pain brought her. This look was enough to bring me to my knees. My smile faltered, a growl slipping through my clenched jaw. I could see her bite back a scream, only a gurgle escaping. It was a sound that broke my heart, and I struggled against the discord that was still tearing through my mind. Del was holding the tears back, trying to stay strong, and I couldn't help the swell of pride I had for her. It was mixed with the feeling of weakness that I couldn't reach her, that this unseen power was viciously destroying me while Discord forced me to watch as he tortured her.

"You fucking touch her again, and so help me, I will tear your fucking arm off and strangle you with it."

"You are nothing but a weak, powerless god. A child god at that. Your threats don't frighten me. None of you frighten me. And I will hurt her all I want. Does that make you jealous, Turning?"

I gritted my teeth, fighting against the power that was still holding me at bay. Theo was screaming, his voice raw by this point, banging so hard against the barrier that trapped him that he had bloodied his arm.

Del gave me a slight smile, mouthing, "It's okay," to me before turning her head as much as she could to Theo.

"Shhh, Theo," she said softly. "It's okay. You can't always protect me."

"What do you want from me?" I asked, not wanting Discord to hurt her any more.

"You will bring me Terror. And if he refuses to come, his sister dies."

Fear raked through me at the thought. My heart bashed within my chest so hard that it brought rivets of pain.

"You're too weak to kill me," Del said, her voice sounding hoarse against the grip he had on her.

He threw her to the ground, her head hitting hard. The move was too much for me to bear, and ignoring the power ravaging my mind, I flew from the ground and knocked him over. I punched him repeatedly until his power tightened on my mind, the voices, the disharmony so loud that my ear drum burst, and blood trickled from my ear and nose. He kicked me from him, and I landed next to Del. She raised her head, blood seeping from the fresh wound on it. Tears were in her eyes, and I knew they weren't for her, not for the pain of her injuries but the injuries I'd received.

"Bring me Terror."

The ground shook as his power hit it. Elder power. Discord was one of the Elders and, as so, had the ability to send us out of the tournament. A black space appeared on the ground. A connection back to the Elders.

"And what will you do to him?" I asked, trying to buy time while I worked out what to do.

"Why, I'll destroy him. He is the reason for my banishment. He is the reason I lost everything. The reason the others stole everything from me. And I will enact my revenge on him and…" but he stopped. I knew what he was going to say, that it wouldn't stop with Jackson, he would destroy us all. "I've been waiting for you to enter the realm. The last ones, trailing behind all the others. But I had to wait."

"Why me?" I asked. "Why not Theo?"

"Because you had her. And Terror will bend backwards to protect his sister as would Pain. And I suspect just as you would. You will bring him, or she dies."

His words were terse and emotionless, and I had no doubt as to the truth of them. He would kill her, but I knew he'd kill every one of us, then make his way to the Elders. I didn't think he could hurt them, not where they were. But if he drew them into this trap he'd lain, he could. They would be powerless, even if their immortality remained.

And I was more than certain he'd find a way around that. He had ordered the murder of my parents after all and recreated the one weapon that could kill a god, the one that his Chaser used in his attempt to kill Claire.

No matter how I looked at it, there was no way out. No way to keep those I loved safe. Unless I changed direction on him and added some chaos to his plan. I would never leave Del with him. If it meant I forfeited my life, then so be it. At least she and Claire would be safe.

"I don't think so. You won't touch her again." Before he

could react, I kicked Del away from me, knowing I'd hurt her—likely breaking a rib with my force—but knowing I needed to get her to safety. Get her to the Elders, to her brother. She flew toward the connection to the hall, her eyes questioning me as she fell away. Discord's scream fled from him, and his power hit me so hard my body went numb, the world fading as darkness set in.

CHAPTER 18

DEL

Discord. Who had seen that coming? I should have. The way my powers had been agitated, the way we'd been blocked from entering my realm, the strange sensation the closer we'd come to both borders. The creature that had not been distinctly Heart's. But I hadn't, nor had Graham. His instinct had been screaming at him, my delusions vying for my attention, yet we hadn't heeded either. Only now, with my mind calm and quiet, was I able to see what I'd been blind to—that the kingdom of Chaos had been compromised.

Discord was ranting at Graham to bring Jacks to him. Blaming Jacks for his own mistakes. I knew the truth, as did Graham. He wouldn't stop with Jacks, he would kill Graham and Claire as he'd wanted to all those years ago. Losing Jacks would shatter me and Theo, and our realm would crumble. But losing Graham would destroy me completely.

My body ached. Without my power and insanity there to welcome the pain, it was hard not to feel weakened by it. As Discord grew more violent, I looked to Graham, seeing the intent that Discord couldn't with the clarity of my sanity. He would never bow to Discord's demands. He didn't take well to commands. Instead, he would protect Jacks, and in turn Claire and me, even if it meant his death.

Graham's kick was sudden and unexpected, shattering my ribcage. The force of it sent me far from him. The pain scorched me, but I knew in my heart that any pain he brought me would never be from anything but love. I met his eyes, mine questioning him until I realized what his motive had been. He would never leave me behind, never leave me in danger. He'd promised to protect me, and that's what he was doing. I felt myself shifting as the connection to the hall took me, my eyes never leaving Graham's until I fell away, hearing my Uncle's frustrated scream.

I landed with a heavy thud, not the usual graceful stance I normally would have had. The impact hurt, especially with the shape I was in, but leaving Graham behind hurt worse. And Theo. For a moment, I couldn't move, too emotionally drained until I heard Jacks' voice.

"Del!" He came running to me, his face before mine as he pulled me into his arms.

For just that moment, I took comfort in his embrace. I didn't have time to relish it, for everything we knew was in jeopardy, everyone we loved…I loved.

Claire was there just as fast as Jacks, her worried eyes overtaken by gold, the brown gone, just as had happened to Graham's right before he'd lost his power. She looked frazzled, and I reached my hand out to touch her arm, feeling the shake in it. Her realm was being torn apart, the impact straining her power and her body without any of them knowing what was causing it. I could only imagine Jacks' mental state at watching her deteriorate. Claire was his world now.

"Del, what happened?" His fingers traced the bruises on my body. Ones I noticed were fading, just as I noticed my delusions were back, the clarity I'd had now buried below their dance again. I smiled at the feel of them, and I was certain I looked as insane as they made me feel.

"Del, where's Graham?" Claire asked, a panic in her voice.

Graham. At the sound of his name, my heart stuttered. I hated being torn from him, leaving him behind whether it had been his choice to stay or not. Hated not having him next to me now that he was mine.

"Discord," I said, feeling my strength return. "He's returned."

The room erupted in a cacophony of voices.

"Hush, let her talk," Jacks commanded, and I saw the faint shiver through Claire. Even in this state, my brother ruled her disposition.

Helping me to a sitting position, Jacks brought his hand to the spot where I'd hit my head, his fingers returning with my blood on it. I'd never seen Jacks frightened until that moment.

"What do you mean Discord's back?" my aunt, Death, asked.

I looked up to see her face, the façade of life interchanging with death quickly then returning to life.

"He's back. He has control of Claire's kingdom. He…" I saw it all now, clearly. How he'd led us all to his trap, forcing us from Nightmare's border to Chaos. But I didn't know how he'd blocked our kingdom, and it was bothering me. My mind was trying to grasp it, but it sat just outside the delusions. The clarity had fled when my power returned.

"Del, what did he do?" Jacks demanded. "Did he do this to you?" He brought his bloody fingers up and grabbed my arm, the bruises barely noticeable now as my immortality healed them. The scrapes and cuts on my other arm had healed, the ache from my dislocated shoulder having faded the moment I'd returned to the hall.

"Yes…no…" I didn't want to tell him it had been Graham.

We didn't need to have that conversation here or now. "Some of it, yes. He has the others. All of them imprisoned behind some shield; he stripped us of our powers."

The gasp was loud and resonated through the hall. "That's not possible," Heart murmured. She'd brought her hand to her chest, the usual pink to her cheeks only a faded blush, making her look almost pale.

"I don't know how he did it, but the minute we stepped into Chaos, it was like my powers were bound within me." I looked up at my brother. "There was clarity and calm."

His eyes softened. He understood what that meant for me in a way only Theo or Graham would know.

"Come on." He helped me stand then sat me on his throne. "Tell us what happened. Start from the beginning and tell us everything."

Everything? I released a laugh, knowing they'd blame it on my madness. There was no way I was giving Jacks or anyone in this room every detail.

Jacks crossed his arms, his eyes narrowing. Claire sat next to me, and I glanced at her after watching Jacks' façade break for a split second when his eyes flicked to her. It was something only I would notice, and perhaps Claire. Jacks hid his emotion below his power. While my power was a mirror to my emotions, Jacks' power was a shield to his.

Claire was pale, those eyes startling even me with the splintered look of the gold that sat in them now. They almost looked like someone had smashed a mirror of gold and the fragments lay strewn through her eyes. As if the destruction of her realm was fracturing her from the inside out.

My mouth dropped as I realized that was it. Creator, how were we to fix this? To save her? Losing her would destroy Jacks in a way from which he could never recover. I'd seen it once before, and they'd only just begun their relationship at that time.

The damage it had done to his control, to his terrors was astounding. If he were to lose her now, after over a century of loving her, there would be no bringing him back. His terrors would overtake the mortal world, casting it into a never-ending nightmare.

"Del. We're waiting." I could see the irritation at my delay in talking.

"I..." My eyes moved back to Claire, and I couldn't tear them from her. Couldn't stop the thought that we would lose her, that Discord's attempt to take back his kingdom would shatter hers and with it, she would break. He didn't need us to bring him Jacks. Didn't need to kill him because losing Claire would devastate him. But maybe we would all be lost. Discord's damage was already bleeding into the other realms.

I looked back at Jacks, the others all around him, worry etched in their faces.

Finally, finding my voice, I replied, "He's destroying Chaos, ripping its foundation and resurrecting his realm from below. The destruction is tearing at the seams of each realm that connects to Chaos."

"That's insane."

"Well, she is Delusion, how can we know if anything she's saying is true," my uncle, Famine, told Night.

I saw the change in Jacks. He swirled to face Famine, about to defend me, but Claire spoke instead. "Because she would know. Of any of us, she would understand what that looked like, what it felt like. And that's exactly what it feels like. Fracturing."

Jacks turned back to her, his anger fading as the concern took over again.

"Go on, Del," she said, squeezing my hand.

I loved Claire. She was like my sister, the chaos in her drawing me to her like it had drawn Jacks to her. It hurt to see her like this, and I knew it was killing Jacks, no matter how he hid it.

"Discord has splintered Chaos, and it's spreading over into the other realms. Whatever he did to break its hold on the realm, it's infecting the other realms. We sensed it the closer we came to the border." I went on to explain the sensation, the darkness that had blanketed the borders into Heart and how it had spread further by that next day, telling them of the strange creature we'd seen.

They remained silent as I spoke, but their expressions belied their thoughts.

"A creature consisting of multiple realms?" Night asked, her ebony skin not shimmering as lovely as it normally did. "That's not possible."

Jacks stood, wiping his hand down his face, and I could see the stress my words had brought. The confirmation that Claire was indeed in danger. "It would be if the realms are truly splintering. If the borders were indeed collapsing to the strain Discord has caused in the Chaos Kingdom, then the magic within each surrounding realm would collide. Once he shatters Chaos completely, Chaos and Discord will run untethered through the surrounding realms as an unstoppable poison. That infection will bring down each realm, one by one, manipulating our lands, our creatures, and bleeding into the mortal realm until it too collapses."

Stunned silence met his revelation, and he looked back at me. Of anyone, Jacks would understand how clearly my insanity would reveal the truth of his words. He'd been the voice of my thoughts. I nodded, giving him a grim smile. There was nothing more to say.

"How is he back?" Death asked me. She looked frazzled, something that was unnerving to see in a goddess who held life in her hands.

I shook my head. "I don't know, but he wants vengeance. He wants me to bring Jacks back...no, he wanted Graham to bring him back. But Graham saved me, he kicked me through the connection Discord opened to the hall. Discord had intended for Graham to come back, using me as bait. He knew, Jacks, that you would find a way back to me, that Graham would bring you because he wouldn't leave me there. Nor would you."

"And the others?" Night asked.

"All powerless, locked behind some kind of shield."

The murmur was sudden, rushing through them. If Discord could render the children of the Elders powerless, he was more of a threat than any of them had envisioned.

"There's no way to break the sequester," Heart said, her pink hair darkening and lighting with her power as if it was unstable. And maybe it was—the corrupt mix of chaos and discord infecting her realm. As it battered against her borders, the corruption was slowly infecting her.

"Creator," I said, seeing the intention behind his plan clearly. "He doesn't want just vengeance against you, Jacks, or even Claire. He wants it against all of you. That's why he scattered Chaos. He knows that as it batters against the borders, it seeps out, infected with discord. It wasn't a side effect of his attempt to take back his realm, it was intentional. He wants that corruption to spread because he knows what it will do, and he knows the corruption will destroy all of the kingdoms and with them, all of us."

The silence was stifling as the power of my realization settled, no one doubting my sanity now. I was the only one who could clearly see the madness in his plan.

"None of you can help. He knew that the tournament would require a sequester. The only sequester that is unbreakable by an Elder. You're trapped until a second-generation makes it to the end of the tournament. He of all people would know this. That's why he planned his move now. He knew that after hearing the story, you would be focused on finding a way to break the sequester without the completion of the tournament. That you wouldn't notice as his destruction laid waste to each realm." I looked around, seeing it now, the subtle signs in the gods whose realms bordered Chaos. "That you wouldn't notice as you shattered like Claire is shattering, until it was too late, and you were all weak. Weak enough for him to walk in here and take each of you down."

I rose and pushed past Jacks, but he grabbed my hand. "Where are you going?"

"To stop him."

"Are you mad?"

I narrowed my eyes at him. I hated when people asked me that, and he knew it. "Yes, I am mad, and that makes me the perfect counter to him. You beat him once, Jacks."

"You're not me, Dellamine."

"No, I'm not, but just as Terror controls chaos, I own it, too."

His eyes flickered in understanding, his grip growing tighter on my hand. "What do you mean by that?" His voice carried a distinct edge to it.

"She means that idiot finally gave in to her," Pen said.

I snapped my head to her, feeling my delusions fighting to flee toward her.

Putting her hand on her hips, she gave me a smug look. It was one I wanted to wipe from her face with a flurry of my delusions. "Don't give me that look, Del."

"I'm confused," Claire said, rubbing her temples. "What does this have to do with Discord?"

"Dellamine's delusions rule Graham's chaos just like Terror rules yours, Claire," Pen said.

"Did he touch you?" Jacks snarled.

"Are you kidding me?" I asked him. "I am your older sister, Jacksonimet."

"Wait, you and Graham?" Claire asked, sitting back in her chair. "Thank God. It's about time."

He turned to her, his eyes wide in astonishment before the creases returned to his forehead. "You knew about this?" Jacks asked.

"Can we get back to the destruction of our realms?" Night asked.

"No," Jacks growled.

"Let it go, Jacks," Pen said, and I jerked my head back to her. "Don't worry, Del, I'm not touching him again. I've been telling him for ages to just take you. And I can guarantee it was you he was picturing every time he took me."

I gripped my hands, trying to keep my power at bay. Jacks, however, was not doing as well, his terror had shadowed the hall.

"You fucked Graham?" Jacks asked her.

"Can we not talk about my brother fucking people," Claire complained.

Pen, never one to learn when to stop, pushed, saying, "I don't remember you complaining when you were fucking me."

The golden streak of chaos that touched my power as it shot past me was quick and wicked. It landed Pen on her ass. Claire had stood, her chaos a maddening fury around her, unstable and uncontrollable.

"Really, Chaos?" Pen said, struggling to free herself.

"Don't talk about fucking any of my men, not my husband or my brother, Penelipen, or I will twist the connection you have to my mother's realm so far that your mind will never quiet the chaos I reap." She snarled the words, and they came out in a deep growl that impressed me.

"Claire," Jacks' voice was controlled and commanding. He was the only one who could handle Claire, the only one who kept her power in check, and I wondered at the connection and how different it was to me and Graham. I didn't control Graham's chaos, nor did he command any part of me, yet he owned me, and I owned him, especially that chaos that simmered below his surface.

Jacks had settled Claire, and Penn was brushing herself off. Cal was staring at her with a disapproving look, his arms crossed.

I couldn't help but laugh. "I think you need to worry about your own man, Pen, and not ours."

"Gladly. He's always been yours, Del. He never wanted me, he only used me because he wouldn't let himself have you. Too afraid of your brothers and...well, I think you know the rest. I told him you two belonged together, but I wasn't going to pass up that body or that aggression when you hadn't claimed it."

I glared at her, but Cal spoke before I could. "I think that's enough, Pen."

"I suppose it is, goading you was fun while it lasted, Del. But cousin, you know I only did it to make you jealous enough to finally make your move. And Claire, he's all yours. Between the two of them, that intensity is too much for me to handle. You and Del are the only ones who can handle either of those broody gods."

There was some awkward throat clearing before Jacks said, "Well, now that we all know how Pen gets around, can we focus on the catastrophic event that's hovering over all of us?"

"Funny, Terror," she quipped.

"Shut up, Pen," I said at the same time as Claire.

I gave Claire a smile, hoping she didn't hate me now that she'd found out about Graham.

"We'll be furthering this discussion when this is over, Dellamine," Jacks said, the command clear in his voice. Saying my brother was overprotective was an understatement.

I rolled my eyes. "I think you have your hands full explaining Pen's comments to Claire when this is over."

I reached up and gave him a kiss on the cheek.

"So, how do we fix this?" Heart asked, picking a strand of her hair up that had turned a vibrant red.

I looked back at Jacks, wondering why there had been no effect on him. Our kingdom bordered Chaos as well, so it made sense that the two of us would experience some impact. But neither of us had. "Chaos."

"Yes, we know that," Jacks said.

"No, chaos is the solution." I looked to Nature and Night, the two other realms that bordered Claire's. Nature's eyes were flickering between brown and green, the gold spreading into the hues. Usually his eyes were a rich hazel. Night's black hair had streaks of gray and the shimmer of her ebony skin hadn't simply dulled like I'd first thought. The ebony itself had actually lightened in places.

"All the kingdoms surrounding Claire's are affected by this, you can see it in the three of them. But Nightmare isn't." I turned back to Jacks. "You and I are tied too close to Chaos, and it's still grounded in our kingdom. Chaos is disturbed but not destroyed. It's only shattered, floating around the kingdom and out into the borders."

And if it could seep through the border when none of us could... if it could stay intact within those fragments, enough to attract the other powers, then it could stay intact if brought back in.

"That's it. The chaos is the answer."

"I'm not following," Jacks said.

"Again, why are we listening to Delusion?" Famine complained.

"Because Delusion is more than you think she is," Death

said. "She is madness, but that madness is exactly what's needed when the situation that hangs over us is one of insanity."

I gave her a smile, seeing why Jacks loved her so much.

Her face flickered, turning to death, and I knew what it meant. "I need to do this. None of you can. I'm the only one who's not sequestered, the only one who can dance with chaos."

Jackson turned me back to him, his face stern. "Del, you will not—"

"I will. This is not a time when chaos needs to be commanded. It needs to be guided, to run free with the only power it does that with, mine. There's a reason Claire needs you, Jacks, and there's a reason Graham needs me. You control the chaos, but I free it, I let it dance with mine, and it's amazing when it does. Let me do this."

Worry creased his eyes. "You're not strong enough, Del. I felt you fall, sensed you touch my Terror."

I smiled, bringing my hand to his cheek. "Yes, and Graham pulled me out from under it. I'm not afraid. Let me go, Jacks. You have Claire to protect, and she needs you desperately now. I don't need protection. I never have. My delusions protect that broken piece of me, and now…well now, Graham does."

His eyes softened. "What is it you intend to do?"

"There's one piece of chaos that's still intact, that Discord hasn't shattered. It's the reason you and I haven't been impacted like the other neighboring realms have, like Claire has."

"The chaos in our kingdom."

"Yes, the piece you and Claire left. It wasn't yours to move. It was mine to claim, mine to dance with because it belongs to Graham. And I'm going to let it dance with my delusions, let it keep them safe as I pass over the border. Then I'm going to give it to Graham and let it wake that part of him that only I can dance with."

"That's dangerous, Del. There's no guarantee your powers won't be stripped."

"Yes, there is. The chaos will protect it, and...you may rule discord, but chaos is its equal, and delusion revels in it. I revel in the unraveling of minds, what is discord, but the strand that begins to unwind those minds. I am the fire that burns it down."

"Let her go, Jackson," Claire said, putting her hand on his arm.

"She's right, Nephew. It's time to let her go," Death said.

He nodded, bringing me in and giving me a gentle kiss on my head. My little brother who had kept me safe and had been my guard since the day Violence had ripped the innocence from me, the day my delusions had shielded that part of me, hiding it far below the harsh words of others. He had protected me, he and Theo, shielding me as much as my power did. I wrapped my arms around him tight and hugged him, taking what strength I could from him, letting the connection we shared to our realm and the tie of our powers bolster me before I stepped back.

We didn't have to say we loved each other, we knew. We'd always been close enough.

Be careful, Del, his voice whispered through my mind.

I love you, too, little brother, I said.

He gave me a crooked smile.

"Bring Graham home," Claire said. "Bring them all home and let Discord feel your wrath."

"I plan to." I rolled my neck and turned from them, walking through the Elders and those second generation whose bonding had meant their sequester from the tournament. "I plan to feed well tonight," I said, letting my power whip around me and watching as they stepped back.

I wasn't an Elder, the effects of my powers weren't visible, the damage I caused not seen clearly, but they all feared me.

They feared what they didn't understand. What my brothers, what Claire, what Graham understood and loved me for.

I turned back to them, knowing my power was flickering around me, and seeing Jacks' proud smile. I knew I looked insane. I let my power coat me, let the insanity flood through me, the delusions that whispered through my mind flee from me so that the white haze of them covered me. I knew my eyes reflected nothing but the madness I imbued, and I saw it in their eyes. All but my brother's, Claire's, and Death's. "I am madness incarnate, and no one threatens my family without feeling my wrath."

I shifted from the hall, returning to my kingdom, ready to claim the chaos that we still owned and give it to the man it belonged to, the man who owned the madness within me like none ever had. And if Discord had hurt him any more than he had when I'd left, his death would be slow and debilitating in ways I'd never inflicted.

CHAPTER 19

GRAHAM

Discord was thrashing his power around and ranting at me. His face was red with rage. A stream of power pressed me against the wall, invading my mind again. His magic flooded it with the strings of discord that invoked madness. I gritted my teeth against that madness until I could take no more and dropped my head. Holding my hands over my ears, I tried to block out the noise that was resounding through my head. Trying to block what couldn't be stopped because the discord was locked inside of my mind.

He grabbed me by the collar, and the violence in my head was silenced as his voice cut through it.

"What have you done? You fool!"

"I did what I needed to do to keep her safe. You can't hurt her now."

His punch hit me before I could block it. I ground my teeth at the pain and waited for him to release me. Watching as he walked away from me, I saw an opening and took it. I jumped him, knocking him to the ground and punching him in the ribs. I'd caught him off guard, and I used the chance to bring my weapon around his neck, cutting his airway off. I may have been a god, but I'd begun my life as a fighter. It was a part of me that I would never leave behind, part of my identity.

I heard Theo shouting at me, encouraging me as Discord struggled to free himself. The whip of magic came fast, throwing me from him, my body landing hard against the wall, so hard my teeth shook.

"You are more of a fool than I gave you credit. You annoying spawn of Chaos. Your father was a reckless, irritating man, and your mother followed him around like a puppy. I warned her that he would be her downfall, and he was—"

"Because you had her killed. You had them both murdered!" My anger boiled over at his comment.

"She deserved it! They both did. Just like you and your pest of a sister do. I will kill you both, shred your minds until there is nothing left then gut your sister before that insolent brat Terror. I will make him watch as the blood drains from her body."

I screamed and lunged for him. No one threatened my sister. No one. But my attempt was faulted by my lack of power and his control of it was my downfall. He flung my body against the shield that contained the others. The thud of it reverberating. I slid down, my eyes trailing the blood that skidded down it with my face. My head was pounding, and I wondered if he'd given me a concussion.

"You would have been better off going yourself instead of sending Delusion. The only thing she's good for is the entertainment." I gripped my fists, seeing Theo behind the barrier, his face growing so angry I thought his teeth might shatter from the way they were clenching.

"Why did you bother? Why not go yourself?"

My body was on the ground now so that when I turned I was in a sitting position. I tried to move my legs, to will myself to rise, but my brain didn't feel connected to my body. None of my muscles seemed to be working.

His sharp eyes evaluated me, and a disturbing smile spread. "Why you're fucking the bringer of insanity."

His laugh filled the space, and I heard Theo's muffled reaction behind me.

"Tell me, son of Chaos, does that insanity run amuck in her when you're bending her over? Does she taste as maddening as she looks?"

I fought the disconnect of my mind to my body and forced myself to my legs, jerking my other weapon out and taking a fighter pose. I could feel the blood that was escaping the wound on my head and thought he might have fractured my nose as well, tasting the blood that was running from it. Wiping it away with my arm, I said, "Say another word about her, and I will shove this weapon so far up your ass, you won't be able to sit for weeks."

His eyes glinted. "I invite the attempt, and I see you did more than simply use her body. Is her heart as fractured as her mind is? I always wondered what she'd be like to tame."

I tossed my weapon before he could react, sending it with speed so that it impaled his eye as it lengthened. He screamed in fury and backed away, pulling at it.

"No one tames Delusion. Now shut your mouth while I beat the shit out of you."

I attacked while he was struggling, too distracted with his pain to use his power. I pounded his face with my fists, backing him into a corner as he continued reaching, fighting with his injury. His body was unable to heal until he could remove the weapon, and I was planning to keep him distracted from that task. He stumbled, falling, pulling me down with him and throwing me from him. It gave him the moment he needed, and he yanked the weapon out, leaving an ugly, empty socket that was slowly repairing.

"Damn you!" he screamed, his power encasing me. He bashed the side of my face with the bloodied weapon. My ears were ringing, my head jarred with the force of it. Pain lacerated me so that I laid there stunned for a moment. I saw Theo and the others, pressed against the shield, pounding to get out, but they couldn't help.

I'd pushed Discord too far, looking for an opportunity I didn't have, taking the small one I thought I'd had but quickly being reminded that I was out forced. I rolled over, pushing myself up, my arms shaking with the effort.

"You are a determined one, aren't you? Or perhaps you had one too many tastes of Delusion, and she's ravaged your mind like she does her victims."

I was standing by now, my back to him, and I turned abruptly, backhanding him and grabbing him by the shirt.

"I said to stop talking about her," I growled.

His eye was still bloody, but it had almost healed, giving him a look that was disturbing but one I wouldn't let myself turn from.

"And I said, you are a fool. A determined one, but a fool nonetheless."

I felt the impact of the weapon before I realized he'd shoved it in me, its blade side still activated. It tore through my chest as his power encouraged it, the pain unlike any I'd experienced, nothing like the pain Del's touch had wrought, nothing I welcomed. I stumbled back, trying to grab it but my hands kept sliding from the blood that layered it.

"No!" I heard Theo scream, the other voices carrying with his, but as I fell, they faded, and an image of Del filled my mind as darkness overcame me.

CHAPTER 20

DEL

I stared out at our kingdom, my determination stymied. At a loss for what to do next, I was frozen. My clarity was gone, erased with the return of my power. I needed to get into Chaos, needed to get back to Graham, but first, I had to find the piece of Claire's kingdom she'd left behind. The piece that sat close enough to the border of Chaos to keep Nightmare safe.

The creatures of Nightmare would do me no harm, they would recognize my connection to the realm, but I didn't know if they would heed me. Jacks controlled them, and they obeyed only him. I didn't have control—no part of my power involved it like his did.

"Damn, Del," I muttered. I leaned over the railing of my room and looked into the fog, sending my senses out.

I had an idea of where the piece of Chaos lay but not an exact location. It was beneath the surface of Nightmare, our realm having incorporated it into itself.

"Here goes nothing."

I shifted myself deep into the realm, close to the border of Chaos. I was certain that I would be able to pass through from our realm. Discord had assured Nightmare's border to Heart was barricaded with his magic but not the border to Chaos. There was no reason. His intent had been to ensnare the gods by redirecting the path of the tournament, he only needed to block the one side of our realm.

Keeping my distance from the border, I walked on, not wanting to inadvertently cross over for fear of losing my powers again. Then I'd really be screwed.

The screech of a Molinard caught my attention, and I swung around to see it skittering away with the knowledge that I was a child of Nightmare. I didn't know how far I was from the piece of Chaos, but having a ride would cut down on the little time I feared I had to spare. Graham's life hung in the balance. He was a fighter, and if Discord hadn't already killed him, he would. There was no way Graham wouldn't act rashly and fight him.

"Heed my command!" I screamed at the fleeing Molinard.

It slowed but didn't stop.

"Dammit." I wasn't Jacks. Commands weren't my thing. But maybe they were. After all, I left commands that ravaged the mind and led to insanity when I took my victims. They may not have been commands like Jacks gave, but they were still implicit directions that the victims couldn't ignore. They were weaved too far into their minds to deny.

I let my delusions flee, wrapping the creature in them and feeling them sink into its small, fragile mind.

"You will heed my command. You will obey me."

It stopped and turned to me. I couldn't tell if it was listening or pissed off. The large, spiderlike creatures with spindly legs that wove the webs of nightmares for my brother were difficult to read. There was no need for any thinking, they were instinctual creatures. Its skinny legs made a dancelike motion as it eyed me.

"Come to me. You will take me as far as I need to go."

231

I weaved my delusions deeper into its mind, pulling at what little I could until I perceived the hold. It lurched back, fighting against my mental grip, shaking its spiny head as if it could shake free of my power.

"I am a child of Nightmare. You will obey my command." I used my fiercest voice, unleashing the insanity that fled, layering my delusions with it.

It fought more, falling over, its legs grabbing at the air until it stilled. For a moment, I thought I had killed it, but slowly, it brought itself upright.

"Bow before me," I commanded, unsure how I felt about taking this role.

It lowered itself on its front legs, dipping its head down.

"Perfect. Good boy," I said, moving closer with some hesitation.

This was a creature of Nightmare, there was always a chance it could be playing me. But the connection I held in its mind still told me it was mine to use. I climbed atop it and commanded it to move along as I searched for the piece of Chaos. Sending my delusions out, I knew I would recognize it. Graham and I were tied too closely not to, my delusions too close to his chaos to not perceive a piece of it.

It didn't take long before I sensed the chaos. I spurred the Molinard on, and it sped up, squealing and rising on its hind legs as we drew too close to the border of Chaos. I patted its bristly hide, trying to calm it. Molinards were the most terrifying of nightmare's creatures, but even they knew not to pass into the next realm. I could see the decay stretching far to the left of me, spreading into our realm but not to the degree that it had disturbed me yet. The chaos that sat to the right of me was shielding me, shielding the realm from the infection.

Within minutes, we reached what I'd been looking for. Hopping down from the beast, I coaxed it to stay for me, letting my delusions flitter around it to calm it. I really needed Jacks. He was the one who controlled the creatures of our realm. I could merely convince them with my attempt at command, and sway them with my power as I'd done to this one. It didn't mean they would remain in my control. It skittered nervously around, but, to my relief, it stayed.

I walked to the spot where we'd placed our piece of the original kingdom of Chaos, the kingdom split among all the other realms as a way of remembering Claire and Graham's father. The Elders had left their mother's kingdom intact, Penelipen winning the trials to take over her duties. Graham would relieve her once he'd accepted his place as ruler of the kingdom. The thought of Pen annoyed me. No matter what she'd told me about him being too much for her, she'd still sunk her claws into him and taken what was mine. Of course, Graham hadn't held himself back.

Stop it, Del, and focus. He's yours now, I told myself and sent my senses out.

I could feel the chaos, feel the connection I had now to it, the way my heart recognized it and my delusions stirred at its presence. This was a risk, one I didn't know if I could pull off, but if anyone could, it was me. Biting my lip, I called my powers, sending my delusions out to cover the chaos that had become embedded in the ground over time. It stirred as my power seduced it, waking it. Lifting to greet my delusions, the gold of it swirled in a dance with the white of my magic until I drew my power back. As it heeded my call, returning to me, the chaos followed. It hovered before me, as if testing me, knowing I wasn't its owner but somehow recognizing my connection to it.

"Come," I beckoned. "Let me take you to him. Let me free you."

It slowly coated me, and I closed my eyes to the feel that was so familiar, so like Graham's touch and the way his power danced with mine when we were intimate. I opened myself to it, letting it settle into me, feeling it buck as it realized it wasn't in its correct host. That I only owned its owner and not the power itself.

"Shhh," I said. "Protect me like he does, and I will free you, I will take you to him and set you free to dance the way you should."

The chaos calmed, my delusions seducing it again until it settled softly on the outskirts of my mind, hovering protectively over my delusions and the madness that sat below. Returning to the Molinard, I petted its thick fur, inviting the cuts it gave me from its coarseness.

"I need you to take me into the next realm. I know it will break you, but if I don't, we will all be broken. Including your master," I told it. "Help me save us all, and I promise I will have him recreate you as something even more terrifying than you already are."

It nuzzled its face in my palm in answer, and I climbed onto its back. I could feel the shake in it, the knowledge that our creatures couldn't survive beyond our borders. But I had a feeling with as warped as Discord had made Claire's realm, it would last long enough.

Digging my heel into its hide, I urged it forward, forcing it beyond the haze and through into Chaos, thanking the Creator that Discord hadn't bothered to block this side of the realm, that he'd only thought to block the side the tournament would guide us through, just as I'd thought.

I rode at a pace that was power fueled until I could feel the creature weakening, its consistency decaying, its connection to our realm too far to keep it whole. Until finally it turned to ash, sending me tumbling as it crumbled to dust and slipped away on a breeze that carried it back to Nightmare.

We weren't far in, and Discord hadn't noticed me. To my relief, my powers had remained intact. Whether it was the chaos

I carried or the way I'd entered the realm, I wasn't certain, but I'd take it either way. There was no way I'd make it to Claire's castle on foot, not in time to keep him from hurting Graham more. I didn't think he'd hurt the others...yet. But Graham had sent me through to the hall in his place, complicating Discord's plans.

Time wasn't on my hands, and I knew I had to get to the castle fast. That's where he had everyone, below ground in the dungeons Claire had sealed off when she and Jackson had claimed the castle.

Dungeons. What god used dungeons? We had no use for them. We didn't take prisoners, and we never had mortals in the kingdoms. Even more reason we should have mistrusted Discord from the start.

I rolled my neck, thinking about Claire's main floor and shifted myself to it, hoping Discord didn't notice my presence. The realm outside the large stone balcony where I landed in the hall drew my eyes immediately. The change was dramatic. Claire may have loved my brother, but she didn't live in the darkness he preferred. Her land had once been airy and bright, a nod to both her parents. The chaos was subtle, but it had covered the realm. It was seen in the way the clouds moved, the fragmenting of the sunlight, the shifting of the grass and the way the colors of it flickered as if never quite knowing which color to settle on. It could be seen in the trees, the way they bashed into each other in the wind which whipped them in every direction, and the insects that flitted in confused directions, bumping into each other and spilling nectar or pollen everywhere.

Now, the realm was layered in darkness, shadows that seeped from spaces like snakes with whispers on their tongues. Words carried on the wind holding anger and discrepancy, the wind itself disharmonious to the ears, stinging as it drifted over me. The darkness was blurred, my eyes trying to make out definition, but there was none there to grasp. And above it all, fragments of chaos, glittering pieces of gold and light, were scattered along as if trying to find a landing spot but confused by what had settled below it.

Even Claire's castle was distorted, a strange blend of discord and chaos as if the two were struggling for dominance. It taunted my delusions, the insanity in me spurred by it. Within my power, the chaos stirred, knowing its other pieces were out there.

I slipped through the castle, dodging the streams of discord that lurked, careful not to alert him to my presence. I wasn't certain I had a plan; the only thing on my mind was getting to Graham before Discord killed him. Slowly, I tiptoed down the spiral stone staircase that led to the lower levels of the castle. As I neared the landing, I could hear Discord muttering. I peeked around the corner, my heart crashing as I spied Graham. His body was slumped on the ground, blood seeping from where Discord had embedded one of Graham's weapons in his chest. I threw my hand over my mouth to stifle my cry, bending over from the pain of it.

The madness in me was breaking free, the chaos fighting against it but slowly giving in as the delusions pushed for release. I needed to confront Discord, to stop him before he hurt anyone else. I had to believe Graham was still alive, that the blood meant nothing, that the way he was slumped over meant nothing.

I closed my eyes, reaching for the insanity in me, letting it mix with my emotions. My anguish and anger fed it until it took control of me, shoving the chaos aside.

"Discord!" I screamed, my voice shaking the foundation of the castle. Stepping into the room, I set my delusions free before he could reach for his power. Ensnaring him in them, I drove them into his mind in such a way that any mortal would have imploded. He fought, his power freeing and hitting me, pushing me back but not stopping me.

"You were always a weird child, Delusion. Slinking around with your madness, talking to yourself, and imposing on everyone else's sanity." He was trying to weaken me, to hurt that part of me that I hid, the discord in him knowing it could undo me. "No one wanted you. Do you know why?"

"Shut up and let the others go," I ordered him, trying to use the authoritative tone with which I'd controlled the Molinard.

"Ha! You dare command me, you insignificant useless waste of power. There is no place for you. You sit nestled between pain and terror, the two trumping you. Even your little brother is more powerful than you."

He was moving closer, and with each step, his power pushed me back, his words breaking me. I could feel them, slowly unraveling my hold on my power, weakening my delusions and reaching for the vulnerable part of me they protected.

"You have no power here, you meek, weak-minded child. No one cowers to you, no one prays to you, no one even knows you. Terror they fear, pain they know, but delusion…well, delusion is something they swat away like an annoying bug. You are nothing."

I heard Theo shouting in the background, but Discord's words drowned him out, the power of them, the way they twisted into my mind, validating the thoughts of that small part of me that needed sheltering, that hurt with every word.

"Dellamine!" Violence yelled, but I ignored her, knowing she'd likely just add to the insults.

My power was giving, my delusions pulling back to shelter me, having fled earlier to fight and in doing so left my mind vulnerable.

"Dellamine, do not listen to him!" she screamed. I glanced at her, furrowing my brow as I attempted to grasp why she wouldn't be adding to the taunts, relishing in my insecurity. "You are terrifying. You always have been. That's why we never played with you, why we teased you. Why I teased you. It was my defense because I couldn't admit that I was afraid of you and jealous of you."

"Me?" I said, and Discord's power stung me, sending me back a few more steps, the wall hitting my back.

"Yes, now show him who you really are. Kick his ass like you did mine when we were kids."

"Get him, Del," Theo said. "Show him why mortals fear you so."

"Shut up!" he screamed at them. "And you, worthless goddess, it's time for you to die."

He took another step, but he teetered then fell, his head smacking against the ground with a loud *thwack*.

"I told you not to insult her, asshole," Graham said, his voice weak.

He was alive, and my heart somersaulted. My delusions danced across the space as he lifted his head slightly and met my eyes.

"Kick his ass, sweetheart."

I let out a giddy giggle that I knew was in stark contrast to the situation we were in. I didn't care—Graham was alive, and my heart was happy again.

"I thought you were dead, but I guess I need to ensure it this time." Discord stood quickly and brought his foot up to kick Graham in the head, and I snapped.

My power snatched his foot, holding it steady while my delusions swarmed him. He stumbled back, my move unbalancing him.

"Don't you touch my god, you traitorous shithead."

His eyes glared at me with a lethal intensity. Pushing himself from the floor, he roared, "You can't defeat me, you crazy bitch."

"I think traitorous shithead was more creative," Graham said in a pained laugh, causing another flip of my heart.

"Why you—"

He sent his power rushing at us both, but mine pushed it back, streams of my delusions ensnaring it.

"My brother defeated you and so will I."

"Your brother is stronger than you. You are nothing compared to either of them."

He fought, his discord whipping around my delusions in a frenzy that filled the room with the gray of his magic and the white of mine.

"Do you know why I love my brothers so, Discord?" I asked as my power slipped over his, wrapping around it. "It's because I'm a disjointed blend of them. I may not be Pain, but it takes me to the edge, feeding my insanity. I revel in it. I may not be Terror, but it feeds my delusions, strengthening them and me. Mortals may not fear me like they do my brothers, but they should." I commanded my delusions to do what they did best. "Terror may command discord, but that doesn't mean I don't have power over you. I am your worst nightmare, Discord. I am madness incarnate, the bringer of insanity and my delusions unravel the sanest of minds. I take pleasure from chaos, and I wreak havoc in discord."

He'd backed up by now, my delusions holding his streams of power prisoner, rendering them useless. "I dance in the disharmony you create, in the disjointed aggression you cause, the friction you bend. And I twist it until it becomes something different, something insane."

With each tug at his power, it unraveled more, feeding my madness so that I knew I looked every bit like Terror's equal. "Can you feel it?" I asked him as I drew closer, seeing the fear in his eyes as my delusions sank into his mind. "Can you feel me? Because I can taste your fear."

With my last word, I unleashed the insanity that had been swirling in my mind waiting for its turn to play. I poured it into him, watching the final strands of his power fade as I invaded his mind. He slipped to the floor, his eyes darting back and forth like they were looking for a way to escape my punishment.

I knelt in front of him, sending my commands into his mind with the wisps of delusions that remained. The final soft seduction to ensure his mind would remain locked in the prison where I'd placed it. "You are a weak man, not a god. You have no power but what I afford you. You bend to my will because I am your master. You are mortal. You are nothing. You are but a series of delusions that you cannot escape and the more you try, the more they will seep into your consciousness until they have fed on all they can, leaving you nothing more than a shell of the man you were."

He was cowering on the floor now, his hands covering his head as I infected every corner of his mind, feeding from the insanity I was wreaking. I closed my eyes to the sensation of it, feeling my body respond and losing myself to it as the ecstasy built…until a hand grabbed my ankle and jerked it.

I looked down quickly, my power ready to strike.

"Save that for me, Del," Graham said, the curve of his lip lifting despite his pain. I could see his arm shaking with the effort it had taken for him to stop me, and the sight brought me back to reality.

My power fled back to me, tingling through my body, leaving it unsatisfied. He was right. He'd protected me once again, stopping me from reveling in my feed and showing my most vulnerable side.

"I think Turning and I are going to have a long talk when we're out of here," Theo said through the barricade that still held them prisoner.

"Shut up, Theo," I said, moving to Graham and kissing him.

"A serious talk!" he yelled.

"Save it, Theo. I'll be glad to kick your ass when I'm healed," Graham retorted, and Theo let out a bellowing laugh. "Any idea how to get us out of here now that you've defeated the bad guy?"

"Nope, I didn't quite think that through."

"Of course you didn't."

"She's delusion, she doesn't think. It hurts her head too much," Violence teased.

I threw her a look which she returned with a smile. "I can leave all of you there, you know," I threatened.

"Del," Graham scolded. I turned to him, lifting my brow, but then my eyes dropped to the blood that had soaked his shirt, the weapon still lodged in his chest. That joy in my heart faded, rapid fear-laced beats replacing it. Now that my focus was on him, I could see how pale his face was. "What do you need to do now?"

I took his hand, wishing I could give him the immortality I'd regained with my visit back to the hall. "The Elders are trying…"

"What?" His voice sounded weak, and the worry in my chest grew.

The chaos pushed against my hold. I'd forgotten it was there in my madness. "Claire."

"What about Claire?" His expression had turned, his pained features now marred with worry lines.

He was trying to sit up, but I stopped him with my hand.

"No, don't. You need to fix the kingdom, to restore it and restore her. Discord corrupted it, and with his actions, it's been fragmenting her. The gods in the neighboring kingdoms are affected, too."

"Fuck, I don't know how to fix this."

"I do. Here." I took his hand. "Go to him," I told the chaos in me.

"To whom? You know muttering doesn't look good after what you just did, although I find it quite adorable."

I glared at him then watched his expression change as the chaos slipped from my hold and floated in the air before us.

"Command it, Graham. It's your piece of your father's kingdom, the one Claire left in my kingdom. It's mine to give to you, and I'm returning it to you."

"Shit," I heard Theo mutter.

"I have no power," he said, his eyes wider and searching mine for understanding.

"That is your power. It will answer only to you."

"Says the goddess who just held it."

"Eh, I have a bit of sway over it."

The smile he gave me warmed my heart. "That you do."

He held his hand out, and it surrounded him, sinking into his skin. Never taking his eyes from mine, he put his hand against the ground and commanded it. The chaos fled him, pouring into the ground which turned a brilliant gold. The fragments of chaos floating around us heeded its call and drifted to it, settling around it. There was a change in the air, the discord lifting. The chaos spread, repairing the damage Discord had done, righting the kingdom. The heavy, oppressive feel, the darkness, lifted and Discord's hold fell. The barrier dropped and the others filed out of their prison, flexing their hands at the return of their power. I sensed it in Graham as well, the chaos that connected us under the surface of his other powers.

Theo hoisted me into his arms, giving me a bear hug that stole my breath before saying, "You, little sister, are terrifying and amazing."

"Thanks Theo. Any idea how to get us out of here without finishing the tournament?"

"Yeah, Turning's not looking too good," Angst said as they moved him to a sitting position.

"Damn, no, he's not."

"I'm good," Graham said, his teeth gritted. But he wasn't. His color had faded even more, and I could see him straining to stay conscious. Their powers may have returned, but their immortality was still gone until we returned to the hall.

"No, you're not, and you're the only one who can get us to the hall of gods without finishing the tournament."

"What?" he and I said together.

Theo shrugged. "He has his own realm. He's the only one of any of us who does, and that technically makes him an Elder."

"But Pen has the realm still. She hasn't passed it back to me completely." I could see the pain talking was causing him.

"Why would she?" I said, shooting him a look.

"Really? Going back to that, Del? Don't make me punish you." He grimaced, and I dropped it.

Theo gave him a look, however. "Serious talk when we get back, Graham. And no, Pen returned it to you when she accepted Cal's offer to bond. The kingdom's yours, which means you have the power to take us back."

"Are you shitting me?" he grumbled. "All this time I could have been out of this idiotic challenge, and nobody bothered to tell me?"

"You're the baby god. We didn't want to make it easy on you," Angst joked.

"Yeah, you had to prove your worth," Theo said with a laugh.

"You're fucking kidding me."

"Eh, you needed to earn your place among us."

"Bunch of jackass gods," he muttered. "How do I do this?"

As Theo and Angst talked him through it, I walked over to Discord and stooped back in front of him.

"Pretty impressive," Violence said, stooping next to me.

243

"It's nothing really."

She stared at me, and I shrugged, not sure what to say as Graham's magic touched the air.

"Nothing she says of ravaging the mind of an Elder god in a matter of minutes. Terrifying is more like it."

"That's my brother's role. I'm just the crazy one." She shook her head and rose, offering me her hand. Taking it, I said, "You're really jealous of me?"

"Don't push it, Del. I said that in a moment of desperation. I won't admit it again."

"Come on you two," Theo said; he and Angst had Graham up on his feet. He looked terrible. His appearance made my heart hurt, and I wanted to run to him, but I couldn't. We were surrounded, and Theo was right, he needed to get back. "We need to get this one to the hall so he can heal."

As I moved closer to the connection he'd summoned, the pull of the hall beckoned until I was standing once again in it. The Elder gods rushed to us the moment the magic dissipated.

"Graham!" Claire screamed, running to his side.

I was pushed back in the throng of questions and reunions, the Elders wanting answers. All of them forgetting I was there, forgetting what I'd done. I was fine with it, attention like that wasn't my thing anyway.

I backed up further and hit a solid form. Looking up, I met Jacks' eyes, which were smiling proudly at me.

"So Delusion saved the day," he said.

I turned around, and he folded me into his arms. "I'm proud of you, Del. You saved them, you saved Claire, brought her back when I couldn't."

The kiss he gave my head warmed me along with his words. I stayed in his embrace, the protective hold of my little brother until the attention I didn't want turned to me. The Elders wrenched Discord from Claire's realm and deposited him in the middle of the hall. He was crumpled in a ball, babbling and shaking. He didn't look like a god because he wasn't. I'd stripped him of that. Sure, he still had the power, the immortality, but his mind didn't believe he did, and so it would trick his body into believing he didn't.

The Elders all turned to me. Jacks' hand rested on my shoulders, ready to protect me from their glares, the fear and the mistrust that lay in their eyes.

"Let her fight her own battle, Jackson," Graham said, stepping past them all.

With our return to the hall, he had healed, and my heart leaped in joy. He was still covered in blood and looked a little rough around the edges, but I didn't care. I loved him and only wanted to run to him, to kiss him, to have him hold me and take me.

"You and I will be having a talk when we're through, Graham," Jacks said, but he removed his hands from my shoulders and walked to Claire's side. I watched as he pulled her to him possessively. Her eyes had settled, the gold lining the brown of them again, the specks barely discernible.

"I already told him that," Theo said, his arms crossed.

I stepped forward, ignoring my brothers.

"What have you done to Discord?" Night asked.

"I did what I do to any of my prey."

"He is a god, not a mortal," Conflict said.

"He was a god and is now a mortal," I said defiantly.

There was a gasp and murmuring.

"Look, I did what I needed to do to save Graham, to save Claire and the others. I did what none of you could. Maybe that scares you. Maybe that makes me a threat, but I've always had the power to do that. I am Delusion, I am insanity, the warping of a mind. I will use my power to protect those I love. Discord was a threat, and he has been indisposed. If you'd prefer I free him of my power, I'd be happy to do so and let you lot deal with him."

I folded my arms over my chest and stood my ground.

"How did you make him mortal?" Death asked, and I could see no malice in her eyes, only curiosity as her form shifted back to life for a moment.

"I didn't. His mind did. I simply planted the seed, the delusion that he was a weak mortal man. His mind took the spell and slowly unraveled his identity. Lock him away in an institution in the mortal world, and he'll die an old man, rambling about how he once had the power to destroy nations."

She studied me and gave me a warm smile. "You are quite an imposing force, aren't you?"

"Just having a little fun," I replied with my own smile.

"Someone take him somewhere until we figure out what to do with him," Nature said. "Elders, we should discuss this, but I think we're all a bit tired of this hall. Since an Elder came through from the tournament side, the tournament is forfeit and the sequester dissolved. Thank the Creator."

"You mean if I'd done that earlier in that blasted tournament, the entire thing would have ended?"

Nature gave Graham a disapproving look before continuing, "Shall we reconvene in the morn?"

There was agreement, to my relief. I was looking forward to making Graham mine again. But Death changed my plans. "We need to linger just a few minutes longer. Graham and Penelipen will stay, the rest of the second generation may go."

"But—" I started, but she gave me a look that told me to mind my place.

"Come on, Del," Theo said, taking my arm. "Let them talk."

I wasn't fond of leaving Pen alone with Graham, but I knew that was foolish. He loved me, and she was bonding with Cal. Although that hadn't stopped them from fucking before.

Graham glanced at me, and as if he could tell what I was thinking, he narrowed his eyes, giving me a sour look. I stuck my tongue out at him, thinking it the only reasonable response, and he gave me a sly grin, his eyes twinkling. That look reassured me that my thoughts had been foolish, and his mind was on me and what my tongue would do to him rather than what Pen would do to him.

"A seriously long talk," Theo muttered, grabbing my arm and shifting me back to our kingdom. "Go clean up while I think of how I'm going to beat the shit out of Turning for touching you."

"Seriously?"

"Seriously."

"You never beat the shit out of anyone else who touched me."

His eyes narrowed. "That you know of."

With that, he stormed off. I couldn't help but laugh at my overprotective big brother until my mind turned back to everything that had happened. As I bathed and changed, I went through the events, replaying them. My mind played out how it could have gone differently, how I could have been too late, how I could have lost Graham. It hurt just to think about it.

Stretching out on my bed, I pushed it all away, feeling the exhaustion, the weariness settle over me. I hadn't realized the tournament and the events that had followed had wiped me out so drastically, both emotionally and physically. Drained, I closed my eyes, thoughts of Graham on my mind calming my delusions as I drifted to sleep, waiting for his return.

CHAPTER 21
GRAHAM

The realm was mine. I still couldn't believe it even if I shouldn't have been surprised. I knew Pen had just been hanging around for the company and the sex. Knew Cal had been bending her ear, trying to convince her to step down and hand it to me. That he wanted her to himself even if they couldn't stop bickering—the last fight they'd had spurred quite a night of aggressive sex that I'd been unable to pass up.

That was a thing of the past. Del was the only one I wanted now, and I would pass up sex with any goddess to have her.

I stepped into the main hall of my castle, having cleaned and changed. I was eager to return to Del. I had needed time though. Time to talk with the Elders, to discuss the final transfer of the realm since I'd accepted it when I'd triggered the connection to the hall. The transfer should have required the passing of a trial before the realm became mine, one like Jackson had faced before he'd taken over the Nightmare Kingdom. They were perplexed at how I'd stepped in without the official transfer, perplexed at how Theo had known I didn't need one. I had no answers, but then even after all these years, I still didn't completely understand my new world.

"I'll miss this view," Pen said, coming to stand next to me.

"The realm or my ass?" I asked, giving her a smile.

"Don't let Del see you flirting with me. She scared me before but terrifies me more than Jacks does now."

"She should. A woman that beguiling and deranged should never be underestimated."

"I'm glad you finally told her how you feel."

I raised a brow as I glanced at her. "Are you sure about that?"

"I will miss that aggression of yours, but I'm not up to your level, Graham. We fit well together, but you need more, I could always sense you holding back. I have a feeling you don't hold back with Del."

"No, I don't." The need for Del grew at just the thought.

"And as fun as it was, it's hard to take someone fucking you when they're wishing your body was someone else's."

"Like that time we fucked after you and Cal fought?"

"Oh no, he was nowhere in my mind that time. That was all you, Turning." Her eyes took on a hungry look, and I laughed.

"Go find Cal and devour him. You touch me, and Del will ensure your mind is suitably ravaged."

A shiver ran through her. "True. No goddess will be coming near you now. I hope you know that."

"Fine with me. There's only one I want. Only one I ever wanted."

"I know," she said, rising on her toes and kissing my cheek. "It's been fun, Graham. Take care of the kingdom and try not to bruise Del too much. I saw those handprints on her before she healed. Jacks and Theo see that, and you'll have to regrow your hands every time you touch her because they'll be cutting them off."

"That's disturbing."

"But true. Go claim her before I decide to take advantage of you one last time."

I laughed, shaking my head. "I already have claimed her, and you had your last time."

"That I did, and it was memorable. Goodbye, Graham." She gave me a smile before she disappeared.

It had been memorable, and any other time, I would have taken her once more, but I had Del now. I no longer needed to reach for Pen to fill the need I had to touch Del. I could touch her all I wanted, take her all I wanted for eternity.

I looked back over my realm once more, taking it in as I thought my mother must have when she'd been alive. Wondering if she and my father had stood here in their early years together, before they'd left the world of the gods behind for a life in the mortal world. They'd known they were meant for each other just as I knew Del was the one for me. I'd lost so much in my life— my parents, the truth of my existence, of who I was. I'd lost my identity and replaced it with a life I'd enjoyed, one I would never change for I had loved Angie and our children. They were a part of my life that I would always cherish. But I'd lost them, too.

I didn't want to lose anyone else, and I realized as I'd been lying on the floor, clinging to life, that I didn't want to die because I would lose again if I did. I'd fought, knowing I didn't want to lose Del, that I wanted to touch her again, to see her, feel her, be with her, and if I let go, I would never have that chance again. She had kept me alive, the very thought of her. And now it was time to make her mine completely because I never wanted her away from my side again.

Rolling my neck, I took a breath, knowing I'd have to face Jackson and Theo first, to prove to them that I was good for Del, that I would keep her safe. That I would protect her even though she'd proven today that she was quite capable of protecting herself. I thought of her, the spirit in her as she stood up to

Discord. She'd been achingly beautiful, a picture of madness in a body that could break any man. And often did…something she'd have to give up. Watching that man take her in the alley had torn me up and the thought of anyone touching her like that again, anyone but me was enough to send me over the edge. I'd save that conversation for another time because tonight I was going to ravage that body and watch as it crumbled in my arms, and against my mouth.

With that thought, I shifted to the Nightmare realm, ready to claim my goddess.

"GRAHAM!" Claire's voice pulled me from my thoughts as I walked through the castle on my way to Del's quarters.

She ran to me, jumping into my arms. I hugged her tight; Claire's hugs were always restoring. I wasn't certain if it was our closeness or the connection between our power, but they always left me feeling better than I had.

"Hey there. How are you feeling?" I asked, putting my hands on her face and looking at her eyes. They'd returned to the way they'd always been, the brown that matched mine, the circle of gold and the slight blue that sat just below the brown. The layer of color only Jackson and I could detect.

"Much better. I've never seen Jackson so upset, and I couldn't tell him what was wrong because I didn't know."

I kissed her forehead, relieved she was back to normal. Del's words back in the dungeon had scared me. Claire was mine to protect, no matter that she was Jackson's now. She was still my little sister, and just like he and Theo watched out for Del, I watched out for Claire.

"So...you and Del, huh?" she asked, giving me a knowing look.

"Word spreads fast," I grumbled.

She hit my arm. "Took you long enough."

"What are you talking about?"

Rolling her eyes, she replied, "You've been crazy about her for years."

Her words surprised me. "Crazy is a relative word around here."

"So? You had sex?" she said it in such a low whisper that I couldn't resist my laugh.

"Why are you whispering?"

"Because Jackson is not happy."

"You're kidding me."

"Nope." She shook her head to emphasize the word. "Theo's a bit grouchy about it, too."

"She's how many centuries old?"

She shrugged. "They're no different than you, Graham."

"They're a lot different than me."

She reached up and gave my cheek a kiss. "Well, I'm happy about it. I love Del. I've been waiting for you to finally give in. Now, Pen on the other hand."

I put my hand to her mouth. "Enough. Don't lecture me about my sex life. I am your older brother, and I'm allowed to have sex with whomever I want."

She gave me a sour look but dropped it.

"Anyway, it wasn't anything serious, and it's over...although there was never anything there in the first place but raw sex."

"Ewww, that's too much information, Graham."

"I have to get even for all the shit you and Jackson make me see. Seriously, Claire, do you have to do that shiver thing when he barks a command? It makes me want to punch him."

"Mmm, I love his commands."

"Yeah, that's not something that sits well with me."

"I'm not sure those handprints on Del's arms sat well with Jackson, so don't lecture me on what turns me on, Graham."

"Touché. Where is the commander anyway?"

"I think he went to talk to Del."

"Great," I grumbled, looking down the hall and knowing the conversation that awaited me when I got to her. If they let me through to see her.

"Go. He doesn't bite."

"Good, because I do, and I don't want someone doing that to my sister." I gave her a wink as her face morphed to one of disgust.

I made my escape before she could hit me again.

"You're disturbing, Graham!" she shouted at me as I walked down the hall.

"No more than you are, Sis. Love you, too!"

I left her, knowing she was throwing me dirty looks. As I rounded the corner of Del's wing, I realized I hadn't ever been to Del's quarters. We'd always been in the main areas of the castle. Excitement slithered through me, and I rubbed my hands in anticipation at all the things I wanted to do in her quarters to stake my claim on them and her.

Upon meeting Jackson and Theo, my excitement diminished. They were standing in front of the opening to what I assumed was Del's room. Theo had his arms crossed, and Jackson was surrounded in his moody power. They weren't planning to make this easy on me, and that aggravated me. I stared them both down.

"I suppose you two are here to give me the talk."

"Talk?" Theo said, turning to Jackson. "Are we talking?"

"I haven't decided yet. I was debating on letting you beat the shit out of him first."

"I'm pretty sure Theo can confirm that it takes a lot to beat the shit out of me."

"True," Theo said, grinding his fist into his hand.

"Then talk it is."

Just to piss them off, I pushed past them both and walked into Del's room. To my disappointment, she wasn't there. I took the time to glance over the room. It was spacious, covered in grays with a few delicate pops of pink. A long pink chaise sat to the side, and I couldn't help picturing how I'd bend her over it and take her from behind.

"Get the dirty thoughts of my sister out of your head," Jackson growled.

"I could say the same to you, Jackson."

He slammed me against the wall, pinning me before I had a chance to fight back. "Stronger than you look," I joked. "You ever do that to my sister, and I'll kill you."

"I can assure you I do that quite often to your sister, and she enjoys it."

"You two need to stop," Theo said. "I'm highly disturbed by both of you right now."

Jackson shoved me once more before letting me go, but the death stare he was giving me didn't subside. He didn't scare me, although I knew he should have.

"What do you want with Del?" he asked.

"I want to fuck her—"

Theo's punch landed before Jackson's could.

I rolled my neck and rubbed my jaw. "Nice hook you've got there."

"Don't talk about my sister like that."

"She likes it when I talk dirty to her. You two clearly don't know the same Dellamine as I do."

Jackson's eyes could not have been more deadly.

Clenching his jaw, Theo said, "You hurt her, and I'll break your balls so fast you won't be fucking anything for months."

"But she likes it when I hurt her." Jackson started to move. "And don't even come at me, Jackson. Don't think those commands you give Claire don't bother me. She invites it just like Del invites what I give her."

Theo rubbed his hand over his face, and I could tell the conversation was disturbing him again, but Jackson and I had been like this from the beginning. Two dominant alpha males with Claire in the middle. I'd wanted him nowhere near my sister when they'd first met. I knew now how good he was for her, how that commanding side of him kept her reined in, but it didn't mean it didn't still bother me.

"Are you just using her?" Theo asked. "Because that's what we don't want. Neither of us wants to see Del hurt that way. She's fragile."

"Bullshit. She's stronger than both of you. She's a force to be reckoned with."

"Only when she's confident. Delusion in a wounded state is something that will only hurt the mortal world." Jackson's anger had faded, his concern overtaking it. He loved his sister, they both did, and neither of them wanted her broken.

"I won't let that happen. I won't hurt her that way, I won't break her...well, I'll break her but only in a pleasurable way."

Jackson gritted his teeth, and Theo's muscles flexed larger than they already were.

"I only want her to be happy, just like you two do. She's... she's everything to me now."

"And Pen?"

Would the Pen conversation ever stop?

"There was nothing ever there, just sex. And don't even try to go there because I heard about how you two went at it during the last tournament."

Jackson furrowed his brow, hiding his surprise. "Don't mention that around Claire. She's not particularly fond of Pen after she mentioned I'd had a go with her."

I couldn't help but laugh. "Gets around, doesn't she?"

"She does, much to Cal's dismay. The boy's too soft for her. She needs a firm hand."

We held each other's gaze, a look of understanding passing between us.

"Fine, you can have Del, but if you hurt her, if you wound her or leave her heartbroken, I don't care what Claire says, I will torment you until you're the shell of the man you are today."

"And I'll still beat the shit out of you," Theo added.

"Point taken. You have my word, her heart is safe with me. The rest of her body, however, is mine to use and abuse any way I choose."

"That's fine by me," I heard Del say as she came from the balcony. Her blonde hair was blowing gently in the breeze. The material of the curtains that draped the balcony billowed around her with each step she took. She wore a light pink dress that did little to cover the body that lay below. It was hard to hide my reaction to her, much harder than it had been before I knew what that body felt and tasted like.

Jackson shoved me. "Stop looking at her like that."

"Enough you two. Leave him be, and, Jacks, as often as I've watched you undress Claire with your greedy eyes, you can deal with Graham doing it to me. Now leave, otherwise, you'll have to watch him undress me with his hands."

There was no holding the rise in my pants at that promise, regardless of the growl that escaped Theo or the flare of Jackson's power.

She pointed her hand at the doorway and stood, defiant.

"Fine, but remember—"

"I know," I said, "now do as she says before I rip that dress from her, and you two really lose your shit."

Del's giggle was just what I needed to shove them both out of the way. I heard their grumbles and eventually the closing of the door, but she was in my arms by then, returning the ravenous kiss I was giving her.

"So, you're going to use and abuse my body, are you?" she said against my mouth.

"Damn right I am."

I skimmed my hands up her body, lingering on her hips and giving them a hard squeeze. Her gasp was enough to send my dick lurching.

"Are you fond of this dress?" I asked, nipping at her neck.

The way her answer sounded, drawn out and breathless, was like a rush of currents through my body. "Not particularly. Why?"

My hands had reached her breasts and were coaxing her nipples out. "Because that means I have no qualms about doing this." I gripped the material and tore it from her body, her breasts bouncing free in a way that caused my dick to jump in expectation.

As I pushed the material away, she fought to take my shirt off, her nails scratching against my chest, sending a flash of need through me. I grabbed the shirt and pulled it over my head, pushing her body across the room as I did.

"I thought I'd lost you," she said between kisses.

"You thought wrong and now you're stuck with me."

"Gladly," she replied with a sigh.

I grabbed her ass and lifted her, moving her against the wall. The force caused a beautiful cry to leave her lips. I stifled it with my kiss, my hands touching and pinching every inch of her.

She reached for my pants, but I stopped her, pinning her hand against the wall. I pushed against her, my length pressing painfully into her, and let go of her ass, leaving her legs to hold her up. Legs she gripped around me so that a shock of pain hit me. I took her other hand and brought both above her head, lifting my mouth and watching her expression. Holding both wrists firmly in one hand I gripped them tighter, knowing her skin was bruising and delighting in the way her eyes lit with excitement.

"Hurt me, Graham," she said hoarsely, stirring the chaos in me.

I smashed my mouth against hers with the hunger that she'd spurred in me, grinding into her and feeling her arch further into me.

"Do you want to come for me, Del?" I muttered, drawing my tongue down her lip and taking it between my teeth.

"Desperately."

I let my hand glide down her body, stopping to squeeze her breasts, loving the way they spilled over my hand, and the way the nipples dug into my flesh. Running my thumb across one, I drew back to watch her. Her eyes were rich sage, the slivers in them frolicking in anticipation. I gave her what she wanted, pinching it between my fingers and seeing the flinch that accompanied her moan.

"Damn, I love you, Del," I said, my dick throbbing aggressively against the material of my pants.

Her lips parted as I rubbed her nipple harder between my fingers. She threw her head back, a deeper moan tearing from her. "Make me come, Turning, and stop being mushy."

I shook my head and laughed, dropping my mouth to her breast. Grabbing her ass, I lifted her higher. My teeth skimmed her nipple, my tongue flicking over it as she ground her dampness into me.

"Silk or leather?" I asked against her skin. The growl she gave me was enough to make me come undone. "Don't growl like that unless you want me to spill all over my pants and not inside of you." Her body bucked. "Now answer the question."

"Demands, Turning. I don't answer—"

I bit her hard, her groan cutting her words off. "Answer the damn question, Del."

"Leather," she said, "It burns more."

Good God, she was killing me, and she knew it. I walked her to her bed and threw her down, enjoying the bounce of her breasts. Pulling the belt I'd worn just for this purpose from my pants, I watched her eyes flash with excitement, that glorious smile forming as I straddled her.

"Move those damn arms above your head before I use this another way," I said, snapping it and watching her legs clench at the sound. I would never use it on that soft skin, just knowing how the thought turned her on was enough.

She brought her arms up, slowly letting her fingers drift along her chest, letting them caress her breasts seductively before she moved them over her head. And like the sadistic angel she was, she crossed her wrists for me.

Shit, if she kept this up, I wouldn't get far enough to pleasure her before I took care of myself. I tied her wrists, like I'd imagined doing. The way she shivered as I smoothed my hands down her arms, feeling the softness of her skin before moving them down her breasts caused my breath to catch. I took one in my hand, bringing my mouth to it and licking in circles around her nipple. The moan that escaped her was deep and sensual, stirring my need for her. My other hand cupped her other breast, and I dragged my thumb across the other nipple while I bit the one, letting my teeth scrape across it. Her muscles quivered below me. Her legs clenched tighter, and I forced my knee between them, shoving it hard against her wetness. She was soaked and it seeped into my pants.

I dropped my head at the feel, trying to hold myself together.

"Please, Turning, fill me. Please."

"I do like it when you beg, Del," I growled, the rumble from deep in my chest.

I stood, knowing I needed to step away from her to calm myself. Taking her in, I marveled at how the muscles in her legs shook, my mind picturing them wrapped around me. I took one, my hand following the curve until I reached her wetness. Sinking my fingers into her I groaned at the same time she did. My length was screaming at me to slide into her and satisfy myself, but I wanted to see her break first. To have her do so multiple times.

I removed my fingers, her whine making me smile. Then I wrapped my hands around her waist, squeezing them so hard she cried out, her pleasured shriek only spurring me on.

"By the Creator, Graham, if you don't make me come—" I stopped her with a kiss, demanding her attention, my tongue shoving in to force hers in a dance for dominance. Pushing my leg against her arousal again, I brought my hand back to her nipple, relishing at how hard it now was. With each twist and pull, she moved herself against my leg. Her body shook as I drew back to watch her, nipping her lip on my way up.

Grabbing her thighs, I forced them apart, removing my soaked thigh and penetrating her with two fingers, the thrust sending her head back, her breasts forward. I took one in my mouth and bit before I let it go. Her groan was feral this time and it was music to my ears. I licked the blood and brought myself up to watch her again. Removing my fingers, I cruelly hovered over her, just out of reach while I licked each one. The taste of her sent my dick jerking to be free.

"Turning," she growled. She was close to climaxing, the flush of her cheeks told me so.

"Something wrong, Del?" I asked, standing again, and removing my pants. Her legs squeezed shut as my aching dick bounced free. She eyed it hungrily, but I didn't let her have it yet. Instead, I took her legs and separated them again, bringing my arms around them as I plunged my tongue into her, relishing the sweetness of her.

Her body lurched, and a scream tore from her. I licked along her warmth until I reached her clit, flicking against it rapidly at the same time I thrust my fingers back into her. A deeper scream tore from her as I brought her over the cliff of ecstasy and her climax ripped through her. Her delusions escaped, whipping around in a frenzy, and I could no longer resist. I snatched my fingers from her and penetrated her so hard her body lurched again. She was tight, her muscles spasming around me as I drove into her. Holding her hips in a grip I knew was causing pain, I met her eyes, which were laced with a glorious mix of arousal and madness, calling the chaos that fled from me in answer.

I reached up and freed her wrists, and her hands came to my back, raking across it. The sharp pain only further pushed me toward my climbing release. She yanked my head down, her lips smashing against mine aggressively. She was rising again, a second climax building, and I slowed my pace, wanting to fall apart with her this time.

I pushed her ass further into me, the depth only tormenting me more. Her moan was worth the risk of losing my hold on the need for release that was pummeling me. Her legs tightened, almost stealing my breath. As her head went back, I took the moment to take her breast in my mouth again, sucking her nipple so hard she let out a delightful squeal. I continued to thrust, our bodies slapping against each other in a rhythm that was undeni-able. Unable to hold back the rising tide, I broke, my orgasm hitting me with an intensity that had me roaring. Within seconds she was joining me, her body thrusting up to meet mine at her loss of control. Around us our power erupted in a blend of gold and white haze that coated the room.

I thrust a final time, feeling the tremors in her legs from her release, the residual quivers of it pulsing around my length.

"I love you, Graham," she said, bringing my head up to look at her.

She was beautiful, her cheeks flushed with the remnants of her climax. The white haze of her power was still touching the blonde of her hair, the slivers in her eyes calm amid the lush green. She was every bit the goddess I'd always loved, the one who I'd love for eternity.

"Stop being mushy, Del," I teased her, nuzzling my nose against hers. "Or I'll have to make love to you next time."

"Mmm, that would be a shame because I need you to bring me clarity."

A rush of desire swam through me because I knew exactly what gave her clarity.

"You went too light on me last time," she said, walking her fingers down my chest. "I need you to go rough on me."

The rumble from my core was low and aggressive. "Are you calling me weak?"

"I'm calling you soft, Turning. Now fuck me like I deserve to be fucked. I want you to leave marks this time."

"Is that a command?"

"Yes."

"Then that's a command I'll accept and answer."

And I did, taking her like she wanted, like she needed and reveling in the sounds of her pleasure. I would always answer her call, always obey that command. She owned me as no one had before. She was the madness to my chaos, the storm that stirred my aggression. As I lost myself to her delusions, I knew I would let them ravage me because they belonged to me, just as she did. Just as she always had, and she now would for eternity. Chaos and delusion intertwined in a dance of pain and ecstasy until the end of time.

ABOUT THE AUTHOR

 J. L. Jackola discovered her passion for writing in grade school when she wrote a short story that earned her a spot in a local writing workshop. She has been creating fantasy worlds ever since. When she's not weaving tales, she can be found logging miles in her running shoes, watching movies with her family, or curled up with a book. She resides in Delaware with her husband and three children.

To learn more, visit her website at
www.jljackola.com

Made in the USA
Middletown, DE
03 June 2023